the wife
&
the dancing girl

Anuja Chandramouli is a bestselling author, writer, and new-age Indian classicist. She has published 12 books across the mythology, historical fiction and fantasy genres. She followed up her highly acclaimed debut novel, *Arjuna: Saga of a Pandava Warrior-Prince*, which was named as one of the top five sellers in the Indian writing category for the year 2012 by Amazon India, with *Kamadeva: The God of Desire, Shakti: The Divine Feminine, Yama's Lieutenant* and its sequel, *Yama's Lieutenant and the Stone Witch*. Her articles, short stories and book reviews appear in various publications like *The New Indian Express*, *The Hindu*, *Scroll.in* and *Femina*.

Some of Anuja's other books are *Kartikeya: The Destroyer's Son, Prithviraj Chauhan: The Emperor of Hearts, Padmavati: The Burning Queen, Ganga: The Constant Goddess* and *Muhammad Bin Tughlaq: Tale of a Tyrant*. Her book *Mohini: The Enchantress* was the winner of the JK Papers and Times of India Popular Choice AutHer award for the year 2021. Her books are also available as audiobooks and have been translated into Hindi. Her last book *Abhimanyu: Son of Arjuna* was shortlisted for the 2022 Atta Galatta – Bangalore Literature Festival Book Prize.

An accomplished TEDx speaker and storyteller, Anuja regularly conducts workshops on creative writing, mythology and empowerment in schools and colleges across the country. Her 'Mahabharata and Ramayana with Anuja' storytelling series is now available on YouTube and Spotify. She is a trained Bharatanatyam dancer. This mother of two girls lives in Sivakasi, Tamil Nadu.

Email: anujamouli@gmail.com
X handle: @anujamouli
Instagram: @anujamouli
Website: www.anujachandramouli.com
YouTube Channel: https://bit.ly/storywithanuja
FB page: https://www.facebook.com/authoranujachandramouli/

the wife
&
the dancing girl

anuja chandramouli

Published by
Rupa Publications India Pvt. Ltd 2024
7/16, Ansari Road, Daryaganj
New Delhi 110002

Sales centres:
Bengaluru Chennai
Hyderabad Jaipur Kathmandu
Kolkata Mumbai Prayagraj

Copyright © Anuja Chandramouli 2024

This is a work of fiction. Names, characters, places and incidents are either the product of the author's imagination or are used fictitiously and any resemblance to any actual person, living or dead, events or locales is entirely coincidental.

All rights reserved.

No part of this publication may be reproduced, transmitted, or stored in a retrieval system, in any form or by any means, electronic, mechanical, photocopying, recording or otherwise, without the prior permission of the publisher.

P-ISBN: 978-93-6156-042-2
E-ISBN: 978-93-6156-174-0

First impression 2024

10 9 8 7 6 5 4 3 2 1

The moral right of the author has been asserted.

Printed in India

This book is sold subject to the condition that it shall not, by way of trade or otherwise, be lent, resold, hired out, or otherwise circulated, without the publisher's prior consent, in any form of binding or cover other than that in which it is published.

To all who have loved. And lost.
But continue to love anyway.

∽

PROLOGUE

The Wailing Wife

I LAY WRITHING AND thrashing on the red soil, trying desperately, and failing, to process the magnitude of the loss that had befallen me. How was it possible to lose everything worth having within the span of a few wretched moments? All my life I had been patient, kind and hopeful. Only to lose the love I had so desperately dreamed of regaining.

I could feel the raw rage charring my insides as it poured forth, eager to unleash the wrath of the thousand hells of Yama, until there was nothing left but the devastation and desolation that mirrored the desecrated ruins of my heart and soul, once filled to bursting with love for him. *Him*. Dearest husband who had been mine to love and lose and love and lose, again and again.

Was there anyone in the annals of time who had been as sorely tested as I? All I ever wanted was to love and be loved in return. Gold, silks, jewels, and the so-called good things in life never held any allure for me. Yet, the Gods and Fates had judged me greedy for loving him too much and snatched him away for good. Damn them all to the same loveless existence they had condemned me to!

How happy he had made me. Now he was gone and had taken with him all the joy I had ever known. All that remained were the memories I could shore up before they too were snatched up by time. These played out in my throbbing head in a giddy rush as I relived every precious moment with him, as potent passion and pain surged through my insides. Rocked violently by love and laughter, but also by loss, and the languishing I endured when he disappeared into the dancing girl's embrace. It was a cruel carousel that made me laugh and cry as I was tossed hither and thither on the relentless tides of remembrance. It was *all* I had aside from the vengeful anger that kept me alive for the sole purpose of righting a wrong.

I refuse to retreat into the comforts and terrors of solitude that loom over my life. Not this time. The time for licking my wounds in unwavering silence is long gone. I refuse to hold my tongue and suffer in silence. Rage has given me wings and my husband's killers will be brought to their knees. Justice shall be served. For his sake. Everything in my life had revolved around him. Why should that change? For I loved him more than anyone or anything else in this accursed world. I will go on loving him. In life. And death.

He shall be avenged. With blood and fire. This I swear on the enduring strength of my eternal love. For Kovalan, my beloved husband. Gone, but not forever. Not if I can help it. And when my work is finished, it will truly be over. For without him, I am already dead.

A Dancer's Dirge

I lost him, long before he was lost to me. Even so, it was a death blow. When the news of his death reached me, they said I fainted and when I came to, I lay like a woman who had lost her mind. Unseeing and lifeless, almost a corpse. No food or water passed my lips for days. They said I had lost the will to live. And they had begged me to live for the sake of my daughter. Our daughter.

All I had were the memories of what I had lost. I held onto them for all I was worth. Despite everything, relentless remembrance of a happier time with him made me smile. It was enough to bring back the futile hope that lulled me into believing that he would somehow find his way back to me. From death and beyond.

I hoped and hoped, determined to hope until I could hope no more. But they told me he was gone forever. That I could never have him back. All the love in the three worlds which was less than the minutest morsel compared to the grand passion I had nurtured for him would not bring him back.

Our love had been perfect, while it lasted. When we lay entwined on flower-strewn beds, our senses swimming with a surfeit of sensuous sustenance, warmed by the raging flames of passion and cooled by the soothing breeze of affection. At the time, I had truly believed that things would always be that way between us. Now it was all gone and the only thing that remained was the aching emptiness where he had been, which nothing could ever fill. Not food, music, dance, good conversation, none of the things I had loved when I had shared them with him.

It hurt when they blamed me for the tragedy that had claimed him. It hurt worse when in the throes of my grief, I realized they were right. He had met his fate while fleeing from my embrace—our shared bed stuffed with the feathers of mating swans. It hurt worst of all, knowing that none of it could be undone.

What will become of me without him? I suppose I know the answer to that. He may have gone past recall. And his wife, with him. But my term of punishment was far from over. I was fully convinced that this was the price exacted for the flawless love we had shared. And I still had to pay my dues and pay them I will. Even if it means enduring more torment of the spirit and the flesh, I welcome the pain.

Even knowing how it all turned out, I never regretted a moment of the time I spent with him. The delights borne of our love outweighed the pain it had bred. Even if it was not entirely true. And I will bear it all. For him. My Kovalan. A part of him shall always belong to me and I will hold on to my beloved with all my strength. Never to let go. Through death, which has already claimed me with him gone. And beyond. Because our love story was epic. And it always will be.

KANNAGI

My One and Only

I COULD NEVER RESIST my feelings for the nice boy who became my husband. It was a bit too much for my mother to handle. Amma blamed my father for it. She complained that he was encouraging his only daughter, who had become hopelessly besotted with the son of his closest friend. In my head, I was already scripting and rescripting our love story, which was going to be one for the ages, and insisted on disappearing into my perfect storyland.

This annoyed Amma no end. And she might have been right about Appa as well. For he was my only scale drawing of how a man ought to be. He was always the nicest of men. Appa was also one of the most successful merchants in Puhar, the capital city of the mighty Cholas, and was the foremost trader of grains and spices. People always said that it was not his formidable acumen for trading that set him apart, but his benevolence and generosity. I loved that everyone loved my father. And that he loved me, best of all.

Amma did not mind that. 'Men are silly creatures,' she remarked. 'Your father is better than most, but he is still a man. It suits me perfectly that his only child has claimed his heart and not some foul *vesha* or exquisite *dasi*. And don't you ask me what those things mean. You will know when you do.'

Appa would carry me on his shoulders when I was younger,

or I would hold his hand as we walked along the promenade of our beloved Puhar, every time his ships came in. The harbour, Maruvurpakkam, was our pride and joy, for this was the point where the River Goddess Kaveri merged herself into the sea with a silvery rush of exquisite recklessness, their ardent union forming an estuary that was so extensive and deep, the biggest ships in the world could come and go, safe as you please. Or so my father said.

'The River Goddess is the greatest,' the sailors and fishermen, swaying and somewhat unsteady on their feet, sang to each other, well within my hearing, chuckling all the while, with the casual familiarity and veneration they had for the river that was their life, 'but like all women she is half a whore, which augurs well for us mere mortals, except when she is pitching an unholy fit and flooding the banks, destroying our boats, baying for our blood to drink and our bones to chew on.'

'She wouldn't mind our embrace. Provided we have tools the size of a palmyra tree!'

My father would frown, and that was the end of that.

At the time, I had no idea what 'half a whore' or even an 'entire whore' meant but I knew enough not to ask my father or mother about it. Besides, hadn't Amma said that I would know what I wanted to know when I did? I preserved the words carefully in my head until I was old enough to figure out the meaning on my own. And then I wished I had remained ignorant because forevermore, I would worry endlessly about the half of me that was supposedly a whore. Like the great river Kaveri, on whose lap I was raised, I wondered if I was half goddess and half whore. The thought of being either was terrifying.

Puhar was originally called Kaveripattinam because it was built on the bank of our beloved Kaveri of schizophrenic disposition. The people referred to it as Puhar, an endearment, that sprang forth from their great affection for this greatest among cities. And it was beautiful.

Our King Karikalan's enormous palace was at the heart of Puhar, and it was grand indeed. I remember it well enough, but I can't recall the particulars about the bustling streets, the many temples, or even the neatly ordered marketplaces hawking everything from gold and gems to freshly caught fish. My memory plays tricks on me, leaving me utterly confounded about what is real and what isn't, what happened and what didn't, the things I buried and those I conjured up.

Whenever I think of my Puhar, I can only recall the details of my parents' residence where I spent my childhood and the home I made for myself. To be fair, messy memory alone isn't to blame. I knew these parts of Puhar best because I seldom stepped out and away from the familiar comforts of my home. Which is why my little sojourns to the port with my father hold such a special place in my heart.

It was one of my favourite things in the world to feel the sea breeze in my hair and take in the sights and smells as he told me about the ships standing proud and tall in the harbour. The big ones with the strong beams of timber lashed together, formidable prows and majestic sails were intimidating and most impressive. They were the ones that sailed to places with exotic names like Eezham, Nagapuram and distant Burma, returning with precious cargo stored in large warehouses on the shorefront.

'A demon guards the warehouses,' father told me with mock solemnity. 'If anybody were foolish enough to lay their grasping paws on the valuables that bear the tiger stamp of our King Karikalan, they would find their eyeballs have been gouged out by the vigilant demon with bloodshot eyes and a lolling tongue. And he also carries a club. He is not to be confused with the one who stands guard at the crossroads and devours those with falseness in their hearts—swindlers, cheats, and loose women—before spitting out their bones.'

I hated this story. It frightened me no end to think of demons prowling about looking for swindlers, cheats and loose women in my Puhar, which always seemed so warm and welcoming, filled with all manner of marvels that soothed the senses and stirred the soul. How could the most beautiful and bountiful place in the three worlds harbour anything at all that might be construed as beastly? Naturally, I was a foolish little girl who grew up to be an even more foolish woman.

We watched the bare-chested men unload the cargo from their ships as the sea frothed against the hull and lashed them affectionately with salty spray. They sang songs for our amusement that told of the strange things they had seen on their journey. I liked being there and treasured the memories years later when mother deemed that I was too old to be seen in the company of rough sailors. It was a pity. They had been so kind and always had something pretty for me.

All the walking and the bracing scent of the sea always made me hungry. Appa would buy me some snacks from the vendors who had little stalls by the sea, and I would savour the spicy peanuts and raw mangoes rubbed with a dash of lime and chilli powder, listening as my father chatted with his friends and acquaintances. Some of the men on the ships did not look anything at all like our people. Appa said they were *Yavana*s, from a faraway land in the West, and they spoke a strange language. I was fascinated by the wild, unruly facial hair they flaunted and their barking laughter. Apparently, they brought wine, horses, perfumes, lamps and sculptures for trading. Appa seemed to be on friendly terms with them the way he was with everyone else.

They patted my head or pulled my cheek in a familiar manner, which I didn't like, but they always brought dolls for me, wearing pretty garments and with the shiniest, golden hair you could imagine. For Appa, there were amphorae of wine, some of which he stored at home, much to my mother's annoyance. She said drinking it made him sillier than usual.

'It makes you silly too, but you don't hear me complain, do you?' Appa would tease her.

Amma would be incensed. 'You know I only have a sip or two for its medicinal properties. Living with you has ensured that I suffer from a chronic headache.'

He let me have a sip one time and mother was most irritated when I spat it all over my emerald-green *paavadai*. It had tasted terrible, like grapes gone bad, but I was most pleased that my father had shared it with me.

∽

On that memorable day from my childhood, Amma did not understand why I was so restless. She was trying to plait my hair, having anointed it with an exquisitely scented oil brought on one of my father's ships. I was filled to the brim with excitement and feverish energy. Amma thought I was being trying. For not keeping still while she worked on my hair, sighing repeatedly in exasperation.

'Why are you so worked up, child?' she scolded, working the ivory comb with unnecessary force to untangle my tresses. 'You will wrinkle your *pattu* paavadai and end up looking like one of those street urchins whose mothers let them run wild. Do you have any idea how difficult it was to procure this exact shade of blue? Sometimes I am convinced that men are colour-blind. You ask for sky blue or *kungumam* red and they bring back a bolt of cloth that is clearly green as grass.'

I knew all about the effort that had gone into the making of my blue pattu paavadai. Amma had been so pleased when my father managed to procure it for her. His earlier efforts had not been very successful because it wasn't the exact shade she wanted. Amma was a very exacting woman and even a merchant prince dared not cross her. The rare *mayil kazhuthu* or peacock-blue silk streaked with green and gold threads had finally pleased her, and she wanted the satisfaction of seeing me wear it.

It was difficult, but I managed to keep still while she plaited my hair, weaving fresh flowers and jewelled pins into it. Then she fastened a pair of ruby earrings and a heavy gold chain with a carefully engraved image of Shri, the Goddess of Prosperity. She gave me a stern glare when I squirmed in discomfort. Amma knew I hated all the ostentatious ornaments she was forever making me wear. They weighed me down and were next to useless when one was trying to clamber up a tree to help oneself to fruits or chase after chickens who didn't seem to understand that I only wanted to feed them some grains. But she insisted I wear them for reasons I was told would become clear once I was older.

'You are a strange child, aren't you?' she peered at me, pleased with the results of her labour. 'Quiet as a mouse, but quite the little monkey on occasion. Why, there isn't a tree you can walk past without attempting to scramble your way up to the very top. Whatever will your future in-laws say if you keep this up?'

'My mother climbed trees too,' Appa piped in, risking her ire. 'In fact, when she passed away, my father swore that he could feel her presence, perched on her favourite tree, keeping a watchful eye on the two of us. She only ever climbed trees in secret, after my grandmother clutched her chest and dropped to the floor, when she saw Amma sitting pretty on one of the topmost branches of a mango tree. So she took to climbing trees in the dead of the night, when nobody was skulking around. Sometimes, she would just sit on a branch in silence till dawn broke and then she would come down and resume her duties with none being the wiser.'

Amma's gaze softened as her husband, who made her impatient most days, retreated deep into the embrace of his mother's memory, but she muttered something about monkeys and madmen before grabbing me by the shoulder. 'Don't you dare ruin the silk by shimmying up trees, do you hear? As you know, we are having guests today and I want you to be on your best behaviour.'

'Has she ever ruined her clothes even while at play? Has she ever behaved in a manner that might be construed as anything less than perfection?' my father rushed to my defence.

Amma allowed herself a smile in agreement. 'You are a good girl, there is no denying that. In fact, you are so perfect it is not good for you.' She fussed over my hair unnecessarily. 'Even when you are too excited to keep still, you are still a good little girl. So I will let you go out and play. Perhaps it is best if you remain out of sight while your father entertains his friend. I am sure they will wish to converse about their saintly mothers and their strange antics without interruption.'

I embraced father before leaving the room, my silk skirt held in my hand so the folds wouldn't trail. But I strained to listen to their conversation as I made my way out as slowly as possible.

'Masattuvan will want to see his daughter-in-law-to-be,' my father remonstrated with her. 'That dear boy, Kovalan, might accompany him, and it won't hurt them to get to know each other. Kannagi is intended for him after all. The matter was decided almost immediately after she was born. My friend took one look at her...'

'...while she was still a baby in her cradle and made you promise that you will give her hand in marriage to his son because she was the prettiest little thing he had had the good fortune of laying his eyes upon. I have heard this story many times. In fact, I was right there when he said those words, remember? And while I agree that the match is a good one, it is too early to be talking about these things. There are long years to go before they are of marriageable age and a lot can happen in the interim. And I really wish your friend would stop referring to her as his daughter-in-law, it is most indiscreet, not to mention highly inappropriate...'

'But Masattuvan is the very picture of discretion,' father protested. 'He only calls her his daughter-in-law in my presence. There is nothing wrong with that. I am his oldest and closest friend, after all. Why, we grew up together and when we were Kannagi's age...'

'...you built boats with wood you salvaged from the ports and dreamed of owning a fleet that would traverse the high seas and return with riches past imagining. The two of you planned to set sail and have many a grand adventure that usually involved rescuing nubile young women from the clutches of demons and marauders so that you could ravish them yourselves, or something every bit as indecorous. And since you are both the sons of wealthy merchant princes, fate blessed you with the fortune to make your more sensible dreams come true.'

'Valli! The things you say!' Appa admonished her, but there was a world of affection in his voice.

I didn't know what 'ravish' meant at the time, but I guessed it was something unseemly. I crouched beneath a jewelled couch gifted to my father by one of his admirers, feeling very naughty and more than a little guilty for eavesdropping on my parents. But I couldn't help myself.

Amma went on firmly, 'Closest friend or not, it is just not done for him to go around saying these things.'

'Why not? What are you so afraid of?' I knew that Appa was smoothing down his moustache. He always did that when he was agitated. 'He is just so eager for this match because he knows that our Kannagi has been taught the ancient traditions, customs and proper ways to conduct herself. Masattuvan disapproves of these new-fangled practices where married women leave the sanctum of their homes to participate in *samana*s. The sole purpose of these dens of vice seems to be to engage in indecorous conduct and find lovers. Then these women shed crocodile tears when their husbands travel for work, and the moment the master of the house has departed, arrange for illicit trysts with the men they have befriended. If the women keep this up, I fear the end of the three worlds is close.'

Amma rolled her eyes impatiently. 'Most husbands are away from home not because they are hard at work but because they are besotted with some courtesan or dancing girl. It is these same men who accuse women of loose morals simply because they wish to educate themselves about current affairs and enjoy some good conversation with knowledgeable men.'

I knew that Amma was getting worked up. Her breathing had become more rapid as she continued haranguing Appa. 'Be that as it may, I am more concerned that people will talk when they are not casting an evil eye at the impending union by marriage, of the houses of the foremost merchant princes of Puhar—Masattuvan and Manaykan.'

I was certain she was giving him the evil eye herself. She hated it when he disagreed with her.

'It is not like you to care about what people will say, and the union is a blessed one. How can anyone do anything but rejoice when the two purest souls in this land are united in marriage?'

'Don't be naive,' Amma scolded him, 'there are plenty of folks who resent the success of the pair of you, especially since our King himself holds you both in high esteem. They praise you to your face and pray for your downfall behind your back. Besides, it is not only about baleful influences. Your friend's son is a good-looking fellow and he comes from a noble lineage famed for their peerless conduct, but I have my concerns. He has a slight, almost frail build and seems to be a highly strung and sensitive creature. I don't trust men like that. At least with the oafs and boors, one knows what to expect. The sweet-natured ones are more dangerous because you can't be certain whether they will break your heart by taking off on a reckless flight of fantasy or dying young and breaking your heart anyway.'

'Valli! The things you say!' Appa rebuked her again and I could hear his strained tone as he fought to keep from voicing the outrage my mother's words had provoked in him.

I wished she would stop saying those dreadful things too, but I strained even harder to listen, particularly since I couldn't understand some of the things that were being discussed. All I knew was that their adult words thrilled and frightened me in equal measure. And I was determined to memorize the words for when I was grown up and could comprehend what had been said.

'It needs to be said. If your friend goes on in this manner, even if it is only to you, let me remind you that even the walls have ears and if something untoward were to happen, it will be hard for us to make another match for our only daughter if people feel she is already spoken for. People can be vicious and spiteful that way.'

'For a practical woman, you have the most morbid fancies,' Appa informed her in that superior tone I know she hated. 'Be assured, we have consulted the astrologers and the soothsayers. They have informed us that our Kannagi and Kovalan have shared many lifetimes together. And theirs is a timeless bond that shall never be sundered. For so it is written in the stars. They are meant to be. You need not worry on that account.'

Amma held her tongue though she was usually vocal about the ineptness of astrologers and the rest of their ilk.

'I don't know about all that. But if that stripling dares to break my daughter's heart, he shall answer to me. All your talk has resulted in her falling deeply in love with your friend's son, though she is still a child, and as anybody with sense knows, loving your spouse is a fool's move.'

'You say the most extraordinary things, Valli,' Appa sounded discomfited, 'and despite everything you say, it was love that helped our marriage weather many a storm.'

Amma snorted in response, but he persisted, 'They are going to be very happy together, you will see.'

'It is a long way in the future, is all I am saying. As for our Kannagi, if she is lurking about in the vicinity listening to conversations not meant for her ears or hoping for a glimpse of our young visitor, believe me when I say she is going to be deprived of her favourite *payasam* for a month, and I may forget myself, pick up a stick and…'

I fled. But of course, I *had known* all along. Amma was right about that, though I agreed with my father that she was worrying unnecessarily. While it was true that I could not always make sense of what they were saying, I understood enough. For instance, I knew for certain that he was the one I would marry, one day. Kovalan. Even his name was perfect. I hugged myself with excitement.

It was always lovely when he visited with his father. Whenever possible, I would try to catch a glimpse of him. Sometimes I studied him from a distance and listened hard to what he spoke or the things that were said about him. I wanted to understand him so that I could be the best possible wife to him. They said he was handsomer than Manmatha and Muruga, and that was true, although I must admit that I had no idea what either of them looked like. All I knew was that one was the God of Desire and the other a Warrior God who destroyed at will. But in my opinion, neither of them looked as good as my husband-to-be. Just thinking about it made me blush some more.

I ran along the long winding corridor, past the marble pillars with their intricate carvings, navigating my way past the many sculptures and objets d'art Appa's ships had brought back from faraway lands, past the enormous kitchen where the maids were slaving over their wooden stoves, pausing only to grab a handful of puffed rice, and out the back. Slowing down only as I scooted past the lotus pond to feed the fish, I hastened to the shady mango grove and clambered up the branches of my favourite mango tree. Given the commotion about the palatial house, I knew his father had arrived. From my vantage point, I could see the two old friends embrace and settle down in the courtyard, which was nice and cool for a long chat. Amma would serve them an assortment of delicacies that had been especially prepared for the occasion and that ought to keep them busy for a while. But where was the boy I was going to marry? There was no sign of him. What if he hadn't come? I suddenly found myself dangerously close to tears.

'I didn't know girls could climb trees.' His voice made me flinch and I almost fell off the branch I was precariously perched on. At that moment, I was so happy I could barely stand it. He had come. And he had found me.

'My grandmother could climb trees too,' I blurted out before I could stop myself.

'She sounds nice,' he replied, 'mine is always threatening to break my leg if I climb trees because she is scared I will fall and break my head.'

I smiled at that, and we both lapsed into silence as shyness overcame me again. Did he know that we were to be married and live happily ever after? I would have liked to ask him, but I couldn't. But surely he knew? And did the thought make him delirious with joy, the way it did for me? I glanced at him from beneath my lashes. He seemed so relaxed, and his entire being wasn't focused on me, that much was certain, while he was the sole object of my attention as well as affection. His eyes were fastened on the antics of two squirrels on another tree, and then he would glance at his father occasionally. I would have been disappointed at the disparity between our feelings for each other, had I been capable of feeling anything less than love for him.

We sat that way for the longest time while our fathers conversed, which made up a good part of the day. But it seemed to have flown by in a heartbeat, and yet again, I wished he would never leave my side. He smiled at me before he left, and I was giddy with happiness. Of all my memories of him, this one stands out—I don't know why. Up there among the branches, it was as if we had disappeared into a world that was just ours, and I suppose I liked having him to myself. Being with him felt so right and I was convinced that there was none in the three worlds as fortunate as I.

I lived for his visits. Or the chance to feel his presence close by when he was in the temple or the harbour. Every time he left, my heart grew heavy, and I longed to see him again. The days of my childhood were spent envisioning the perfect life with him. I played out entire situations and conversations in my head, and they were always flawless. But I knew that when we were married, it would be even better than the visions conjured up by fantasy, and I could hardly wait. Amma always shook her head in disapproval when she caught me daydreaming or smiling the secret smile that she knew meant I was thinking of him, which was all the time. But I paid her no heed. Her approval or the lack thereof did not matter to me. Only he did. And soon we would be together. Kovalan and Kannagi. Forever.

MADHAVI

Only One Rule: Never Fall in Love

MY MOTHER INSISTED that I call her by her name, Chitrapati, not Amma. She was very firm on this point, though she never bothered to elaborate on the reasoning behind her extremely unusual stance, especially since we lived in a land where the Amma sentiment ruled all and mothers were worshipped every bit as ardently as goddesses. It was one of the few times in my life I obliged her.

Although she detested everything about motherhood, Chitrapati was determined to play the role to the hilt and demanded implicit obedience from me. Unfortunately for her, I was born a rebel and determined to die as one. No wonder she always felt the need to emphasize that being my mother was the most trying aspect of a life that had already taxed her to the limits of her formidable will.

Paati, her mother and my dear grandmother, had been scathing. 'Chitrapati always assumed that she would stay young forever. For someone who thinks she is clever, your mother can be so stupid. As if making her own daughter refer to her by her name instead of using a more respectful form of address is somehow going to change the fact that men are not going to lose their wits over her fading beauty, or that her face and form are no longer her fortune.'

Paati would chortle loudly afterwards, deliriously satisfied with her efforts to shred her daughter's nerves to smithereens.

I called my mother Chittu. As a child, my tongue refused to wrap itself around the demanding syllables of her cumbersome name. She decided that the moniker was perfectly acceptable.

'How wonderful!' Paati would chime in sarcastically. 'Now people will most certainly be fooled into thinking that Chittu is Madhavi's sister, not her mother. After all these years, you are every bit as foolish as you always were. It is just pathetic that you refuse to age as gracefully as I did.'

Chittu frowned but said nothing. She had a healthy respect for Paati's temper and acid tongue. The two were constantly at each other's throats. But this was just the way things were between them. It was worse when they were really fighting and gave each other the cold shoulder. Their frosty silence terrified the entire household, and we would all cower under the storm clouds of their mutual animosity, waiting for the hostility to blow over. Chittu was always the one who caved. Paati would then go back to needling her, while her daughter responded in kind, doing anything at all that would earn her the grand old matriarch's instant disapproval.

I, on the other hand, got along very well with Paati, probably because she was far more approving of me than her daughter. But that was not the only reason. She was the *thaikizhavi* of our family and ran our rather extensive household like her personal fiefdom, which I suppose it was. Paati was fiercely proud of her ancestry and was keen to impress upon me the monumental stature of our lineage.

'We enjoy the patronage of our King Karikalan, who once remarked that we are like the gleaming rubies of his crown, adorning his kingdom with our auspicious presence and resplendent talent. It is he who built the massive temple for Pasupata in our

Poompuhar, to celebrate his many successful campaigns. Devotees come from far and wide for worship and to witness the divine spectacle of the best dancers in all the land, performing their hearts out, so that the Gods honour them by bearing witness and showering the land with blessings.'

Naturally, this turned out to be a boon for our sprawling community of dancers, musicians and others associated with the craft, who benefited from the King's munificence.

'We are closely associated with the temple thanks to my efforts, but no thanks to your mother, we have fallen out of favour with the temple authorities because she is a wild, wilful creature, who doesn't have the sense to listen to her mother. Fortunately, my reputation still counts for something in Puhar, and we were able to manage. Our future is going to be a magnificent one, because it lies entirely in your capable hands. And unlike Chitrapati, you take after me.'

All I knew of the lamentable business was that at the pinnacle of her career, mother had received a highly coveted honour—an invitation to join the royal household and serve the King himself. It was also known that she was forced to leave the palace under a cloud of secrecy and ignominy. Neither Paati nor Chittu would say more on the subject. It was most perplexing as despite everything, we had not completely fallen out of the sunshine of King Karikalan's favour, and he continued to extend his patronage albeit from a distance. Paati considered this a victory under the circumstances. Chittu, on the other hand, thought otherwise.

The same could not be said of the temple authorities who had slammed the door in our faces for whatever it was that Chittu had done to offend them. Years later, I learned from admittedly dubious sources that a little girl was involved. And she had died screaming under the weight of the pujari who had violated her.

The pujari was put to death, by order of the King. But the temple authorities seemed to be convinced that it was Chittu who had somehow been involved in the King's decision-making process and harboured a grudge against her for life.

I laughed out loud when I heard this story. It sounded most unlike Chittu. Especially since Chittu tended not to stand up for anyone or anything. Not even her own daughter.

Fortunately, God's depraved representatives in this world were no match for the might of a good king. Things would have gone very differently for us had it not been for Karikalan's benevolence.

By order of the King, our small community of dancers was bequeathed the whole street right outside the great Pasupata Temple. When Chittu was in her prime, Paati made sure that she received adequate recompense every time she performed. Thanks to her shrewd bargaining and perennial charm, we were allocated generous funds for running our household as well as land from the temple coffers and King Karikalan's overflowing treasury. They were not our only benefactors; many highly placed men in the kingdom vied with each other for Chittu's affection and generously showered her with jewellery, silks, bronze sculptures and more gifts than she knew what to do with. Even so, my mother seldom smiled, simply because she felt like it. Mostly, her smile, with its artfully concealed artifice, was merely a means of getting her what she wanted, and it usually worked. I wondered why she seemed to think there was so little to smile about. And why she felt she had nothing even when she had everything.

Poor Chittu was a bitter woman. She felt she had not lived up to her full potential, and her conviction in the matter gave her a sour look that detracted considerably from her charms and aged her before time, unlike Paati, who still retained much of her beauty, grace, cheerful demeanour, and all her cleverness.

In the astute manner that defined her, Paati had salted away sufficient money to ensure that our lifestyle would not have to suffer drastic changes when Chittu could no longer perform at the *sadhir katcheri*s and I was still training and couldn't contribute to the family's finances. However, there were other dancers Paati had taken under her wing and paid the expenses for their training. None made it to the heights of glory Paati and Chittu had achieved but they did well enough for themselves. The dancers were loyal, handing over their entire earnings to the thaikizhavi, knowing that they would be cared for.

Paati held the reins, and no decisions were made without consulting her, whether it was about booking performances, finding patrons, hiring the right musicians, commissioning works of art, the proper manner for disbursing funds, or just about anything else. The place was always a beehive of activity. Paati and Chittu were forever entertaining a stream of visitors, ranging from high-ranking dignitaries to people from humbler backgrounds who came to them for financial assistance.

No matter how busy Paati and Chittu were, they never took their eyes off me. From the moment I was born, it was impressed upon me that everything depended on my success as a dancer.

ꞌ

Paati had ordered the construction of a *silambu koodam* for my training. The most famous *nattuvanar*s and *vidwan*s of the time had been lured thither. Thanks to the combined efforts of Paati and Chittu, I would get the best instructors. The former was considered a living legend and so famed for her many talents and great generosity that none dreamed of refusing her. She regularly donated gifts of jewels, plates, bells and lamps of pure gold to the many temples that adorned the land and commissioned skilled *sthapathi*s to sculpt bronze idols, presented silver and gold to adorn the homes of connoisseurs and places of worship, and contributed to the maintenance of pleasure parks and gardens that dotted Puhar.

Her greatest joy was feeding the needy who flocked to the *chatram* she had built near our home, and the grateful poor blessed her with every mouthful. Later, Chittu would perform these same duties with diligence, for she knew that even though Paati was no longer among the living, she still had the power to strike her down for gross negligence of all the things that were sacred to her.

On the other hand, the vengeful temple authorities who had no qualms about accepting Paati's many gifts over the years nevertheless rejected her application to dedicate her granddaughter to the temple. Chittu was most distraught, but Paati was undeterred. 'We have served the Chola kings for generations and our ancestry can be traced back to Urvashi, the greatest of the *Apsara*s. I will be damned before I let those debauched old goats determine the fate of the jewel of our clan.'

Paati demanded and was given an audience with the King. She took me along for the momentous meeting. 'Keep still and don't you stare at his leg...' she warned me.

Naturally, I knew the story. Everyone did. Paati had told me the details often enough and I always listened with bated breath, because no one could narrate a story as beautifully as she did. She held me spellbound with her mesmerizing eyes that took on a life of their own and transported me across space and time so that I could live the stories. Later, people would say that my dancing transported them to fantastical realms or helped them to blissfully merge with the divine, and they would hold my hands with reverence and weep with joy, more grateful than they could adequately convey for the experience. In those sweet moments, I always thought of Paati.

'Before our King became the greatest of them all, he was merely a young prince whose father, Ilamcetcenni, was killed by a cowardly assassin and Bhoomi Devi, the Earth Goddess, drank her fill of a king's blood.' Paati spoke in hushed tones, and you could practically see the glistening blood, smell its sickly-sweet odour, and taste it at the back of your throat.

'His father's cowardly enemies tried to have him killed too. Heartless creatures who were so evil they paid no heed to the fact that Karikalan was merely a boy who had lost his father and stood to lose his inheritance as well...' she went on and I would shiver with dread, 'but he was too clever and tough for them. They set fire to his tent under cover of darkness while he was on the run, but he escaped though his legs were badly charred. Eventually, he destroyed all his enemies and staked his claim to the throne. Bhoomi Devi grew drunk on the blood of those who had wronged him.'

She would pause at this point, and I would pick up the narrative thread: 'In the two battles fought at Venni, he defeated a massive confederacy comprising the Cheras, the Pandyas and eleven rival chieftains. The Chera King, Perum Cheralathan, was so humiliated by the crushing defeat inflicted on him by the incomparable Karikalan that he killed himself. And Bhoomi Devi bathed in the blood of this unworthy King. Why do we revere those who fall on their swords and die, Paati? Surely, the sensible thing would be to live and fight another day? As long as there is life, there is always hope, isn't there?'

Paati would chortle in response, 'That is because men are seldom the tigers they fancy themselves to be. And are forever overcompensating for their very real inadequacies and overall impotence by hiring poets who work hard to bolster their egos by singing their praises and hyping their inconsequential acts in exchange for money.'

Paati looked at me with suddenly narrowed eyes to see how far I had understood and nodded in satisfaction before continuing with her story about our King who, unlike others of his sex, was very much a tiger among men. 'Following Karikalan's military triumphs, which culminated in him planting the Tiger Flag of the Cholas on the highest peak of the Himalayas, he turned to trade, which flourished under him. Our King is no bloodthirsty brute who leaves nothing but a trail of destruction in his wake. He built the engineering marvel that is the Kallidam along our Kaveri, saving us from the accursed floods and diverting the excess water into the newly constructed irrigation canals, making Thanjavur the most fertile and prosperous rice bowl in this land. And as you know, he also built and beautified Puhar, which is our pride and joy, making it the foremost centre for art, culture and learning. We are fortunate to have a King like him. May he live forever!'

∫

Karikalan cut an impressive figure, but what made a bigger impression on me were his courteous ways and surprisingly gentle manner. He gave me a broad smile which revealed his crooked and stained teeth. I looked at him surreptitiously, noticing that he was ancient, and his hair was snow-white, but it was thick and bristling with the same fierce energy reflected in his eyes. A pendulous belly swung up to his knees, but he held himself erect on legs which were still sturdy, despite the grievous burns he had suffered as a stripling.

Remembering Paati's strict instructions, I did my best not to stare, and the King obligingly sent for a platter of sweetmeats which I busied myself with while he conversed at length with Paati. I had no idea what they were talking about as their voices were low and it was too much of a strain to eavesdrop. I did as I was told and tried not to let my curiosity get the better of me.

After they had talked at length, Paati rose to her feet with an air of satisfaction. The King made the slightest gesture, and an attendant arrived with presents for us to take home to Chittu. To my delight, the sweets I had relished the most from the platter were among them. Paati watched closely as I went to the King to thank him for his kindness. I had planned to convey my gratitude most prettily but when I looked into his bulging eyes, which seemed on the verge of spilling out of their sockets, I could not find the right words. Instead, the most impertinent question popped out of my mouth before I could swallow it.

'It must have hurt a lot when your legs were on fire, your royal majesty!' I could have bitten my tongue off right then. Of course it would have hurt. It was a foolish thing to say to anyone, let alone the King, and I feared he would think I was a silly girl.

His eyes took on a faraway look, and I could feel the searing heat, hear the cackling of burning flesh and animalistic howls of pain, and feel his agony as the flames threatened to devour him. None of us was prepared for what he did next. He lifted his royal raiment a little and showed me a glimpse of the dreadful burns that nevertheless could not detract from the sturdiness and power of those limbs. The King watched my expression keenly.

'What a charming creature you are!' Those captivating eyes beneath his monstrous eyebrows were twinkling with merriment and I remember thinking he was not only courageous, but kind too. I immediately resolved to find someone like him to be my paramour in the future.

'I was fortunate to escape in the manner I did,' he chuckled.

'Believe me, it was a narrow escape. I crawled out of my tent in a rage that burned hotter than the flames, determined to give those thrice-damned assassins exactly what they deserved. But then I lost my balance and went tumbling down a slope. That saved my life. That and the whore who snuffed out the remains of the flames with her own sari.'

What is a whore? I wanted to ask, but held my tongue. Of course, I had heard the term before, but I wasn't sure what exactly it meant. All I knew was that a dasi was never to be confused with a common whore. Everyone in our household harped on this point incessantly, though they were less willing to tell me what it was that a whore did that made her so reviled. Paati was marginally more forthcoming: 'They provide a much sought-after service and get paid for it, but in the process they lose everything else that is valued in women, so they are always worth so much less than the coin expended for what they offer. In short, they are foolish women and inauspicious creatures.'

The King was still talking, and I could tell that he had revisited a painful place he hadn't been to in years, and I regretted having taken him there. 'I did manage to track down every single person involved in the heinous deeds perpetrated that night. I watched as the Fire God feasted on the flesh, blood and bones of the filthy traitors. Surprisingly, it wasn't as satisfying as you would imagine…and the stench was awful. I remember how dissatisfied I was that, despite my best efforts, I could not find the kindly whore who had saved my life. Because she was the only one among us who was worth her weight in gold. She alone did the right thing without worrying about rewards or punishments or being remembered as a hero.'

'You haven't forgotten her…' Paati said softly, 'and that counts for something. We won't forget her either, for the gift of our King.'

'I won't forget you and this little charmer here either,' the King said warmly. 'Our Madhavi is going to be the most beautiful, accomplished, and noblest of women. The poets will compose elaborate paeans in her honour. Her name and achievements will live long after our bones have fed the Fire God's insatiable appetite. I shall be watching her progress with keen interest.'

When we left, loaded with presents, Paati was beaming with pride and aglow with satisfaction. 'You did well, little one. It is almost like you are incapable of setting a wrong foot forward, even when your foot is in your mouth.'

∫

Chittu was somewhat less than overwhelmed with joy when we told her the glad tidings. I was to be trained as a *ganika,* a royal dancer, by order of the King and be exempt from temple service.

'What do you mean she is not to be dedicated to the temple? Then she will never have the status of a rajadasi!? It will not be possible if she is not given in marriage to our *ishta deivata* and branded with the Sacred Trisula, as you and I and all the dasis before us did to establish our exalted status as the Wives of God! If the proper rituals are not observed and she is not consecrated, how will she be revered as a *nityasumangali*, one who is eternally auspicious? People will think her a common courtesan and a mere dancing girl. They will heap infamy on her and she will be ruined.'

'Hold your tongue and cease your infernal prattling,' Paati snapped, 'it will be as I said. She will enjoy the patronage of the King, but she will not be tied to his court or to those evil creatures who run the temples, and she will have the autonomy to determine the shape her career will take.'

The grand old lady was dangerously close to losing her temper and Chittu quailed.

'You are a fool if you think people delude themselves into thinking that we are chaste, auspicious women just because the perverted priests perform their damnable rites and rituals for the ostensible purpose of uniting us in marriage with God, when in reality they merely wish to barter our bodies to the highest bidder. We *are* courtesans and dancing girls who have one or more patrons, and this is a truth we must accept with pride if we seek to use our exalted status to its best advantage. Madhavi here will be more famous than your typical *devadasi*s, and mark my word, people will remember her glorious achievements and celebrate her long after we are gone. The King himself said so, and I recognized the truth of it the moment I beheld her. Her training shall commence in earnest, and it is your duty to make sure she reaches her full potential.' Paati's eyes were flashing, and I knew that no one could contradict her.

At the time I was just glad that I would be trained as a dancer and didn't have to be branded with those silver stamps bearing the *trisula* (trident), the weapon of Pasupata. Some of the other dasis had the *sanku* and *chakra* mark on their forearms, indicating that their divine husband was Narayana, wielder of the conch and spinning discus. Everyone agreed that it was a painful procedure that left the dancers feverish and unwell for days. Later, all this just seemed fitting given the way my life turned out. Everyone believed I belonged to them all, but no one considered me as the only one to have and hold forever.

Meanwhile, Paati had the final word. In defiance of the temple authorities, she conducted a grand *sadhaka puja* to mark the commencement of my training as a dancer. The initiation rituals and ceremonial requirements were strictly followed. By now, everyone knew that Paati had secured the King's consent despite the efforts of the temple authorities to prevent my initiation. The head priest was very unctuous and officiated the event himself as a peace offering. To my surprise, Paati was most gracious to the odious man and almost buried him under a shower of gold coins.

Not to be outdone, Chittu was the epitome of warmth as she welcomed the priest and thanked him in language so ornamental it made my stomach turn. I lowered my eyes, looked demure and blushed as Paati had instructed me to do every time someone heaped excessive praise on my talent, which many said would supposedly make me outshine the celestial nymphs—the Apsaras—who adorned the sabha of Indra, the King of the Devas.

There were so many vacuous sentiments and insincere compliments on display that my ears burned from all the falseness. These were people who had delighted in the tidings that the end of Paati and Chittu's reign was near, and now that there was recent evidence of royal favour, they were falling all over themselves to ingratiate themselves with our family. What I didn't understand was why my mother and grandmother were putting up with all this, by smiling and speaking falsely in turn.

It was my first glimpse of the unscrupulous manoeuvring, duplicity, and the crafty ways that characterized what I thought was a simple community that prided itself on being nothing more and nothing less than purveyors of fine art. Paati, Chittu and the priest clearly revelled in the sport of it all. Even then, I knew I would find the devious scheming that would be part of my training distasteful. Not that I was ever a saint, but back then I foolishly believed I was above such things and was convinced that talent, hard work, honesty and an open heart would be sufficient to make all my dreams come true.

After the ceaseless worship concluded, we adjourned to the *koodam*. Chittu wanted to make sure I looked my best. After a bath where my hair and skin were scrubbed with herbal unguents and a paste made of turmeric, sandalwood and rose water to make my skin glow, I was dressed in a traditional green and gold costume. My hair had been oiled, plaited and adorned with jewels and strands of fresh flowers. My earlobes had to bear the weight of heavy gold *jhimki*s. The nose pins and rings were even worse, making me feel like the snot had hardened painfully in my nasal passages, but Paati said I would get used to it.

I wore strings of rubies and pearls around my neck and waist. Chittu carefully applied the kajal she had made herself to outline my eyes. 'Don't rub them, even if they make your eyes itch so badly you might be tempted to rip them out and toss them far away. Do you hear? Or cry,' she said tersely, 'no dancer worth her salt ever shows up anywhere with her eyes looking anything less than perfect.'

'Is that right?' Paati demanded caustically. 'As I recall, one of your lovers woke up in your arms, took one look at the black furrows streaked across your face and ran screaming into the street convinced he had lain with a *pisaasu*.'

I giggled at this, and Chittu frowned. Paati, meanwhile, was guffawing fit to burst.

The silambu koodam was a large hall, propped up by massive pillars that opened onto a carefully tended garden on one side. Stalks of paddy were scattered on the floor, which had been carefully prepared with compressed clay and dried cow dung, with water sprinkled over it. Over the course of the next seven years, this floor became an extension of my body, and I came to know it intimately.

A nine-yard sari was twisted and tied to two of the wooden pillars and I held it with both hands for support, although I had told Chittu earlier that I could balance perfectly well without such an unwieldy contraption. 'I used to imitate the steps of the older dancers and know the advanced *adavu*s pretty well,' I reminded her, but she quelled me with a reproving glare.

'Just do as you are told and keep your mouth shut!' she hissed.

My guru Sundaram Pillai, whom I always addressed respectfully as Ayya, had taken his place with the *thattukali*—a wooden block comprising a stick and base to direct the rhythm of the dancer in his hand—and commenced my first lesson as he chanted the *sorkattu* '*Theyya theyyi, theyya theyyi.*' Paati sat behind me, holding my feet by the ankles, moving them up and down to the rhythm in her firm and steady way. Ayya led us through the four speeds and neither Paati nor I faltered. He nodded approvingly and spontaneous applause broke out as I prostrated at his feet, received his blessings and presented my *gurudakshina* to him, which included gifts of gold and silver, along with the traditional offering of coconuts, betel leaves, flowers and fruits.

I didn't know it at the time, but I was very fortunate to have been trained by the best in the business. And when I look back, those were some of the greatest days of my life. The years I spent under the watchful eyes of my guru and nattuvanar par excellence, Sundaram Pillai, were immensely demanding, but richly fulfilling and deeply satisfying. I had never worked harder, but the effort was worth it. Chittu was delighted that I had taken to the rigorous training without feeling the need to rebel.

The next few years passed in a haze of frenetic activity. Vasantamala, who had been assigned the task of assisting the budding dancer, would wake me up long before sunrise, and help me bathe and dress for lessons. After I had offered my respects to Ayya, he would commence the singing and music lessons. There would be exercises for the throat and vocals, which Ayya would guide me through as I sang the scales repeatedly until he pronounced himself satisfied with the smallest of nods. At first light, there would be a short break and then Ayya would begin my dance training, along with exercises that had to be repeated endlessly to increase strength, stamina and flexibility. This went on for hours, but I did not mind because it felt good to move my limbs.

Outside of the beat, all I heard were Ayya's staccato instructions—a reprimand if my form was anything less than perfect or if my concentration wavered, and a crisp word of praise when he was pleased with my work. I revelled in the latter, as it was always sufficient to shake off my exhaustion and motivate me to work even harder to earn Ayya's always seemingly grudging approval.

Ayya would take a break during the hottest part of the day, when he would have his meal and settle down for a siesta. After a little refreshment, I would present myself for lessons with the other masters hired to help me play the musical instruments. I learned to play the *yaal*, flute, *nadaswaram* and drums. In the process, I absorbed the essence of *raga* and *tala* into my very bones and bloodstream. What an exhilarating experience that was.

My lessons would continue with Ayya in the evenings when the shadows had lengthened, and the lamps were lit. There would be lengthy discourses on the philosophical, mythological, spiritual and sensual elements we would explore and experience through the ancient art that had been bequeathed to us.

'All it takes is surrender,' Ayya would say repeatedly. 'Never forget that you are less than insignificant. Bow down to the superior might and majesty of music. Creation began to the divine beats that emerged when Shiva struck his *damaru*. Our destruction too will be to the beat of the damaru. The music was here before us, it will be around long after we are gone. Never forget that. We are privileged to be able to immerse ourselves in its vast splendour. To become one with its ebb and flow. Allow it to take you where it will… Enjoy the process, become one with it and revel in the union with the divine that will see you soar as something more fully realized than the sum of its parts.'

He was a soft-spoken man, but his words were filled with passion, and they inflamed the senses. Sometimes his discourses were so engrossing, none of us budged as he spoke, even when the time for meals came and went. Chittu would then serve us snacks in the silambu koodam, a departure from tradition that Ayya occasionally allowed, and we would carry on conversing but in a more informal manner. Ayya would share anecdotes about dancers, musicians and important dignitaries whom he had come across during his travels over the course of a storied career. I loved those meals we shared together and thought of them often, so I never forgot his words.

Within two years, Ayya decreed that it was time for my *salangai puja*.

It was a grand occasion, conducted in the silambu koodam. Paati sent for the greatest vidwans of the age and not even one declined her invitation. Their presence was important for they would assess my talent and pronounce judgement. If I managed to win their approval, my advanced training would begin in the more esoteric forms of *natyam* as well as its more elaborate and challenging pieces that only the most proficient dancers could perform.

Lord Ganesha, the destroyer of obstacles, was duly propitiated. Chittu carried around a golden tray with my new garments, *salangai*—the anklet of bells she had commissioned from a famous jeweller—as well as the customary coconuts, flowers, fruits, turmeric and betel nuts for the visitors to touch and offer their blessings. The tray was then placed on the altar. Paati tied the bells around my feet, and I prostrated before Ayya and the matriarch to obtain their blessings.

I then performed for the guests. Ayya had his thattukali and conducted the *nattuvangam* assisted by the vocalists and the rest of the *periya melam* comprising the musicians playing the lute, flute, nadaswaram and drum. I struck the floor firmly with my right foot and began dancing. Time ceased to matter as my heart surrendered to the music and my body followed. I danced in a feverish ecstasy to the timeless rhythms, revelling in the joy of performing the exquisite pieces Ayya had taught me. When I finished, the applause was thunderous.

The vidwans compared me to a light-footed gazelle, complimenting the perfection of my form, my exquisite grace, the intricacy and speed of my footwork, and soulful expressions which had wrung their hearts and left even the most jaded of them teary-eyed. To my surprise, Paati was weeping too. Ayya placed his hand on my head as I fell at his feet, 'I have never had a worthier student. May your fame last forever!'

It had been a glorious day, and I was immensely happy and satisfied. However, even the most beautiful emotions were transient. I woke up in the morning feeling curiously flat and emptied of all feeling. If that was not bad enough, Paati passed away peacefully in her sleep shortly afterwards.

Chittu was distraught. 'Her health had been failing for a while now. She could no longer see or hear as well as she used to. But she was determined to stay with us long enough to experience the joy of tying those bells around your feet. And when you reduced those proud vidwans to ardent admirers who worshipped at your feet, she could not have been prouder. If only she had lived to see your *arangetram*.'

I was devastated by her loss. My training had consumed me entirely and I had ended up barely spending any time with her. There was so much I had wanted to share and discuss with her.

I would have liked to ask her about the identity of my father, whom I never knew. No one said a word about him, uncaring that a daughter deserved to know the truth about her father. Or at least whether he was a prince or a pauper or something in between. I wanted to tell her of my growing disdain for remote Gods with stony hearts, callous men and callow love, and seek her advice. It had been my intention to discuss my observations with her regarding the slyness and superficiality of the many people who came into our lives. But now I would never have the chance to listen to that sardonic voice full of wisdom and wit.

I buried myself in training. Chittu took a more active role in certain aspects of my instruction which she felt was lacking. She taught me how to dress and adorn myself so that I could appear alluring to men. Naturally, I could not have been less interested, and it was Vasantamala who heeded mother's nattering and took on the responsibility of making sure I was suitably attired and always groomed, despite my lack of cooperation. She learned how to string flowers to adorn my hair, paint my breasts, and make fragrant unguents to perfume the body.

Chittu also insisted that I learn to comport myself with refinement and converse with charm. As soon as my training with Ayya was over for the day, Chittu would whisk me away so that some of the older girls could teach me the art of lovemaking and ways to please a man so that I could become an expert in the sensual arts. This time around, Vasantamala was not allowed to learn these things on my behalf. I hated being taught to flutter my lashes or walk by swaying my hips from side to side. I rebelled so often that Chittu was heartily sick of me and insisted that I would be the death of her.

Then there was the preparation of the *thamboolam*. I hated this elaborate ritual with a passion. Roasted and perfumed areca nuts, ground together with a spice or two, were wrapped in betel leaves and served to men with a dash of *chunnambu*, which was slaked lime and had accidentally blinded more than one curious child. It also reddened the lips and was favoured as a tool of seduction. It was a disgusting habit where people resembled cows chewing cud as they chomped on the lousy leaves with an imbecilic air, and they would spit it out into dishes placed everywhere for the purpose, though most missed and made an awful mess. Chittu, and Paati before her, would carry the *vetrilai potti*, a heavy silver box that contained all the ingredients for making these damn things, which I firmly refused to chew.

In dance, I found solace from Chittu and her attempts to make a seductress out of me, and it was my intention to submerge myself so deeply into the depths of my art that I would never resurface again in a world where I was expected to please men and take them as lovers. The notion did not appeal to me in the least and I wanted nothing to do with it.

At the time, I believed that my life was mine and that I could do what I wished. It was my plan to learn everything I possibly could from Ayya and carry on dancing for as long as my limbs were in working order. What a magical existence that would be. Who needed love or men when art offered so much more?

Ayya always shook his head when I shared my feelings with him. 'Be careful, child! Fate determines everything. It has endowed you with the gifts of beauty, talent and charm. In any case, I would suggest that you keep your mind clear of preferences and proclivities for they will lead you astray. And no matter what happens, do not tempt fate.'

I should have listened to him, but even if I had, there was no escaping the inevitable. For Kovalan was always going to be my fate. And I, his.

KANNAGI
Wedded Bliss?

Nothing had prepared me for how irrevocably dreadful it was going to be. Or how awkward. As for the embarrassment, even after all these years, I blush to tell of it. Amma did try to warn me and insisted that I get my head on straight and temper my excitement and expectations before everything spun out of control. In hindsight, I realize her advice was sound, but I had been in no mood to listen. I should have. It is too bad, that one must endure the bumbling process of being hopelessly stupid before belatedly stumbling upon wisdom. And I was hopeless. Hopelessly in love and bubbling over with happiness.

'I am glad you are delighted with our choice of spouse for you, but it is indecent to be this happy. The Gods frown on such unseemly displays of ecstasy.' Amma was frowning, but it was impossible for me to stop smiling, even though my cheeks and jawbone creaked in protest. But I didn't care in the least. It was finally going to happen.

Kovalan and I were to be united in matrimony. Henceforth, we would be together for the rest of our lives, and I just knew that it was going to be even better than my greatest hopes and fondest expectations. I could hardly wait for our life to begin and had little patience to listen to Amma's well-meaning advice or sit still as she made me try on one piece of jewellery after another and drape myself in the silky soft yet stiff silks that had arrived on Appa's ships, while haranguing me at length on how best to comport myself with care and prudence across what she stressed was the rocky terrain of marriage.

'Would you please wipe that smile off your face,' she scolded me. 'You are building up the impending union too much in that fanciful head of yours and setting yourself up for some serious disappointment. Not even a God can live up to such high expectations. Marriage is no different than anything else life has to offer. There will be good moments, but the sad truth is that these will be few and far between compared to the bad and ugly elements that are more liberally sprinkled across most marriages.'

I said nothing, but I felt Amma was worrying unnecessarily. She may be right about how challenging it was to make a marriage work, but it would be different for me. My dreams had been full of Kovalan for as long as I could remember, and they held out the promise of everlasting joy, and I could barely wait for them to come to fruition. The reality of a long-cherished dream must surely be better than the dream itself... I was sure of it.

My needs were simple, unlike those of my only friend, Devundi, who lived next door to us. Without her company, my childhood would have been so lonely, and I was very fond of her. She liked to talk and since I was a good listener, we got along very well. Devundi wanted to marry into the royal family and dreamed of becoming the Queen. 'You will always be my boon companion, Kannagi. In all of Tamilagam and the lands that lie beyond, you will be the only girl who is not dying to seduce the King and steal him away from me. So, I shall keep you close, and we will have so much fun.'

She always said things like this even around my mother and was undeterred when Amma snorted with laughter at her grandiose plans. As for me, I did not want anything at all except to be with him. All the time. *That was not a lot to ask for, was it?*

Our wedding day was fixed after Appa had consulted the astrologers. They had suggested the most auspicious of days, when the moon was closest to his beloved Rohini, the star and wife he loved most, and we were assured that those whose nuptials were concluded on such a perfect day would enjoy a lifetime of marital bliss and harmony. Appa and I were thrilled.

Frenetic preparations were underway, and both our households were a bustle of frantic activity, although it was impossible for me to process anything that was happening because my head and heart had room for nothing save thoughts of my husband-to-be. Both our mothers were insistent that the bride and groom not see each other before the wedding, and I missed seeing his dear face.

Devundi, who popped up all the time, wanted me to write pages and pages of passionate poetry which we would then smuggle to him, but I balked at the suggestion, not only because every idea of hers was guaranteed to be more outrageous than the one before.

'You are too timid!' Devundi scoffed. 'I think men like bold women. Why else do they all run behind those brazen devadasis with their deliberately coquettish ways? My mother says it is too bad that we respectable women can't compete with these trained seductresses in the arena of love. I probably would have a better chance of becoming the paramour of a king or prince were I a dancing girl!'

She struck a pose like a dancing girl, and that made me laugh. Personally, I cared nothing for what other men wanted. Appa told Amma and me that his friend had broached the official marriage proposal when he did because they had noticed that Kovalan could not take his eyes off me every time I happened to be anywhere near him, and that they would remain curiously alight for hours afterwards. His words had filled me with so much happiness that I could barely breathe. My husband loved me too, and that was all that mattered.

'This is no laughing matter,' Devundi chided me sternly, 'my mother says we would have been as rich as you, if my father had not squandered our fortune on some grasping dasi who had him dancing to her tune while pretending to dance to his. Amma says it's a good thing the girl found herself a younger and richer paramour after she had successfully abrogated my father's riches.'

It was typical of Devundi to say the most scandalous things, and I was shocked but, as always, I couldn't help noticing that my response seemed to encourage her to say more horrifying things.

In the meantime, there was a whirlwind of wedding-related activity around me as the most momentous day of my life drew closer. I was near breathless with pleasurable anticipation. Appa and Amma were determined to spare no expense to ensure that I had the perfect wedding. They even paid an exorbitant fortune to fetch the finest jeweller from Vanji, the famed capital of the Cheras, to our very own Puhar on one of Appa's ships to make my wedding ornaments. And the master craftsman worked hard for months to produce some truly exquisite pieces that became the talk of the town. Folks were constantly visiting us and Amma would show them the wedding jewellery and silks she was putting together for me. There would be loud exclamations of admiration, and the kind ladies would bless me and urge Amma to ward off the evil eye from the young bride-to-be before they left.

Amma was pleased with her own efforts and particularly enchanted by a pair of solid gold anklets that were so enormous and heavy, I could barely lift them.

'You will grow into them,' Amma exulted, 'and they will be the pride of your collection. Not even the Queens in our

The Wife and the Dancing Girl

Tamilagam and the whole of Bharatavarsha can boast of owning such a magnificent pair. Would you look at the delicate tracery and the engraved floral pattern, embossed with flawless rubies and diamonds? It looks so exquisite, I could have sworn that Vishwakarma, the architect of the Gods, made it for you himself. It looks so ornate and solid, but it is hollow inside and filled with precious little jewels. Can you hear them tinkling? It is the finest music you will ever hear.'

She waved them in front of me and I tried to respond enthusiastically, but without much success.

'Now pay attention, Kannagi!' Amma went on sternly. 'Your father wanted you to have something truly unique and extraordinary, so he asked his good friend Mikaman, the Sinhala chief of the Karaiyar community, to procure the rare Nagamani gems for you. It takes a special cobra with unique markings and hundreds of years to create this jewel from concentrated venom, which must not be expelled while this delicate task is being undertaken. And it is an even riskier enterprise for mortals to get their hands on these precious stones, but Mikaman delivered the goods. I stood vigil while the jeweller placed the Nagamani gems, which were obtained at great risk to life and limb, inside both your anklets, made from the purest *kilichirai* gold, named for the parrot's wing on account of the greenish hue. It was painstaking business, for the potent venom distilled in these gems must be handled with great care. The smallest mistake can lead to instant, agonizing death. That old man wept after he made the anklets and said that they were his finest work and that he would die happy having made something so incredibly beautiful!'

Appa was very pleased with the anklets, and he chimed in to tell me the story himself: 'Mikaman built ships with timber granted to him by the King of Eezham and he waged a war with his traditional enemies, the Mukkuvars. He fought their chief as well as his brothers before making it to Nagadipa, where he was able to procure many fabled treasures, but none as rare and valuable as the Nagamani gems. Endowed with the power of Lord Shiva, they are highly potent, and they will bestow fame as well as fortune on their owner and protect you from baleful influences and the venom of enemies. They can cause harm as well to those who have harmed the owner, which is nothing less than can be expected from a gift imbued with the essence of the Destroyer. My daughter is the best among women, and she shall have nothing but the best.'

His childlike enthusiasm was contagious, and I could not help thinking that I was truly fortunate to be my father's daughter. But it troubled me that a battle had been fought to obtain the Nagamani gems. 'Did so many have to die in order to make these anklets?' I asked hesitantly. It would have been ungrateful of me to say it, but I wished there had not been so much bloodshed to obtain these precious stones.

Amma frowned, troubled by the dark turn my thoughts had taken. 'A blood price must be paid for anything that is worth having, child. Look at all the beauty that surrounds you... Puhar's palaces, temples and our own home and fortunes were built on the blood and bones of the less fortunate. That's the way things are. There is no need to lose sleep over it, because that is how things will always be. This is the reason I keep telling you not to wander about with your head in the clouds, when you should be working on cultivating a more practical mindset.'

'She has the kindest heart and the sweetest disposition,' said Appa softly. 'I should have known better than to tell this particular tale given how much my daughter abhors violence. Erase it from your memory, child, and focus on the bright, shining future that awaits you. I know that all the treasures in the world would not impress you, because you are one among the rarest of noble souls, born without covetousness, but you are my only daughter, and I want to do everything I can to ensure that you never lack anything.'

I would always be grateful to my father for his generosity and thoughtfulness when it came to my wellbeing, but I could never forget the story he told me about the Nagamanis safely ensconced in my anklets. Amma made me wear them on my wedding day, force fitting them to my feet using fine gold wire to hold them in place. They were so heavy and beautiful, no doubt, but they were monstrously uncomfortable to wear.

While Amma was putting together the most enviable collection of gold and gems in the three worlds, wedding invitations were being delivered. Young girls from Kovalan's family and mine, mounted on richly caparisoned elephants, were sent out to do the job. They were accompanied by musicians who made sure that the news of the impending nuptials was carried across the length and breadth of the land.

Devundi was one of them, and she told me it was the most fun she had ever had. 'I kept an eye out for prospective grooms for yours truly, in case neither kings nor princes are willing to do the sensible thing and marry me, but I was surprised at the dearth of good-looking and wealthy men in our land. They are all too old, too fat, too ugly, too short, too stupid, too thin or too poor. It is a disgrace! And Puhar is crawling with beautiful women. I don't think that's fair at all. Everyone agrees that you have snatched up the best of the lot in terms of looks and wealth. And the best part is you managed the feat without even trying. You don't need to look so appalled, Kannagi. It is the truth.'

A huge pavilion was erected in front of our house and Devundi said, 'Your home has been transformed into Devaloka. The canopy is made of that brilliant mayil kazhuthu silk that your mother is obsessed with, and embroidered with the biggest, fattest and most flawless pearls I have ever seen. It is held up by gem-encrusted pillars, bedecked with strings of fresh flowers. It is going to be the wedding of the *yuga*. The people of Puhar will talk about the sumptuous arrangements for years to come.' She blathered on and on, but I was only listening with half an ear.

As for the rest, I can't seem to recall too many details of my own wedding. I remember being unsettled by the trickiness of time. Sometimes it felt like time had slowed down to a crawl in the months leading up to the big day, and yet it all seemed to have passed in the blink of an eye. Bits and pieces of ephemeral events remain vivid, but it is hard to tell the difference between the things that happened and the things I was constantly daydreaming about. I remember my heightened emotional state as I swung from giddy happiness to rank terror and back again. There were a lot of prayers, ritual baths, chanting, anointing with fragrant pastes and unguents, and endless dressing up. The ladies sang hymns while getting me ready and paid me excessively flowery compliments that made me cringe in embarrassment. 'She is so beautiful and virtuous. The very epitome of Arundhati, that jewel among women. This is why married women are asked to look to the heavens on their first night and seek her blessings to inspire them to similar heights of chastity.'

Despite everything they said, I had doubts about my attractiveness and fervently hoped that Kovalan would find me beautiful. My body was hardly special either and I thought I looked somewhat repulsive without my clothes. What if he felt the same way? It was not like I had the greatest of personalities either. I was not vivacious like Devundi or clever and charming as Amma, who had the ability to say and do as she pleased while staying adored. It took effort for me to talk, and it was near impossible for me to laugh out loud. Mostly, I preferred the comfort of silence. Would he think I was boring and dull? I prayed that wouldn't be the case and swore to myself that I would be the best wife I could possibly be and devote my life to taking care of his every need. Surely those qualities were more important than beauty or charm?

The wedding passed by in a blur. I must have looked as solemn as I felt, because Amma nodded approvingly as the priests droned on and on, chanting the holy incantations. I stood still like a statue carved in stone and nearly sank into a state of dazed stupor while the interminable wedding rites were performed. It was painful for me to feel the eyes of everyone in the crowd on me, jabbing at my sensitive skin with the intensity of hot needles, but I bore it with all the stoicism I could muster, knowing that I had a lifetime of happiness to look forward to.

Weighed down with jewellery, flowers and the heavy sari of pure gold and crimson silk threads, I dared not look up at my beloved. My eyes welled up without warning as I was assailed by a storm of heady emotions and sudden dread. That was when he took my trembling hand in his. I still remember how comforted I felt as he gently stroked it while leading me around the sacred fire seven times. And suddenly, the way he made me feel was the only thing that mattered, and just like that, my nervous foreboding vanished, and I was happier than I could stand.

∽

Some things are best forgotten. Unfortunately, these are the things you remember despite your best efforts not to. After the wedding festivities, we were taken to his home. My in-laws had graciously prepared the middle floor of their palatial mansion for us to stay in. It had been thoughtfully filled with every possible comfort, but it is the couch that I remember.

The couch was made in a time before memory, and it was said that Maya, the architect of the *asura*s, had carved it expending all the skill and prowess that marked him as the best of the best. The legs of this couch were studded with dazzling gems, and we reposed on it often, as a prelude to our lovemaking, which I came to dread.

He would take my hand and lead me out onto the terrace, where a petal-strewn bed was laid out as per his specifications, since he loved to gaze at the night sky bedecked with a profusion of silver stars and the golden moon as he enjoyed the breeze. He loved undressing me and I submitted, suppressing my own distaste for this kind of intimacy simply because he was so eager and enthusiastic.

Our clumsy fumbling seemed to give him joy and that made me happy. And he was so eager to please me. If it wasn't for the fact that the physical act of making love made me sick to the stomach with a combination of dread, fear and outright revulsion, I might have enjoyed it too. He would trace patterns on my bare shoulders, chew on my earlobes, and plant soft, wet kisses on my neck and across the length and breadth of my body, pausing every time I stiffened in reflexive alarm, massaging my limbs until my protesting flesh became pliant again. With his lips and tongue, he familiarized himself with every nook and cranny of my person, much to my chagrin, which I could not disguise despite my best efforts. Sometimes I cried because it was just too overwhelming, and he rocked me in his arms until I calmed down. He would go on holding me until I fell asleep.

Sometimes, when I woke up, he would be grunting and

heaving on top of my body while inside me, his face suddenly bestial with animalistic lust. I would become paralyzed with terror, so I held still and let him do whatever he wished to because I loved him, even if I hated what he was doing. I hated my body's shameful responses even more and loathed the sticky secretions that trickled down my legs like a dreadful accusation. Surely there were more decent ways to love, be loved and make love?

It was even worse when I woke up a little later than usual after a night of vigorous, extremely painful lovemaking that left me sore and aching, and he was nowhere to be seen. I bawled my eyes out because I couldn't bear the thought of being parted from him.

As it turned out, he had merely gone for a walk to stretch his limbs. He was most solicitous when he saw the state I was in. 'Did something happen to frighten you?' he enquired, wiping away my tears with his hands and pulling me close to him. Relieved, I let myself fall into his embrace and tried to find the right words.

'You were not there…' I managed to sputter, and he was incredulous with amazement.

'But it was just for a minute, and I came back, didn't I?' he soothed me. 'Please don't cry. It was so thoughtless of me.'

I hugged him fiercely, wanting to disappear into him. It was a mistake. Encouraged by my actions, he pushed me back onto the crumpled bed with the crushed petals and insisted on taking me right then and there, under the harsh glare of the sun. I felt the gaze of our attendants on the telltale marks of his passion on my face and form, and I was mortified.

The truth I can admit to myself now is that I wanted nothing at all to do with the love play that he was so keen on. It was messy, sticky and filled with smelly bodily fluids that overpowered the intoxicating scent of all those newly opened buds that wafted over our entwined, writhing forms on the terrace over the course of those balmy nights that were too long for my liking and too short for his.

It was impossible for me to derive pleasure from prurience. I wish it were not so. Eventually I would learn to tell the two apart and perversely, when all hope of pleasure was snuffed out, I yearned for it till I hurt all over. But by then it was already too late.

I liked our quiet moments together. Or when he shared his thoughts with me. Like Devundi, he thought I was a good listener. 'I know that my father would like me to follow in his footsteps and relieve him of some of the responsibilities of running the family business. And it makes me happy to ease his burden, but the truth is, I have neither the inclination nor aptitude for business.'

'What would you rather do?' I asked him.

He would shake his head with the restlessness I could sense uncoiling deep inside him. 'That's the thing, I am not sure… Sometimes, when I hear a particular haunting melody, I want to follow the tune and explore the worlds it transports me to. When I hear the siren call of the waves, I want to depart on one of the ships and travel to the far corners of the world and beyond. On rainy nights, when the wind howls in my ear and the thunder roars across the stormy sky, I want to ride the lightning and make my way past the stars to the heavens above.'

Of course, his talk alarmed me. None of these journeys sounded remotely close to feasible or appealing. Worse, I could not help but realize that he had no place for me, his wife, in these wild, improbable dreams. I pushed these disturbing thoughts away and smiled at him. 'I hope you get to experience all these things, and more importantly, I hope they make you happy,' I said instead.

He smiled in response, 'I am so blessed. A man could not ask for a more understanding wife. Anybody else would tell me to stop raving like a lunatic and embrace the good fortune I was born into, instead of hankering after that which may just turn out to be my ruin. And they would be right, you know...'

I never knew how to respond to that, but it didn't seem to bother him. Instead, he would hum his favourite tunes and when he got bored with that, he would tickle my armpits or suck my toes and fingers or twiddle my nipples and playfully tug my hair while I would swallow the words that rose up unbidden, insisting that he stop playing with my body parts because I did not enjoy it in the least.

'You are too serious!' he would tease me constantly. 'An old soul in a ravishing young girl's body.' Then he would chase me around the house and scoop me up in his arms in front of the entire household and I would bury my face in my hands, unable to bear the soul-crushing humiliation.

For someone who made me so happy, he also had a penchant for making me miserable. It was confusing for me then and still is. I liked it when he pampered me with attention, provided it was not amorous in nature. He would always buy some fancy trinket for me while going about his business in the port. A bronze lamp, a piece of jewellery, a new sari, a string of flowers, or my favourite sweets and snacks. It warmed my heart to know that he had thought of me and cared enough to find out what would make me happy. I loved him every time he made me smile. But then he would pinch my cheeks or press his lips against mine as his tongue snaked its way inside my mouth, and the merriment would fade from my features and the joy drain from my soul.

Sometimes, he would be moody and lost in his own thoughts. I would sit quietly at a distance, eager to help him in any way

I could. But when I felt the irritation and curious animosity my presence stirred in him, I would wince inwardly as if he had struck me with a whip. And so we would remain, trapped in that awkward silence until he drifted off into troubled slumber, and I would stay awake, anxious about the distance that had sprung up between us, dreaming of the intimate moments we used to share when I had felt so close to him, wishing for things to go back to the way they had been. A few days would pass like this and suddenly he would be himself again, making me so happy, I would immediately forget how cold and remote he had been, until it happened again.

Still, there was nothing I loved better than caring for him. Anticipating his needs and taking care of his every wish before he could articulate them made me feel good. Nursing him back to health when he was unwell filled me with contentment. It was immensely satisfying to prepare his favourite meal with my own hands and serve it to him. 'It tastes heavenly!' he would smack his lips in delectation and insist that his parents try my cooking and pronounce the same judgement. I would lower my eyes in embarrassment, while they obliged and indulgently praised me. On learning that I had not eaten, he would feed me with his own hands, despite my protests.

'We have attendants to take care of the cooking,' my Athai would tell me, but not unkindly, 'you mustn't tire yourself. A slight creature like you must focus all her attention on bearing children. I thought that would have happened by now, given the ruckus the two of you raise every single night to rival the most raucous of crows, but there is no need to worry unduly. Sometimes, these things take time. And patience.'

Athai took no notice of my mounting agitation at this frank exchange. 'I had my Kovalan after years of prayers and unceasing toil in the marriage bed. Mercifully, he was a healthy boy, and I ceased all my labours in that direction immediately, though everyone told me I was a fool for not trying to have more children. I had the good sense to ignore such talk, and I haven't regretted it since. I suggest you do the same.'

'There is no need to rush things,' Kovalan said with his characteristic light-hearted laugh, when he came looking for me and realized that his mother had cornered me first. 'Why can't we focus on each other for a while? In fact, I think *you* should redouble your efforts, Amma, to give me the sibling I have always wanted. And Appa does occasionally talk about how he has always wanted a daughter. A Mahalakshmi like our Kannagi here.'

'That is a brilliant idea!' my father-in-law chimed in with a bark of laughter, delighted with his son's insouciance and characteristic disregard for his mother's strict ideas about perfect decorum.

Athai frowned irritably and I flinched involuntarily. Father and son did not notice because they were clutching their sides and screaming with laughter.

'Boys never grow up,' Athai said with dignity. 'That way they can torment their mothers and wives and get away with it for the rest of their lives. So it is entirely up to you, my dear, to honour my wishes.'

I wanted to please her, but the birthing bed held even more terrors for me than the marital bed, if that was even possible, and I shuddered at the prospect of more pain that supposedly promised pleasure.

In about three years, Athai and Mama decided that the time had come for us to have a home of our own. Initially, I was nervous about running a household, but Athai said I had been a good student and had learned everything she could teach me about managing a home. That was most generous of her.

My dear in-laws took care of everything between themselves to make sure that all our needs were more than adequately met. The new house had three floors and spacious terraces thoughtfully designed so that their beloved son could bask in the moonlight and salty sea breeze that he loved so much. The wooden balconies had beautifully rendered carvings. From the third floor, we had a breathtaking view of the bustling streets of our great city, the magnificent temple dedicated to Pasupata, and our King's palace, all the way out to the blue sea.

My Athai took care of the furnishings with loving attention to detail. She even made me a present of polished silver and bronze vessels exclusively for my use, a new wardrobe and some treasured pieces from her own jewellery collection, in addition to hand-picking a retinue of attendants and maids to help me run the household.

Every bit as considerate, my Mama handed over vast stores of wealth he had set aside for his only son, to manage our expenses and invest it as Kovalan saw fit. I loved that the family logo, which featured fantastical beasts of the sea set against a profusion of flowers and trees, had been painted or engraved in various parts of the house. It was truly a blessing to have been married into such a wonderful family, and I was more grateful than I could convey to my loving in-laws. With a full heart, I prostrated myself at their feet and received their blessings.

Kovalan insisted on carrying me over the threshold, ignoring my muted protests, but not even that could dampen my enthusiasm at having a place of my own. I was determined to take my duties as wife and hostess seriously. Amma, Appa, Devundi and all my relatives would visit often, and I would receive them with dignity and serve refreshments as per their preferences, which I took careful note of.

Athai had trained me well, and Amma said she was pleased with my newfound sensible approach to life. 'You are no longer the giddy girl whose head is stuffed to the brim with fanciful dreams. How dignified you have become. Your father is so proud because several of his acquaintances have been telling him that his daughter is the best of wives and a credit to her father. Your Athai was also full of praise for you and said she is pleased with the amount of effort you put in to practise time-honoured traditions that are a boon to both our families. Of course, her happiness and mine would be complete if you hurried up and brought forth a baby girl or boy.'

My cheeks turned crimson, but naturally that did not stop Amma from expounding at length about the ideal sexual positions for childbearing, the medicinal potions I should take to maximize fertility, the Gods I should invoke, and so on and so forth, until I felt physically sick with repugnance at the direction the conversation had taken. She shook her head sadly, 'And here I was, afraid that you had grown up too quickly, but you are still the silly girl who tries my patience almost as much as her father does.'

Devundi was almost as bad. She did not pressure me to get pregnant at the earliest, but she insisted on sharing salacious details about the most intimate aspect of the husband–wife relationship, much to my discomfort. She had married shortly after me and had already produced three children in quick succession. Fortunately, she wasn't too disappointed that she hadn't married a member of the royal family, although she always exulted that her husband was a merchant prince like mine.

'He may be older and grotesquely overweight, but he is most generous when it comes to paying heed to my occasionally extravagant demands, and I couldn't be happier. I am glad I gave him the sons he wanted, but you shouldn't worry too much about getting pregnant. It will happen in good time. Besides, these things are not in our hands,' she pointed out sensibly. 'I only wanted one son myself, but the Gods insist on blessing me with more and more to the point where I wish they would spare me their excessive largesse.'

She ignored my lack of a response and went on talking. 'It is too bad you cannot enjoy connubial bliss without bringing forth babies. I keep promising myself to practise abstinence just to spare myself the evils of birthing and breastfeeding and wiping shit-stained little bottoms, but I just can't seem to control myself. My husband is even worse, so it is certain we will have a thousand children and wind up on the streets having burnt through his massive fortune. That is, if I don't get killed during the gruelling labours of childbirth!'

She waited a moment to see if I would divulge any unseemly details about my own love life and resumed talking when I refused to oblige her curiosity. 'You are fortunate to have a place of your own. The sight of my mother-in-law's accusatory, perpetually critical visage is such a deterrent to the enjoyment of the limitless pleasures afforded by our bodies, but at least she dotes on her grandchildren, so I can leave the brats in her care and tell her I am off to pray in the temple before coming here to see you. How nice it is to see your dear face. You have become too wrapped up in your duties and have forgotten your friend. I would scold you if you weren't such a sweet thing, and I didn't have to rush back before my mother-in-law screamed herself hoarse and actually made good on her threat to throw me out of the house.'

Amma, Athai or Devundi would take me to pray in various temples on festivals, and on one such occasion, I witnessed a young girl being executed before my eyes. I collapsed in a dead faint and woke up to the sight of my mother's worried face looming over mine. Devundi was there too, torn between ascertaining if I was fine and turning back to the gruesome sight of the poor woman, whose body lay twitching in silent protest.

'Why did they do this to her?' I whispered, tears forcing their way out, even though I knew the sight would make Amma impatient.

Devundi rolled her eyes. 'It is obvious enough… A fallen woman has no place in society, especially not in one that places a heavy premium on womanly virtue. I am assuming they told you the same things I heard every single day of my life, from when I had barely learned to wipe my own bum. Rains favour the land adorned with virtuous women who let nothing, and no one, sully their exalted status as pure women. A land where the women's conduct is flawless will never know the evils of drought. The land that is blessed to be populated with nothing but *pattini*s will flourish and the kings who rule over such exemplary female subjects shall never taste of defeat. Of course, such an impossibly high standard of ethics need not be adhered to by men.'

'Keep talking in that wretchedly shrill voice that could shame the crows off their perches and prompt them to shit on your stupid head,' Amma snapped at her before turning her attention back to me, her expression softening when she realized I was still shaking. I tried to be brave like her, but I just couldn't.

'You know the laws of the land…' she said gravely. 'Thieves, loose women, adulterers, false godmen, frauds, murderers and the corrupt will receive capital punishment. This is necessary because we cannot allow immorality and vice to undermine the foundation of our society, despite what your loudmouthed friend has been blabbering.'

'Her only mistake was that she was careless enough to get caught while committing adultery, and being unfortunate enough to have a vindictive husband,' Devundi said carelessly and unapologetically in the face of my mother's mounting irritation. 'The law says that loose women will be executed. But the same law looks the other way when dasis build their fortunes on the strength of their promiscuity and lascivious lifestyles. In fact, many minions of the law at the highest echelons are their patrons and take a share of their ill-gotten gains, and don't even get me started on the brothels and pleasure houses that infest our land. Most men frequent these dens of iniquity and spend lavishly for a taste of illicit and possibly disease-dispensing pleasure because they know they will not be dragged into the streets, accused of adultery and executed. But when a bored housewife finds herself a lover, everyone thinks it is necessary to make an example of her.'

Amma gave her a sharp look. 'We can argue about the unfairness of it, but it would be pointless. The law is different for men and women for reasons that have always escaped me, but all I know is that women can never afford to be as stupid as men. Kama's gift is a dangerous one for a woman, and succumbing to its pleasures is ultimately not worth it. Few men have what it takes to satisfy a woman physically or emotionally, and embarking on a quest to find one at the risk of losing life and limb calls for a degree of stupidity that deserves to be punished with disgrace and death.'

'My husband is worth it,' I said quietly, 'he is my everything and always will be. No matter what.' Amma and Devundi seemed taken aback by my sudden vehemence, so I quieted down.

The incident left me deeply disturbed and Devundi's views filled me with horror. For days afterwards I suffered nightmares, and Kovalan soothed me like a child until I stopped shaking. In those hateful dreams, I was always naked on the street, indifferent to the rude gaze of onlookers, and I was fondling my own breasts in a brazen manner that left me sick with disgust before they chopped them off, and my head as well, while flames raged in the background. Then I would wake up screaming and shuddering, while my perplexed husband did everything he could to calm me down, even though I refused to tell him what was troubling me. When he tried to make love to me, the violent shaking and trembling would return in earnest, along with the tears, and he would stop at once. For that alone, I owe him my very life and more.

Comforted by his forbearance, I began to assert myself more. My attendants were instructed to prepare meals that would be served to ascetics, travelling monks, mendicants as well as the poor and the needy. Feeding hungry people made me happy and I was determined to make sure that those in need of nourishment would always find a hot, nutritious meal at my home at all hours. I began observing fasts and practising the strictest abstinence to ensure a long life and prosperity for my husband. Kovalan was rather amused at first. 'You are becoming more and more like my mother,' he would say with a laugh.

There were times when he was hurt by my refusal to accept his embraces on account of religious demands, but when I quietly undressed of my own accord and lay down beside him, making it clear that he mattered more to me than all the Gods in the pantheon, he would apologize and urge me to get dressed and go to sleep. His respect for my feelings made me love him even more, as if that were even possible.

I slept on a mat beside his bed so as not to tempt him unduly, massaging his head and limbs with soothing ointments to calm him down, humming his favourite tunes to lull him to slumber. He surrendered to my ministrations and seemed happy that I still devoted my entire being to taking care of all his other needs. For the first time, I was perfectly content and happy with all aspects of my life. I thought he was too. But of course, I could not have been more wrong.

MADHAVI

Money and Honey

Chittu was impatient for me to grow up. She dreamed of the day when I would successfully perform my arangetram, launch my career as the best and most sought-after dancer in Puhar, find an obscenely wealthy patron, and artfully siphon off his fortune to replenish our own. Once his funds ran out, I was to find another patron, and so the whirligig of wealth wringing would go on and on. The idea, of course, was to find that one man whose wealth and regard for me would never run dry. A few dancers even managed this feat, but for all I knew, they were creatures from the realm of myth and legend conjured up by storytellers, because like our celestial counterparts, the Apsaras, we were all treated like currency meant to pass through many hands. The difference being that in the case of Apsaras, their value remained undiminished.

Mere mortals like Chittu and I would grow older and not wiser, but merely embittered and chewed up. Then it would be my daughter's turn. Just thinking of it made my gut heave, so I always tried to turn my thoughts elsewhere; not that there was any escape—anywhere at all. A fish must swim. And a dancing girl must dance and lead men on a rambunctious romp replete with ribaldry cleverly disguised as refinement. Someday the jig would be up, and then what would be left?

It was a curious thing but despite having grown up cradled in the lap of luxury and opulence, there was always an acute sense of uneasy privation, an overwhelming feeling that there simply wasn't enough money to go around, let alone lavish on the gorgeous things we surrounded ourselves with. Chittu somehow managed to scrounge up the funds to fill our bellies, our bodies and our lives, fit to bursting with every conceivable extravagance that could be imagined, so that we could maintain the high standard of living we were used to, studiously maintaining the tragicomic charade that we could afford to live like royalty.

Did kings feel the same pressure to live like kings? I would never know. Not until our King Manarkilli, the late Karikalan's son, chose me to join the royal *anthapuram* with the rest of his wives and concubines. This was what Chittu wanted. I heard her tell Vasanta when they both thought I was asleep, 'How sweet she looks when she sleeps. Mercifully, Brahma saw fit to lavish on her the invaluable gifts of beauty, talent, and a charming disposition, even though we both know she can be moody and difficult.

'I have tried and failed to teach her the tricks of our trade. It bothered me no end that she refused to learn, but finally my mother rightly pointed out that the only quality valued by men which most dancers lack is innocence, and that can't be taught. And very rarely feigned. Madhavi has this quality, and mother said that this charming cluelessness of hers would help her find the right man, perhaps a king who will become besotted with her for life. And she will become his favourite without even trying, and we will all benefit from this match.'

'That goes without saying,' Vasanta agreed, 'and it will be a foolish man who lets her go, but I am not sure she will be suited for a life in the royal harem. Madhavi is a free-spirited soul, and she will not like the suffocating rules and restrictions that are enforced in court. In addition to that, she idolized Karikalan. His son, Manarkilli, our King does his best but...'

'Don't you let that foul tongue get away with you, foolish girl! My mother would have had your hide for that. This is what I get for being so kind-hearted. The trouble with girls today is that your mouths are a lot bigger than your brains, and to compound this grave limitation, you think you know better than your elders. We will not talk anymore of this, but I know what is best for my daughter, and like it or not, she will do her duty. As long as she does not squander away the gifts she was born with by getting carried away with those fine scruples of hers, which a dancing girl simply cannot afford, we will be protected and looked after for the rest of our lives. Run along now and fetch my vetrilai potti!'

Chittu left too, muttering to herself. I sighed deeply. If she had her way, I would become the King's mistress and resign myself to a life in a gilded cage, watched over day and night by the palace guards, and die a little every single day. Kings, like other ordinary men, were known to be unreasonably possessive about their possessions, and I knew too many dancers who had been prevented from dancing or even leaving the harem because their royal lover was loathe for others to partake of their charms, and they were confined to this prison of affection long after the king had lost interest in them. As far as I was concerned, this was a fate worse than death.

Ayya, meanwhile, had other plans. The head priest of the Pasupata Temple was invited to watch our practice sessions, and contrary to what Chittu believed, I was not entirely clueless. The man was revolting, though he was considered an expert on the Vedas and Shastras, a fine scribe and one of the most powerful men in the land, especially since Manarkilli, who was not quite the man his father was, sought his opinion on all matters of state. Some openly declared that he was the most powerful dignitary in the land. He seldom looked at me, choosing to close his eyes and hum along to the music, but when he left without a backward glance or a word of acknowledgement to me, I nevertheless felt unclean and was dangerously close to tears. Nothing escaped Ayya's notice, but I knew that if he had his way, I would find myself in that creature's bed. This betrayal from the man I had always treated as the father I never had was more than I could bear. And it hurt more because I still craved his love and approval.

Meanwhile, Vasanta was keen for me to take the newly appointed commander-in-chief, Senapati Seyon, as my lover. She had seen him during a victory procession and could not stop gushing about how perfect he was for me and swore he was the handsomest man in the land. I had no wish to have anything at all to do with him. He sounded like a violent man who would sacrifice his own mother, wife and daughters if it meant furthering his authority, and I wanted nothing at all to do with men like that. Too many had died bleeding from every orifice, after these military men got drunk and lost control. The thought of being the lover of a fighting man made me shudder and I shivered uncontrollably.

Surely there was a better way to live? Why couldn't I just dance like there was no tomorrow? Why should my dance serve the sole purpose of attracting men I didn't want in the first place? Some days I wanted to run away and become one of those Jaina or Buddhist monks who looked so beautiful and peaceful, even with the rags they wore and the shorn heads they sported. And why couldn't we live more frugally? Then we would not feel compelled to do the things we did. But Chittu would only say that I knew nothing.

All I knew was that we ate like kings and entertained like emperors, even though we could scarcely afford to live that way.

Our association with temples continued, and like a bottomless pit of ever-present need, the decadent dwellings of the Gods and Goddesses demanded massive contributions from us in the form of gold and silver. The more we gave, the more was required. Chittu never demurred. Many a *gopuram* was covered in gold and pillared *mandapam*s studded with precious gems thanks to her unstinting largesse, paid for by the blood, sweat and vaginal discharge of the dancing girls in her care. These were my sisters, and we often trained together. They were full of bawdy stories and laughter, but I could not help but notice that with every passing day their smiles grew wider, but they seldom reached the eyes, where only sadness lurked.

A dancer was supposedly chosen for training on the strength of her beauty, brains, talent for dance, aptitude for music, and robust health. I knew that Paati would check and see if a potential dancer's breath smelled sweet first thing in the morning. She said this was the surest indicator of good health, and many a hopeful was turned away because they failed this exacting test. Paati would scrunch up her nose in distaste and remark acidly, 'Her mouth stank of decomposition. She is well on her way to becoming a corpse sooner rather than later. Get her out of my sight.'

But it was hard to find girls who met all these stringent requirements. Not everyone was blessed with both beauty and blinding natural talent. Even then, there was no guarantee of success. Some were lazy and lacked the discipline to endure and get the most out of the rigorous training that relentlessly demanded all we had to give and more. Every single day. Most were stupid, content to settle for middling returns from performances on street corners or in bawdy houses of ill-repute and mediocre men of measly means. Others were merely unfortunate. They might be blessed with the looks, the requisite talent, and the ability to work hard but fame and fortune eluded them. Either way, too few had what it took to dance their way into the hearts of thousands and secure not just their future, but also that of all who depended on them. It was a high-pressure situation, and many crumbled under it. But not Paati, or even Chittu, for that matter.

Given the dearth of talent, or because these were mostly desperate times, Paati, Chittu and other dancers who were past their prime sometimes purchased dancers from destitute families. These unfortunates gave away their girl babies in exchange for a few coins, assuaging their conscience with the hope that the discarded daughters would have a better life. Superstitious upper-class folks were also known to do the same, because unscrupulous fortune tellers had predicted that a hapless newborn girl baby was ill-omened and destined to drive the house of her birth to dire straits unless she was dedicated to the temple and left to the tender mercies of depraved priests and perverted pimps.

My best friend, Vasantamala, had been abandoned at our doorstep. Chittu, who did not have a sensitive bone in her body, was happy to inform Vasanta that whoever had done this had not even waited long enough for the gift of a bag of coins or ensure that the baby was not carried off by stray dogs. Vasanta would cry herself to sleep whenever Chittu chose to regale us with this story, and it would be years before my attempts to soothe her would work.

Of all these girls, some did manage to carve out a decent career for themselves if they managed to learn fast and survive the cut-throat competition. A rare few managed to thrive, going on to become women of substance and means. They were famed across the length and breadth of the land for their expertise in music, dance, poetry, and scholarly treatises they composed on matters ranging from love and good health to the proper pursuit of spirituality, as well as their charitable work.

But the vast majority were ground down beneath a punishing system where the dancer was condemned to institutionalized servitude in order to serve the carnal appetites of men, mercilessly exploited, and cast out to the fringes of society, where the slavery they sought to escape mercilessly closed in on them. But we did not acknowledge or talk about these things. We distracted ourselves with pretty things, wore the finest clothes, adorned ourselves with the costliest jewellery, smiled sweetly, and danced our way into a state of pure bliss and oblivion, determinedly allowing the superficial glare of glamour to blind us to the inequity that was the hallmark of our lives.

The older girls who made their homes with us and trained in our silambu koodam worked hard to fulfil the financial needs of the household. Paati, and after her Chittu, had singled them out for the training and bore most of the expenses. After their arangetrams, Chittu made sure the debt was fully repaid. They worked hard on their feet and backs but couldn't satisfy my mother, who extracted all their earnings, giving them only the barest minimum to keep body and soul together.

The competition was fierce and all the dancers from our community vied for the limited spots in the royal *sabha*s, temple festivities, performances at weddings, and private salons. They fought each other to win the hearts of the miniscule percentage of men of true means who could afford to keep them in the style they were accustomed to. These men were infuriatingly faithless. The dasis and ganikas vying for their affections were every bit as fickle, trained as they had been by mentors as conniving as my mother. All were notoriously adept at swindling their patrons out of their considerable fortunes. It was a dizzying carnival of limitless lust and crass commodification of womanly charm.

'Never forget,' Chittu would tell us sternly during our training sessions with her, 'that only a fool gives away her most alluring attributes for free. That's why even the wives belonging to the higher echelons of society enjoy the exact same status as slaves. And a whore is one who settles on a throwaway price, that is the only degrading thing about her profession. A dasi or a ganika is neither. Therefore, she, 'the eternally auspicious one', is worth many times her weight in gold. And those who procure her services will be blessed in this lifetime and the next.'

Here she would pause to glance surreptitiously at me. It was a sore point with her that I had not had the *pottu kattuthal* ceremony dedicating me to the temple and declaring to the world and those fanatically religious enough to believe that I was God's wife. Paati had been right. It didn't really matter. Not everyone opted to go through this sort of thing and get branded with the deity's emblem, but went on to become accomplished dancers anyway. They took the risk to avoid coming under the iron control of the bloody priests and were happy to avoid these pestilences.

Chewing elegantly on the *paan* she had prepared with the costly ingredients she toted around in her precious vetrilai potti, Chittu warmed up to her favourite topic, sighing contentedly with a pseudo-sensual satisfaction that made me gnash my teeth. I knew this was part of her seduction routine and it always made me queasy, but there was no stopping my mother when she was in the process of educating her ignorant charges.

'Lead your lover on a merry dance and commit yourself to every move, the way you do when you perform before an adoring audience,' Chittu paused to spit noisily into a bejewelled spittoon and wipe her mouth delicately with her *pallu* before resuming her chewing and lecturing, 'but the important thing is to let him think that he is the one in charge. Men have fragile egos, and you must be careful never to inflame these temperamental creatures, unless you have an inexplicable desire to be beaten to death or violently raped.'

The more experienced dancers nodded in agreement, for they knew what it was like to run afoul of the male ego. One of them pointed to her broken nose and indicated the hip she had dislocated after being savagely kicked. 'And no matter what you do, never ever laugh at his penis, even if it is littler than your little finger.' Everyone burst out laughing, including Chittu, who said between cutesy chortles, 'You are lucky you were not killed over that precious bit of foolishness... Now stop the tittering and pay attention, girls. I am not sharing the wealth of my experience for my health.

'As I was saying, take care to soothe your man. Stroke his pride and lavish him with your attention, affection and regard. Make your beloved patron feel like the greatest of them all—God among men, an incomparable lover, an invincible warrior and a benevolent philanthropist. Convince him that among the legions of admirers throwing themselves upon the fortress of your virtue, he is the only one for whom you will deign to open your heart and legs, and you will be rewarded for your generosity with his own.'

I had been hearing these things for the longest time and it made me groan out loud, breaking the web she was weaving with the consummate skill of an engorged spider filled with the juices of her prey. Chittu glared at me from under her carefully curled and kohl-darkened eyelashes, adjusting the folds of her sari and rearranging the strands of fat pearls she wore with painstaking care, while plodding on, enumerating the intricacies of seduction:

'With becoming modesty and genuinely contrived coyness, gently prod him into persuading you to discard your upper garments. For this privilege, he must part with a grand sari or two. Or three. Feed him the artfully rolled paan made according to his preference, which you must be familiar with, even if it changes as often as his mood. Chew on it with careful deliberation. Relish the sharp burst of flavour as you place it on the tip of your tongue and slowly nudge it into his mouth. He will not be able to resist the temptation to kiss you. Remember that you are not a needy whore, and so you shall resist, but feebly, as if you were fighting your own desperate urge to kiss him back. For this special favour, he must shower you with exquisite ornaments of the finest workmanship so that you may bedeck yourself from head to toe for your next public performance.

'Connoisseurs may appreciate the multi-layered, manifold manifestation of infinite truth and beauty in our performances, but a great majority of your audience is there to drink in your appearance and to take note of the costume and jewellery you are wearing. And if you wear the same thing repeatedly, they will be reminded of their own poverty and hate you for it. Or worse, they will become fatigued at the familiar sight!'

Chittu shuddered in theatrical horror, as if the idea of repurposing a costume or reusing jewellery repelled her, even though we did do just that out of necessity. 'The Gods don't shower gold coins upon us after a particularly affecting recital honouring them, nor do they bestow us with precious silk fabrics and expensive jewellery. Which is why it behoves us to encourage our paramours to do so, and when they oblige, be sure to let your man know that you are overwhelmed by his generosity and skills as a lover. Convince him that he is the God you worship, who has been welcomed into your heart. Allow your bosom to heave gently when he reaches out to caress it; you must stay his roving hand until he has bestowed upon you treasures worthy of the Goddess of Prosperity herself—golden girdles, diamond necklaces, ruby bangles, strands of the fattest pearls, anklets filled with gems, and bushels of gold coins—to earn the right to indulge his innermost desires. Only then must you make yourself fully amenable to sharing the treasures and pleasures afforded by your body, provided he is ready with further remuneration to sample your lush wares to his lustful heart's content.'

I had no wish to become my mother, but I could see my future writ large on her face and features. It was a depressing sight, prompting me to turn my back on her and shut my ears to her homilies. Mercifully, the preparation for my arangetram took up all my time, and I could not have been happier to lose myself in the familiar beats of the thattukali and let everything else fade into nothingness.

∫

At all hours, ranging from the godly to the ungodly, I trained in the silambu koodam. I sang the scales, practised twice a day the elaborate series of exercises to increase strength, mobility and flexibility, and went through the repertoire of advanced dance movements over and over again until it felt as natural and easy as breathing. Then I would stretch my limbs before settling down to relax and unwind with pranayama and meditation. It was exhilarating.

Ayya recommended that Chittu hire more masters to train me in specific skillsets. Chittu obliged. I learned to play instruments like the yaal and the flute with a vidwan's proficiency. At Ayya's behest, poets Chittu had rounded up would declaim their verses with sparkling eloquence for our pleasure. Scholars would lecture us on the sacred and esoteric texts enumerating the mysteries of the universe, and we would listen spellbound for hours on end. After they were finished, Ayya would signal for me to ask them questions or share my thoughts about everything I had heard. We would discuss the intricacies of interpretation. Again and again, they impressed upon me the truth that there was no fixed way to read the Vedas or the Shastras. They emerged from a bygone era when knowledge, expertise in practical as well as esoteric matters, and lived experiences were passed on freely through the method of oral tradition. What always mattered were the essential truths they contained that could best be adapted to the demands of a changing world, rather than an impractical fixation on exactitude when it came to rhetoric or semantics. I loved these lengthy sessions, which were always fascinating and filled with laughter and wisdom.

Ayya, with calculated disregard for the growing turmoil within me, continued to help me work on *abhinaya*. He would demonstrate how to bring out hidden depths of meaning in all the songs I danced to, not through words or action alone, but by encouraging me to step out of my body and mind, freeing me from their combined weight, so that all that remained for me to do was to surrender to the rhythms and patterns that governed not just dance, but life itself and the mysterious workings of the cosmos.

'Empty out the insides and outsides of the life you have been given and cast aside the treasured trifles you have clung to all these years. It will allow you to travel into the inner recesses of your heart and soul, giving you the impetus to expand outward and explore the secrets of the universe unimpeded.'

I listened and did my best to obey, but some of the things he said were mystifying. 'Don't worry about trying to pin down the meaning behind my words. Trust the process and focus on immersing yourself in the perennial flow of divine grace, which will prove more fulfilling than the stray thoughts that taunt you, the secret anxieties that hound your head, and the vagaries of each passing moment.'

I shut my eyes and silenced the feelings within me that always seemed to be in a state of flux, allowing his words to batter away the remnants of resistance as he continued, 'Your innate talent, beauty and effortless sensuality will take you far, but it is not enough to achieve all that you are capable of. Pour every moment of the life you have lived, every truth you have unearthed, every experience you have cherished, the purity of your burgeoning sexuality, towards sanctifying your dance with exquisite emotions and the spirituality you have worked so hard to extract from the depths of your soul.

'Ultimately, every step you take, every move you make, every pose you strike, every nuance of your facial expression must be consecrated towards achieving oneness with the Divine. If this alone is your intent, then you will have no difficulty in winning the heart of your ishta deivata, your beloved God, and he in turn will protect and guide you out of this *Dukkalaya*—our world plagued by sorrow and suffering—and lead you to his abode, *Sukkalaya*, where there is nothing but *ananda*, eternal bliss. All who watch you will be transported too, provided they have the head and heart to glimpse the sacred truth and arcane mysteries conveyed through your performance, and hope will be kindled in their hearts that one day, they too can achieve *moksha*, the salvation from which God has ensured that none of us will ever be excluded.'

My eyelids flew up of their own volition, and my eyebrows nearly disappeared into my hairline, such was my consternation and doubt. Ayya seemed to have expected my response, because he chortled ever so lightly as he waited for me to say something. At first, I could not find the words as doubt and outrage choked me, but then they gushed out with incontinent abandon, jostling their way out of my mouth, raw and sticky like vomit.

'I know that I will do well to listen to and obey you without question. There is nothing I love better in this life than dance and it will be the perfect blessing to spend my days dancing every single day in temples and on every stage that is offered to me, be it great or humble. And if I receive the remuneration to ensure that all those who depend on me can live in reasonable comfort, that is more than enough. But my mother has other plans for me. You know that too. I could do everything you say and dance with the sole intention of merging with the totality of divine grace, but what is the point if my fate is to be chained to a patron who will move on to the next dancing girl when he has had his fill of me? Chittu will trade me off to another man with money and little else of value, and what if I am powerless to resist? I have never wanted any of that.'

Ayya said nothing for the longest time. His attendants had fallen silent, not daring to breathe. No one looked at me. I had dared to give utterance to the dark thoughts that folks in my community firmly believed were best left unsaid. I was embarrassed by my outburst and tried in vain to still my heaving chest. But I was defiant too. And refused to lower my gaze in mortification. Instead, I held Ayya's gaze, waiting for him to respond.

Vasantamala crept up to me and gently dabbed at my eyes with a soft piece of cloth, taking care not to smudge the kajal, before disappearing as unobtrusively as she had appeared. It was only then I realized I had burst into tears. Ayya relented a little despite his impatience with my hysterical conduct, especially after he had spent years teaching me to be graceful and gracious, cool and composed always, and his voice softened.

'Dance was never intended to serve immoral purposes. Its

function is just the opposite, and the ritual rules pertaining to fluid movement were designed to harness the manifold benefits of a Grand Yagna meant to inspire the composer, the musician, the dancer as well as the audience to conduct their lives in keeping with the tenets of the four *Purusartha*s: Dharma—the moral duties, Artha—the pursuit of prosperity, both monetary and otherwise, Kama—the experience of sensual delights firmly rooted in spirituality, and finally Moksha—the blessed liberation from this vicious, never-ending cycle of birth and rebirth governed by unrelenting karma, where every good deed is rewarded with another and every bad deed is punished with the same over the course of endless lifetimes. But first you must discipline your wandering senses, calm the storms of your terror, and devote yourself only to the immediate demands of dance and music. Trust the skills you are learning, over your own ability to slay the demons that haunt you, and you will be stronger for it.'

I said nothing, though I managed a small nod of acquiescence. Ayya spoke again after placing his hand on my head and blessing me in a precious moment of pure sentiment, 'You will be my worthiest pupil! But you were meant to be worthier still. And you will be. For your courage has allowed you to face your fears and tackle them before they grow too powerful and destroy you. And having done so, you will divest yourself from them. That is enough training for today. I see Vasantamala hovering around with a tray of your favourite treats. I am afraid she blames me for the tears you shed today. Perhaps she is right. I suggest you help yourself to the goodies your friend has brought, and take some time to practise meditation, self-reflection and introspection before enjoying a good night's sleep. At dawn, we will resume your training. This time, nothing will hold you back, and your talent will help you make your way to the happiness and peace you deserve.'

With a final blessing, Ayya left. The rest of his entourage followed in his wake, refusing to look at me, excising my words from their memories so they need not bother themselves with bitter truths. I sank to the floor of the silambu koodam. Vasantamala was at my side in an instant, urging me to eat from the loaded tray she had carried. Surprisingly, I was ravenous. Emotional outbursts do that to you. The two of us gorged on the food she had brought from the kitchen. Rice, lentils, ghee and my favourite *kathirikai puli kulambu* with crispy *appalam*s and a beetroot sweet I could never get enough of. We washed the meal down with sweet curd. I felt better, but there was a lingering sense of unease which refused to dissipate, despite all my efforts to let it go.

Vasanta looked at me with undisguised concern, and I was touched. She was too plain to ever aspire to proper prettiness, but there was something very appealing about her. Perhaps it was her kind heart and her helpful nature. Paati had felt that she lacked the skill to be a dancer and so I was entrusted to her, even though she was only a few years older than me. When I started training, Chittu, who discovered that Vasanta had a pleasing voice, decided that she could be trained to sing—a *paadini* who would accompany me as I sang and danced. Through sheer effort, she had become quite a good singer. We worked very well together as we always synchronized perfectly, which pleased Ayya no end. Her steady presence was also a constant source of comfort and reassurance. In addition, she still watched over me, making sure I lacked nothing while helping Chittu run the household. Honestly, I had no idea what I would do without my best friend.

'You are overthinking things...' Vasanta broke into my thoughts abruptly. I frowned in response. Of course I was overthinking things, but that was not going to stop me from doing it. I hated it when people stated the obvious.

She was enjoying the beetroot sweet, savouring every morsel with grating slowness when I snatched it from her and finished it all off in one giant mouthful. Then I stuck my tongue out at her for good measure.

'Do that at your arangetram,' she said serenely, 'it will kill your mother like nothing else can. She insists that a dancer's every gesture must ooze with grace and pure aesthetic appeal, especially when she is distraught. As I was saying before I was so rudely and unaesthetically interrupted, there is no need for you to work yourself up into a ferment of frustration. You love to dance. So dance! It is that simple. Why worry about whose bed you wind up in? Or not? Besides, your mother controls every single thing in this household, but she never could manage to control you. Though it is not for want of trying. That in itself is an extraordinary achievement because even the Gods have little chance of prevailing against your mother when she wants something.'

To my surprise, I was strangely comforted by her words. For it was true. Chittu could never make me do something I did not want to. Still, I hesitated.

'What is it?' Vasantamala said. 'You might as well get all your incessant worries out of the way, before you burst.'

She handed me the sweet curd, before I could reach out for it. I gulped it down gratefully. 'When I dance, I tune everything out and let myself drift into the far reaches of the cosmos, as Ayya calls it. But you can't stay in those wondrous realms, Vasanta, even if you will give anything to keep on wandering along the endless trails of glittering starburst. You must leave the mystical and return to the mundane. Whether you like it or not. And I am brought back with a shattering crash and a lurch, usually when the music ends. But sometimes it is because I can feel the lust in the rude gaze of the men watching me. They undress me with their eyes, and their lechery pierces through every inch of my skin. All of them do it, even though they pretend to be high-minded and committed to the task of training me. If the so-called vidwans can do this, can you imagine what it will be like when I am ready to make my public debut? Why, it is like surrendering to gang rape by gaze alone! As for the women, they hate me, and I have done nothing to deserve it.'

My best friend nodded thoughtfully. 'I have envied you for your beauty and talent, but I have also pitied you for it, because I know what you are talking about. They can't take their eyes off you or stop their ugly thoughts from roving all over you. But you mustn't let the coarse appetites of men and the jealousy of women get under your skin and make their way into every inch of you. Then you will become party to your own violation. Besides, in the end, despite all their futile attempts, you shall always be above their base desires. Don't let anyone take away the satisfaction you derive from dance, music and the pursuit of your personal quests, whatever they might be.'

She was right again. Why should I give these pigs the power they sought over my person? My body belonged to me, and I will be damned if I ever let anyone lay claim to it.

Vasantamala was staring into the distance, and she continued to do so, even though her words were still directed to me. 'You have always sworn that you will never be enslaved by love. That dance and music is all you will ever need. But I know you dream of finding your soulmate, and you are frightened that you might never find what you so desperately seek.'

She turned her gaze back to me. I smiled ruefully. Of course, she would know the secrets of my heart long before I knew them myself. Vasanta had watched over me since I was a baby, staying up long after I was asleep, her gentle, ever-vigilant presence shadowing me through dream and nightmare alike. I could bare my soul to her, knowing that she would never look away in revulsion.

'I don't care for men of means and power, so valued by Chittu.' It was not easy to confide this even to dear Vasanta, but I did. 'I dream of a man who is smart, sweet, caring and possessed of the kindest pair of eyes in the world. In his arms alone, I will feel loved and safe enough to let go of all of my fears. And I will be truly content. But it is an impossible dream.'

Vasantamala shook her head. 'Love is always within the realm of possibility. You just have to allow yourself not only to want it, but to seek it yourself. And it will be yours. Easy as can be! I have not told you yet, but I never get tired of watching you dance. Because when you move in a way that only you can, I am transported by ecstasy, because the air around you shimmers with the truth, kindness and sincerity you pour into every gesture, movement and expression. All I can see is how much of your inner self you commit to your art. The one who is worthy of you will see what I see, and when he falls in love with these qualities of yours not readily visible to the lusty lepers out there, you will be able to spot him in a crowd of millions, and you will give yourself to him without reservation. And he will be the fulfilment of your dreams!'

She leaned over, and to my horror I realized that I was crying again. Slowly she dried my tears and held me until I stopped sobbing. 'You better be right,' I sniffled. 'If this wonderful man you speak of doesn't find me, or breaks my heart, I will kill him and then you. Death by starvation is going to be your fate. Then I will follow you to the other side of eternity and spend the rest of my time berating you for misleading me.'

'I am right, you will see,' she said airily, as we rose to our feet, and gesturing to her ample hips, she added for good measure, 'Even on starvation rations, I am likely to live for a hundred years thanks to the fat deposits I have lovingly accumulated in my body over the course of many a memorable meal, even though my dearest friend is forever stealing my share.'

We laughed together as we made our way to the kitchen to get our hands on what was left of the beetroot sweet. 'I won't actually kill you,' I assured Vasanta, 'you are the best of friends, and you will always be worth more to me than any man. Even more than the worthy one you talked about. The one with the kind eyes, the soft heart and the strong arms.'

'You say that now…' she teased, 'but when this lucky man shows up at your arangetram and sweeps you off your feet, you won't be able to tell me from a stranger in the street.'

Her words filled me with fresh hope and happiness. My heart was alight with anticipation as I gobbled down the sweet the cook had thoughtfully set aside for me. Vasantamala was still talking about how I must stop with the unnecessary worrying and apply myself wholeheartedly to my art, or something along those lines. By the time she quit prattling and reached for her share, it was all gone. It served her right!

∽

It was time. The years of intensive training for my big day seemed to have passed by in a tearing hurry without pausing for breath, racing past my helplessly clutching fingers to a place well beyond my reach, never to be recaptured. There was no time to dwell on the loss, because I was as ready as I could be. More importantly, I had finally found peace, or something akin to it.

It had cost me everything I had to offer and more, but finally I had submerged myself in the totality of the divine rhythm and surrendered to its potency wholeheartedly without any compunctions at all. Everything across the length and breadth of both the known and unknown worlds is ruled solely by this heavenly music. I could feel its power with every beat of the heart and every breath I drew. Every time I kept beat with my feet and the dancing bells, I felt attuned to the secrets concealed in the emptiness of space and the dark void, safely ensconced in an infinitesimal speck of my eternal soul. Secure in this knowledge, I danced knowing that I need not fear losing my footing and falling for the rest of time, further and further away from grace.

Chittu was busy with the arrangements for my arangetram and she was determined to outdo herself and do Paati proud. She consulted all the astrologers and soothsayers of the known world and parted with a considerable fortune to settle on the most auspicious of days and find the most sacred site in our beloved Puhar. Once this was settled, Chittu moved on to the next stage of preparations, with Vasanta always close at hand to soothe ruffled feathers and undo the damage caused by the matriarch's temper as she argued and haggled with everyone involved, making sure that I was presented to my best advantage.

The Shastras were minutely examined by experts and the stage was erected in accordance with the tenets preserved by centuries of weighty traditions, bearing in mind the most precise measurements. There were two beautifully engraved doors. I would enter through one and exit through the other. Chittu repeatedly drilled into my head the importance of not getting confused between the two doors, assuring me that if I mistook one for the other, I would plummet to the depths of *naraka*, when I should be transporting my audience into the splendours of *swarga*. Normally, her fussing would have driven me to distraction, but

I was past caring about the many irritants I was regularly forced to deal with.

Engineers of proven skill were chosen to place the pillars at the prescribed points on the stage, and goldsmiths worked to cover them with *jambunada*, the finest gold available, embedding the surface with precious stones that would sparkle when the strategically placed lamps were lit. Chittu shouted herself hoarse over these, insisting that there must be no sign of dark shadows on the stage and that every inch of the space was to be brilliantly lit to fully capture the *prakasa* of my dance.

The site was chosen to represent the entirety of the universe. The four *Buta*s, the deities who were the guardians of all, painted with breathtaking skill and lifelike colour were at their demarcated places, in keeping with the cardinal directions identified by the experts. The centre was the *Brahma mandala*, and the ritual space was consecrated by *purohit*s so that it could be enlivened and imbued with the breath of life, *prana*. It was a solemn ritual and strangely moving as I prepared myself mentally and physically to do the best I could for myself and for Paati, who was gone but never forgotten.

Chittu had paid an exorbitant sum to procure the *talaikkol*, the golden staff of an umbrella, studded with jewels at its nine joints, which had stood tall and uncaptured on the battlefield and believed to have belonged to an ancient hero king from a glorious if forgotten past, who himself had received it from a splendiferous deity as a reward for unmatched services. Her wild extravagance was understandable, at least in this respect.

The golden staff represented Jayanta, the son of Indra, wielder of the thunderbolt and Lord of the Heavens. Legend has it that the great Sage Agastya had just finished composing the *Tolkappiyam*, his incomparable text on Tamil grammar, which was supposed to ensure the preservation of the beauty of our mother tongue for posterity. Indra had invited him to Amaravathi as a special guest of honour, where his achievement would be celebrated with feasting, a dance performance, and generous gifts from each one of the thirty-three crore Devas. The recital was to feature the beauteous Urvashi, who was supposedly our ancestor, though I am afraid even children or the extraordinarily unintelligent won't be able to swallow this boastful assertion which could not be supported with a shred of proof.

The dance was well underway, when the Apsara chose an inopportune moment in the middle of her performance to become hopelessly enamoured with Jayanta, who reciprocated in kind. Although she danced without missing a beat, she simultaneously chose to engage in a forbidden flirtation with the handsome Prince, handing over her heart to him in exchange for his. The doyen of dharma and scourge of lovers, Agastya, deemed such conduct unacceptable and unpardonable.

Roaring in aggrieved tones, he made it clear that in his esteemed opinion, a dancer's first duty was to her art, which demanded her heart, soul, mind and body. By failing to fulfil this sacred requirement, she had disgraced herself, the Gods and him, the guest of honour. Agastya cursed the two lovers to take birth on Earth, Urvashi as a dancing girl in Kanchi and Jayanta as a bamboo shoot, destined never to meet. But love always found a way, and Urvashi never danced without placing the talaikkol, a bamboo stick bedecked with gold and gems, at a prominent place on the stage.

∫

On the day of the performance, I was asked to bathe the revered talaikkol adorned with bamboo shoots in the holy waters collected from our sacred rivers in a golden jar, at the *teertha* of our Pasupata Temple, receive the blessings of the priests, wise men and the sacred elephant, and carry it in procession, before placing it on stage at the appointed central position at the back.

Chittu had spared no expense to buy me the finest dance costumes in crimson and gold cloth and a gorgeous yellow pattu sari, shot through with a deep shade of lustrous green. She had procured them from a merchant prince who had conducted his daughter's wedding with great aplomb a few years ago. The event had been the talk of our capital city. Some swore that he was even richer than our King when they witnessed this display of endless wealth. Chittu had been mightily impressed at the time and fell in love with the jewellery worn by the bride. She did her utmost to find the jeweller from Chera Nadu who had demonstrated such exquisite craftmanship, so that she could make similar pieces for me, and became increasingly frustrated when the man could not be traced. Apparently, he had retired and left on a pilgrimage to unknown destinations. Chittu threw a hissy fit and launched into a harangue that I simply couldn't pay attention to.

In the end, even my mule-headed recalcitrance, as she called it, did not stop Chittu from taking pride in the fact that the preparations for my arangetram had gone perfectly, and she was so pleased with herself that it was a discomfiting sight. Our King Manarkilli arrived right on time with the rest of the royal retinue. He was anxious to prove that, like his father, the great Karikala Chola, he was a connoisseur and benefactor of the fine arts. Somewhat on the short and corpulent side, he had a luxuriant moustache which he stroked incessantly, as if to assure himself that it was still there. He eagerly took his seat with the rest of his courtiers and Chittu was beside herself with joy, convinced that all her plans were nearing fruition. Behind him, it seemed

The Wife and the Dancing Girl

to me that all of Puhar had gathered, and I drew a tremulous breath at the sight of the crowd.

In the last few weeks, my thoughts were entirely with Paati, and the thought of her gave me courage and stilled my nerves. In the end, I chose to wear the costume Paati had worn for her own arangetram and the *rudraksha* beads she had favoured in her last days. As a concession to Chittu, I would change into the crimson and gold sari during the first intermission and the yellow and green one during the second, but I insisted on wearing only the jewels Paati had given me. Reluctantly, Chittu accepted defeat, but only after Ayya had told her that the grand matriarch's possessions would ward off the evil eye and ensure that the performance went off without a hitch. It was a relief. I missed Paati, and wearing her things made me feel close to her.

It was with a lone tear in my eye that I sought her blessings and uttered a prayer to the Gods before I placed my right foot firmly on the stage, walking to the pillar on the right, and waited there in the proper posture that Chittu and Ayya had drilled into me. Vasanta sang the two prayers to invoke the blessings of the Gods, seeking their help to allow virtue to prosper and vice to disappear. At the end of the prayers, the respected members of the periya melam played their instruments—the mridangams, flutes, lutes and amantirikai. Ayya struck his thattukali and my body responded of its own accord as I started to sing and dance, with Vasanta's familiar voice accompanying mine, the performance commencing at the appointed hour.

I struck the floor with my feet, leaping and twirling around to execute the intricate choreography I had perfected with Ayya. How can I describe the joy that filled my heart and cascaded outwards to envelop everyone in wonder and excitement? I danced with love flooding my insides, for I was finally free of fear and intoxicated by the roaring deluge of long buried passion that had finally broken free from the shackles of steel. I danced amidst the chaos from which my soul emerged and journeyed to the still calm of its epicentre. I danced across the thousand hurts and heartbreaks I had already encountered, swimming past the eddying currents of grief until they mingled with the waves of the purest elation. Sometimes my movements slowed to a crawl before they exploded in a frenzy of footwork, faster than the swiftest thoughts. The heat generated by my dance burnt my soles, but the flames were quenched in the cool waters of burgeoning love, the food of life itself.

My whole life had been consumed by an obsessive search for what I did not know, which had blinded me to everything else. I was still a seeker, but I was no longer lost, and my mind raced unbounded and free, receptive to the bounties of fate. I would no longer chase after elusive perfection, terrified of catching it, worried that it would inevitably slip through my fingers while leaving me behind, struggling in the clutch of imperfection. For I finally knew that perfection was in my grasp. That my sins of thought, word and deed would be washed clean by the divine forgiveness and the salvation that sin engendered by its very nature. Healing lay on the other side of disease, just as youth lurked behind old age and life after death.

I would no longer allow myself to foolishly hate love, loathe lust or despise desire, as we are encouraged to do by those who should know better but seldom do. There was nothing more important than love or indulging my need for the pleasures of the flesh. I must gorge myself on it and grow corpulent through the demands of my insatiable need. For I could never hope to be free of my need, if I did not first have my fill of it.

I traipsed across the tightrope, borne by the balance and

harmony of the universe in a secure harness, revelling in the subtle reverberation of transcendence and oneness of pure consciousness. Each cell sang out in celebration as one by one, like little drops of water returning to the ocean, they merged into the blessed circle of love and light. Always apart, but together, forever interlocked in the shared hope of perennial peace.

I came to with a start and realized that the music, singing and dancing had stopped. Silence enveloped the stage, even as the applause exploded over our heads. Transported by the magic, intoxicated by the beauty I had imbibed, I stood strong and erect, palms joined together in a grateful salutation as the cries of 'bravo!' '*besh*!' '*sabash*!' and 'well done!' rang out. The crashing waves of ovation reverberated across the heavens as the King rose to his feet, clapping his hands, having set aside his dignity. He placed the floral wreath on my shoulders, as was customary, and presented me with the reward of one thousand and eight gold coins. King Manarkilli stepped back, tears glinting in his eyes.

Silence descended as the King descended from the stage like a man in a daze. With a final bow to the King, the peria melam, and the audience, I retreated to the wings with newfound poise and serenity. Vasantamala was at my side. Impatiently, I searched the crowds with an eager gaze, knowing in my heart that I would finally find everything I had sought so desperately for as long as I could remember. Then I saw him, standing tall amidst the teeming masses. The One. How gloriously handsome he looked. He stood transfixed to the spot, and his kind eyes that glinted with unshed tears and overflowing love met mine. No words needed to be exchanged.

'Over there!' I told Vasantamala, pointing to him, 'Bring him to me. Tell him that Madhavi is his. Now and forevermore.'

KANNAGI

A Splintered Heart

That dancing girl's mother claimed that they were descendants of the Apsara, Urvashi. Amma had told me about it, unable to contain her laughter or disapproval. 'Such a coarse woman, trying to pass herself off as cultured. These people are so delusional, claiming to be the Wives of Gods and descendants of Apsaras. Everyone knows that they come from poor stock, and this entire pottu kattuthal business, marking them off as God's brides, is nothing but a glitzy charade to sell their virginity to the highest bidder. It is disgraceful is what it is, and a shameful blot on civilized society. The day will come when people see through their odious chicanery and that will be the end of this disgraceful business. At least the veshas are honest about what they do and don't pretend to be anything other than the guttersnipe they are.'

It was not a subject I felt comfortable discussing. But when I saw Madhavi dance, I did not doubt her ancestry for a moment. I had not the slightest doubt that she was a celestial being. She was extraordinarily beautiful, moved like a dream, and every pore of her perfectly sculpted body exuded grace. An infectious energy bubbled out of her with gurgling merriment, and we were caught up in its delightful currents, transfixed by the magic she was conjuring up with her exquisite movements and intoxicating charm. But there was more to her than things like mere talent or technical prowess, which was beyond my ability to assess anyway. There was a simplicity and honesty to her performance that marked her out as something special. In the mesmerizing orbs of her eyes which sparkled with fun and laughter when they were not projecting sincere gravitas, one could see a soul that was completely lacking in falsehood.

It was obvious to everyone in the audience that Madhavi was an extraordinary talent and it was a privilege to watch her perform. No one stirred for the entire duration of her arangetram. In unison, we gasped in awe on witnessing her lightning-fast footwork, fluid grace and perfect form. When she smiled, so did we. When she effortlessly conveyed the pathos of enduring the excruciating pain of separation from her beloved heavenly consort, the audience sniffled as one. Agonized by the thought of ever being parted from him, I took Kovalan's suddenly limp hand in mine, feeling very bold and brazen indeed, but unable to control myself.

Kovalan loved music and dance, so we hardly missed any of the sadhir katcheris in temples or grand sabhas. I did not like these performances as much as he did, but I did not protest when he wished to attend these events. We had seen many dancers who were celebrated across the land and considered the very embodiments of beauty, talent and grace. But none of the other dancers had whatever it was that Madhavi had. I don't mean to be harsh, but even to my untrained eyes, it seemed that most of the dasis were either sick with self-love or trying a little too hard to entice with their suggestive dancing and coquettish gestures, which always made me cringe a little and wince a lot.

But this girl had an inner spark that warmed your heart and made you feel a palpable connection with the divine.

As I watched her, my heart ached with curious joy and unidentifiable sorrow. That day, in her company, we soared to rare heights of pure bliss that left us beside ourselves with emotion as we were drawn deep into the embrace of the supreme consciousness. I did not want her performance to end, and when she took her final bow, I found my eyes were flooded with tears. In the few hours she had danced, I had experienced and endured an eternity of life—an affirmation of truth, beauty and spiritual oneness with the *paramatma*.

To my surprise, Kovalan was silent on our way home, and in an unusual role reversal, I was the one who talked endlessly about the marvellous dancer Chola Nadu had birthed.

'Have you ever seen a girl as beautiful and talented as her?' I gushed.

Suddenly, he stared at me as if he didn't know who I was.

'She is just another dancing girl,' he said in a strained voice. 'And she is not as beautiful as you are!'

I laughed at this. 'There is no one in the three worlds as beautiful as Madhavi!'

He did not reply. We were almost home, and I was opening the door when he mumbled something about needing to go out urgently, turned on his heel, and left without waiting for a response. It would be a very long time before I saw his dear face again.

I have never forgotten that day. How deliriously happy I had been! How utterly unaware of the sorrow that awaited me immediately after… For the longest time after that, I had no reason to smile. When I did, it was always with a tinge of apprehension and the irrevocable certainty that happiness was fleeting and sorrow inevitable. Forevermore, perfect bliss would frighten me. For it heralded the impending arrival of tragedy.

Initially, being the silly fool Amma had always feared I would grow into, I did not quite understand what had happened. While waiting for Kovalan to return, I was swaying to the beat and humming some of the beautiful songs Madhavi had sung and danced to. Even her voice was silken and soulful; the cadences reverberated in my head long after the music had stopped, and the dancing bells stopped tinkling. I must have dozed off, but I was startled to realize that Kovalan had not come back to our bed and the hour was late. Sickening anxiety spread through my heart, and my stomach turned over with incessant worry.

I stayed up all night waiting for him to come home, shaking with misery, convinced that something evil had befallen him. I murmured prayers to all the Gods in the pantheon, begging them to protect him from harm. Time slowed to a crawl as I tried to urge myself to be brave and head out into the darkness to look for him. But in my entire life, I had never stepped out of the house on my own, let alone in the dark. The thought of doing so left me paralyzed with terror.

There was no sign of him in the morning either. I was about to run all the way to his parents' house and beg them to help me find Kovalan in case he had been attacked or robbed. A thousand unpleasant scenarios played out in my head, and I thought I was going to lose my mind. At that moment, I heard my maid Ponni's panicked voice. She was addressing Muthumani, who drew in her breath with theatrical shock. Despite the heightened distress, they were trying to speak in hushed tones, but I heard every word.

'You are not going to believe what happened. Those filthy dasis belong in the gutter! Serves us right for letting them invade our temples and the grand sabhas!' Ponni was sputtering with outrage. Dread entered my heart again. She was highly voluble, but it was not her way to speak with so much anger.

'What are you talking about?' Muthumani enquired. She loved to talk almost as much as Ponni did.

'You know very well the master did not come home last night. Do you know why? The reason is none other than Madhavi, the dancing girl everyone is talking about. She had her arangetram last evening. They say she is an enchantress like you have never seen before. She is so surpassingly beautiful and talented that the Gods showered flowers on her. My mother accompanied her mistress, and she swears she saw it with her own eyes.'

'You mother has been drinking again,' Muthumani's voice rose an octave higher, and dripped with scorn. 'The Gods have no use for us mortals and care even less about what we do!'

'I am just telling you what people are saying. Do you want to know what happened or not? Our poor mistress! She is too innocent, and her heart won't be able to withstand it. And she is worth a thousand Madhavis. How patient, cheerful and kind she always is! And no man has a more devoted wife! Yet, this is how the master has repaid her!'

'Sssshhhh…don't talk about the master like that. Kind or not, she will send you away from here if you say such evil things about him. Why don't you just tell me what he has done? Quickly now! She will be here any minute, to prepare his morning meal. Don't tell me he has…'

'But he has… The King presented this creature, Madhavi, with the customary wreath, and I hear that if he hadn't been so dazed he would have taken her to the royal harem that very minute. Had he done so, our mistress would have been spared the evil that has overtaken her. But that did not happen. That Madhavi's mother has a maid, the despicable Kuni, who was seen on the promenade flaunting the wreath like a proud peacock where the noblemen of Puhar head out for their constitutionals. Cackling

The Wife and the Dancing Girl

like the filthy crow that she is, Kuni loudly proclaimed that the man who buys the damn thing for a thousand and eight kalanjus of gold gets to claim Madhavi as his lover. These dasis are always so damnably forward! Imagine tempting decent men in this way... Everyone knows that men, even the so-called respectable ones, can't see past the tips of their dicks!'

'Don't tell me our master bought the wreath!'

'Of course he did... But I don't blame him. These dasis are witches as well as bitches. They prepare love potions from the foulest things...grated garlic to make the blood boil, the menstrual blood of a seasoned whore who has entertained a thousand men to stimulate desire, the flesh of a stillborn baby to disguise their evil intentions and give them a deceptive appearance of innocence, the venom of a snake to make their advances potent. And these are just the ingredients I know. The rest is a deep, dark mystery which these depraved dancing girls guard jealously. With all these skilful machinations, they capture the heart of the rich man they have in their sights, and he becomes their willing captive for the rest of his life! Or as long as he has enough money to afford their services.'

'What will our blameless mistress do? What will become of her? She has no defences against the vile ways of these dasis. It is a cruel fate to be born a woman in this wicked world.' Muthumani was sniffling and Ponni was trying to hush her up. I noted all these details through a stifling fog of disbelief. What they were saying was impossible. Kovalan would not do this to me. And Madhavi was a goddess. Surely, she wouldn't steal a man away from his wife? But why hadn't my husband come home?

What if all this were true? What could I do? What would become of me? I didn't have the faintest notion. All I knew was that I couldn't spend the entire day crying in my room while they pitied me and excoriated Kovalan's conduct. I tied my hair in a knot and went about my duties to the best of my dwindling ability on that day, and the endless days that followed.

∫

Days went by and I prepared countless meals, telling myself that Kovalan would be home soon and that he would be hungry. That I mustn't keep him waiting. They were never consumed. I made and remade our bed, which had not been slept in, because I sat on the floor in the dark every night, alone and afraid, willing him to come home. I folded and refolded his clothes, breathing in his scent and holding the fabric close to my breasts as I wept uncontrollably. Then I would wash the tears from his clothes and mine to make sure they were absolutely spotless, while pretending to ignore the maids who looked on with a mixture of pity and concern.

Hours were spent cleaning a house that was already spotless thanks to the efforts of Muthu and Ponni. Even so, I dusted every corner, swept and swabbed every surface that presented itself, declaring war on non-existent smudges and spots. The meals that were never eaten were distributed to the poor and needy, who always flocked to my doorstep. When I fed the little ones, I felt a certain measure of happiness and peace that had simply disappeared from my life. It was nice to be outside with them for a few minutes and listen to their chatter. When they looked at me, there was no pity or spiteful satisfaction, and I was glad.

I would sit for hours at prayer, slowly performing the rituals, although my hands were shaking. Or at least I sat with my hands folded, pretending to pray, though my mind was too numb, and my heart was too bereft of hope to plead with a stone-hearted deity who, as my handmaiden had pointed out, could scarcely be bothered with the troubles of mortals.

The evenings were twice as hard, because having worked feverishly all day, there was nothing further to be done, despite my best efforts to keep myself occupied. I made sure my appearance was neat and tidy, for when my husband came back to our home. Every day, I would drape my sari and adorn myself with nothing but my *thaali*, hoping that this would be the day he returned to me. Every day a little piece of my heart died, and it became harder to keep up appearances. If fate was cruel, people were even crueller. They kept coming by my doorstep and saying unkind things in loud voices that were intended to carry.

'You can't blame the other woman if the wife is incapable of holding onto her husband's heart. Why, she must have been neglectful in chanting the prayers we were taught to prevent the spouse's attention from straying. These young girls think they know better than their elders and fail to respect the traditions.'

'Hush! Poor thing! She is already dying of a broken heart. I am told she hasn't eaten for days and does nothing but cry.'

'That is not true! She was spotted running and playing with street urchins. I don't know what the world is coming to with women entertaining and performing charity when the husband is not home.'

'I feel sorry for her! They say she is barren. At least a child would have comforted her and spared her the loneliness.'

'Whose fault is that? Why, she could have birthed a dozen children if she had put her mind to it.'

'A curse on those dasis! We decent women cannot compete with them. What can poor Kannagi do but cry?'

I covered my ears, but their pity and contempt flooded my insides, singeing it till it was all I could do not to beat my chest and wail in frustration. When the voices finally faded after inflicting a thousand stinging welts, I was happy to crawl under the little gap in our marital couch, torturing myself with memories of a happier time, tormenting myself with all my failings as a wife who could not hold onto her husband's heart, feeling sorry for myself and crying until I could not cry anymore. The nights were even worse. Because it was more of the same.

It was obvious to me that I should never have denied Kovalan the comfort of my body whenever he sought it. I should have laughed out loud at his wit and said the most amusing things so that he would have been charmed by my company instead of being a quiet, serious and boring person. I should have been responsive and enthusiastic whenever he wanted to try all those strange things in bed, instead of shrinking back in horror and consternation. I should have used carefully chosen and persuasive words to motivate him to become a good merchant and gently persuaded him not to waste his time on dreaming, dancing, and playing music.

I could have told him that I had the worst headache in the world on the day he suggested we go see the famed beauty, Madhavi, dance. I could and should have done so many things differently, but there was no turning back. And it was not for want of trying.

All I wanted was a glimpse of his face. Why didn't he come home? A lot of men visited their mistresses, but they did not actually live with them. They returned home, ate their meals, endured the acid barbs of their wives, had a word with the children and relaxed on their couches, took a bath, and changed their clothes before heading out again. Why didn't Kovalan come home? I wouldn't call him names. I wouldn't accuse him of betraying me. I wouldn't yell at him. I wouldn't even cry in his presence. Why didn't he come home? To at least see if I was still alive? Was I dead to him? Was it true that he was lost to a spell and had completely forgotten about me? Was there anything I could do to make him come home? I would do anything to make him come back to me. But there was nothing that could be done.

Amma was the first to come and see me. I could see she was breathing fire, and I knew that if she said something cruel about Kovalan, it would be just the excuse I needed to kill myself. Except I had no idea how to go about it. The thought of slashing my wrists, swallowing poison or hanging myself were acts of violence I was not capable of acting upon.

To her credit, Amma didn't say anything hurtful about my husband. Instead, she unpacked all the food and snacks she had brought for me. They were all my favourites. For the first time in what felt like aeons, I had an appetite, and I ate hungrily. She talked about this and that, telling me of their travels and that Appa was doing well.

As I ate, I wondered if Kovalan missed my cooking. He always swore that he loved everything I prepared with my own hands. Amma was a woman who appreciated good food and she was a firm believer in eating well. Everything that came out of her kitchen was fit for the Gods, and she had trained me well. I knew I was a good cook. Did he not think of me when he ate? He would always ask if I had eaten, even though he knew I would never eat before he had. Kovalan would become very upset when I replied in the negative. Instead of letting me serve him, he would sit me down and feed me with his own hands, much to my embarrassment. I missed the taste of his fingers in my mouth. What a fool I was! Did Madhavi bother to cook? Did she suck his fingers when he fed her? I felt tears well up in my eyes and choked on my food, unable to take another bite as I concentrated hard on maintaining my composure.

My mother sighed, but not unkindly. 'I was thinking that you might come and live with us, just for a few days. We are your parents, and you are our only child. You seldom visit and refuse to spend the night with us. It is a brave new world where the old customs no longer prevail. A woman's place may be by her husband's side, but how can she do that if he no longer honours her with his presence? It might do you good to stay with us. I know it will make your father happy. You have always been a good listener, and he will be happy to reminisce about the old days.'

'Did he have a falling out with his friend, my father-in-law?' I asked worriedly. This must be hard on his parents too. And mine. What a mess!

'They have not fought or anything,' Amma shrugged. 'We are all civilized people, and we don't really point fingers and yell at each other. They follow the Jain faith, as you know, and it is against their principles to inflict hurt. We are Ajivikas, and you know we have a more practical, fatalistic approach to the inexorable force that determines all of human existence from the beginning to the bitter end. Raging and ranting against fate will not solve or make anything better. Neither will grieving.' As she said this, she looked at me pointedly.

I nodded. 'It would be nice to see Appa, and I will visit you both in a few days.'

Amma rolled her eyes. 'You are a terrible liar, Kannagi! You have no intention of leaving this house and visiting us, let alone coming to live with us. For a good girl, you have always been unreasonably stubborn. But I am not going to force you. It's your life, and you must decide how you will conduct yourself in this difficult time. I know you are stronger than even you give yourself credit for, and that you will handle your troubles with dignity and grace. You don't have to be perfect and work yourself to death every day, especially when you don't have to. And you are not alone. I will give you the space you clearly need, but I won't let you barricade yourself from me either.'

I could not bring myself to say anything. Even trying to arrange my facial muscles into what could pass for a simulacrum of a smile proved to be an impossible task.

'Be brave, sweet child. Life goes on, you will see. Believe me when I say that you will find a reason to smile again. There is joy in your future. I can feel it. A man's love is not entirely worthless, but there are so many other things life has to offer that are more stimulating and satisfying. They will find their way to you. Take care of yourself. Amma will come to visit you again soon!'

I appreciated Amma's kindness and the food, but it was a relief to be by myself.

I spent several evenings and nights on our couch, reminiscing about the love play I hadn't particularly enjoyed while I was experiencing it, but nevertheless missed tremendously now that it was over. I ached and throbbed with desperate need, wanting only to feel Kovalan thrusting on top of me, his smooth back slicked with sweat. I touched myself. Slowly and hesitantly at first, then faster and with frantic need as my body ached to be conjoined with his. I missed everything about him. Even the sickly-sweet smile he would sport while aroused and the animalistic grunting when he made love to me. I had loved his soft kisses and the possessive way he claimed my lips with his own. It had felt nice to feel his tongue on the back of my neck or in the cleft between my breasts. I missed the old days when we made love all the time. If only we could do it again and again, for all of time! I would never deny him again.

My Athai and my Mama, both came to see me. It was extremely awkward. They did not touch any of the food that I served them. Mama could not bring himself to look at me and I was saddened. He was a decent man, and I knew he had strong views about illicit sex. In fact, he talked about it a lot, and although Athai would insist that mealtime was hardly the time or place for him to expound at length on such an inappropriate subject, he would carry on outlining his thoughts.

'It is the heat in the blood,' he insisted, 'which drives men to part with enormous sums of money just to buy disease and infection from the dasis, depriving themselves of health, wealth and peace in the process. That is why we Jains do not include onions, garlic, meat or intoxicants in our diet.'

I had always prepared Kovalan's food without any of the ingredients he had mentioned, but that had clearly done nothing to reduce the heat in his blood that had driven him away from me. Madhavi was Hindu, and my maids had been whispering to themselves that her family paid for goats to be sacrificed at the Koravai temple and themselves partook of meat and alcoholic beverages to please the Goddess. My father occasionally drank a little. Amma would have been angered had it not been for the fact that she drank a lot more than him. She firmly believed that life in this world of sorrow and strife would be intolerable without a little inebriant to move things along more smoothly. Had Kovalan's eating habits changed? Did he enjoy the occasional drink with Madhavi? Was I trying to drive myself mad by constantly thinking these questions?

Athai was most distraught. 'You must have faith, Kannagi. I don't know what has come over my son. It is as if he has forgotten that he has a mother and a father who love him. We are old and he is our only son. But he no longer visits us. How can I bear it?'

She dabbed her eyes. 'If only you had given him a son or a daughter! Kovalan was a lonely child, and he would keep pestering us to give him a brother or sister. I know he wanted lots of children. If only you had obliged! He would not have had the heart to leave the children at least. It is true, I know this about my boy. We raised him with the right morals. There is some witchcraft involved here.'

Mama coughed. He was always such a dear. I fled to fetch water for him and spent the next few minutes enquiring politely about his health. He would try to respond and then he would start coughing again. Eventually, we both gave up as neither of us was particularly inclined to talk about this anyway.

Athai, however, wasn't done. 'I consulted an astrologer. In a past life, you failed to fulfil a vow, which is why this calamity has overtaken this respectable family. You must atone for your sin immediately. To do so, he says you must visit the holy spot where the Kaveri merges with the sea. There are two tanks that have been constructed there in honour of the Sun and the Moon Gods—Suryakundam and Somakundam. After ritual baths in the pools, you must visit the shrine of Kamadeva and propitiate him. You must beseech him to return the lord of your heart to you.'

Mama had another coughing fit, and this time Athai hustled him out of the house, urging me to follow her instructions precisely and save the family from further infamy.

After that, I came down with a fever and was bedridden for a month. It was my responsibility to try to fulfil my Athai's wishes but I could not bring myself to step out and expose myself to the scorn of all the people in the world outside, whose censure and rebukes would feel like a thousand lashes on my back. I welcomed the excuse to remain in bed all day and be as miserable as I pleased. I fervently hoped that the sickness would take me so that it would all end and I would not have to feel so damnably lousy all the time.

Ponni and Muthumani refused to leave my side. They wanted to send me to my mother so that I would receive the best possible care under her roof, but the very thought of leaving the house where Kovalan and I had made a life together gave me palpitations and I wept inconsolably. Why couldn't they see the obvious? When he came back, and he would come back, I must be here to receive him. It was as simple as that. Ponni and Muthu looked alarmed as I pleaded with them not to inform Amma. Reluctantly, they obliged.

In return, they insisted that I drink every drop of the herbal potions they had brewed for me and eat at least a little *rasam saadham* with *vadagam*s. They both knew this was comfort food that I could seldom resist, and I was more grateful to them for sticking by me than I could adequately express. They would apply poultices and cold compresses on my forehead, ministering to me as they would a child. What kind souls they were!

Unfortunately, I survived thanks to their ministrations. My body recovered. The intensity of my grief had lessened, despite my constant efforts to feed the pain. Muthu and Ponni seemed relieved when our household regained a sense of normalcy, and I went back to doing the extremely useless things that were meant to keep me busy and distracted from the fact that my husband was lost to me.

Mercifully, I was still too weak to be sad or cry constantly, so I was able to perform my duties without being overwhelmed by grief. When Devundi came to visit, things brightened up further. She had brought her infant daughter along. Ponni and Muthumani were highly taken with the little one, cooing over her and buzzing around, fetching milk, sweets and savouries they had prepared in an instant, no doubt delighted by the whirlwind of energy and positivity that always followed in the wake of my dearest friend, who seemed to have fully recovered from the horrors of childbirth.

'This is delicious,' Devundi declared as she took a bite. 'Nowadays, I am always hungry and all the food in the world isn't enough to fill the bottomless pit my stomach has become.'

I rocked the little baby on my knee and forgot to be sad. What a sweet little thing she was! The baby gurgled and laughed, delighted with the attention I was lavishing on her. The moppet seemed to enjoy the silver rattle that I had played with as a child, which I dug out of my almirah. But she soon got bored with her new toy, flinging it far away, and started tugging at my hair and ears. I let her have her way, pretending to squeal in pain, which thrilled her to itty-bitty pieces. Soon she was chewing contentedly on my hair, and I cradled her in my arms, holding her warm body close to mine and savouring the delicious baby scent of hers, till she fell asleep in my arms.

Devundi smiled. 'She is a pesky little thing, and when she cries, they can hear her in the deepest pits of hell. Not surprisingly, she likes you, and mercifully, she is behaving and had the good sense to fall asleep so we can talk in peace.'

'There is nothing to talk about.' I said it quickly, continuing to snuggle up against the precious bundle in my arms.

'Of course,' she said soothingly. 'I am just sorry I could not come sooner. Pregnancy is a horribly uncomfortable business. This one was harder than the others and I could not wait for it to be over. You would think I would be used to it by now. Hopefully, this is the last one. It is just too exhausting.'

I always enjoyed Devundi's company, but this time all my attention was on her daughter. 'We named her Arundhati. It was my husband's grandmother's name, and by all accounts she was every bit the paragon of virtue her namesake was.'

'A pretty name for a pretty baby,' I crooned.

'My husband was guilty of a little indiscretion too...' she confided in me. 'I refused to let him touch me when I was pregnant, and you would think the man would understand, instead of acting injured and jumping into the bed of the first girl to welcome him with open legs.'

My eyes widened in horror. Devundi nodded. 'He thought he was being discreet, but he is not clever enough to hide anything from me. I wasn't heartbroken or anything, but I did consider having an affair with someone just to spite him. Nothing happened, mind you. Pregnancy does not do much to improve your already fading attractiveness. But I enjoyed thinking of myself with another man and imagining how nice it would be to teach my loving husband a lesson by putting the cuckold's horns on him. It prevented me from calling him every evil name I could think off and emptying a steaming pan of *sambhar* on his head! And stop gasping like that, Kannagi; if you keep it up, a mosquito will enter your mouth!'

I shut my mouth. And I could not have said anything even if I had wanted to, which I did not.

Devundi was still speaking. 'I don't know why we must pretend we don't fantasize about other men, both real and imagined, more often than anyone cares to admit. I do it all the time, and none of the Gods have struck me down with lightning or their preferred weapon of choice. So it is fine to fancy whomever we please, at least in our heads, wouldn't you say? And stop looking so shocked!'

Ignoring my growing chagrin, she ploughed on, pausing only to polish off a crispy murukku in two bites. 'Or how about the fact that if we rely only on our husbands to satisfy us sexually, we would lose our minds completely, therefore we all count on self-love for appeasement of carnal cravings? Sometimes, I wish those cursed *Gandharva*s hiding among us would just ravish me! But I have heard that they only target virgins. How unfair is that? This male obsession with unbroken hymens is going to prove the death of them and us both! Anyway, my point is that love of the self is the only romance worth having. It is utterly satisfactory, and more importantly, it is entirely safe and disease-free. And the best part is that you do not require husbands or any other man for that matter. If you wish, I could teach you and show you how to fashion some of the implements I have found most handy when it comes to pleasuring…'

'Please stop, Devundi!' I begged her, feeling my cheeks turn crimson.

'You stop it, Kannagi! Why, if what I was doing was so wrong, wouldn't the Gods in their infinite wisdom drop a boulder on my head or ensure that I spontaneously combust? But that did not happen, did it? Besides, my idea of dharmic conduct is very simple…if it feels good, it is good. If it feels bad, it is bad. We would all be happier if we just did the things that make us happy, instead of forever trying to do the right thing as decreed by someone else.'

I swallowed uneasily, remembering my own forays in this direction and said the first thing I could think of to get her off this excruciating subject. 'What happened between your husband and this other person?'

Devundi frowned. 'She really had her claws into him, but fate was on my side. The dissolute friend who had introduced him to this awful creature died shortly afterwards of a painful venereal disease and a deservedly protracted bout of suffering. I won't tell you the details because I am certain you will faint and collapse in a heap. But there were many festering sores, bleeding, rotting of vital organs, and endless cries of agony that could be heard three streets away. My husband immediately saw good sense and broke all ties with that piece of filth. He returned shamefaced to me, fully believing that I had no idea about his misdeeds. The man still doesn't know that I know, and I am not about to tell him. But I am not ready to welcome him in my bed anytime soon. Not until I am fully recovered and have ascertained that he is not infected with some unspeakable disease. That doesn't stop him from whining and pleading to lie with me, and sometimes he is so irritating I have a good mind to kill him.'

Dear Devundi! She was always incorrigible.

'Darling Kannagi! I know that I have little to offer by way of comfort, but no dancing girl will ever measure up to you. Not even one who is as feted as that one. You will see. Men always get tired of their superficial charm and the cheap pleasures they offer. I am sure everything will work out for you.'

I know she was trying to make me feel better. But I didn't think that all dancing girls were carriers of disease. Rather, the dissolute men who demanded these disreputable favours of them were more likely to be the spreaders of infection. As for Madhavi, there was no doubt in my mind that she was disease-free. Moreover, her star was on the ascent. She was performing regularly in temples and sabhas to greater and greater acclaim and, according to my maids, was receiving unprecedented sums of money as the demand for her performances was so high. King Manarkilli insisted that she perform on all state occasions, and she was highly sought after on festival days as well.

They must be very happy together. Why then had I always felt that it was Kovalan and I who were meant to be together forever? Why did I still believe it? Why was it impossible for me to be happy without him? Why couldn't another man steal her away from Kovalan? Was it all too much to ask?

Arundhati gurgled in her sleep, and I took a few deep breaths to calm my nerves. My perpetual state of perturbation was disturbing the child. Devundi reached for her, but I shook my head and rocked her till she fell into deep slumber, this time against the contours of my lap.

'Athai said I should have borne him children to prevent what has happened. That there are certain rites and rituals I can perform to win him back.' My voice was cracking, so I stopped talking.

Devundi clicked her tongue in disapproval. 'Athais talk a lot of nonsense. Babies may be sweet, but they certainly cannot solve anything. In fact, the fact that I am always pregnant and bringing forth children is the reason why my own husband was driven away from my arms.'

I shrugged. 'She probably meant well. But I don't want to bear children. I love them but Kovalan and I were always enough for each other. We were not meant to be parents, and even now I have no regrets. I treasure every one of our moments together, and it may be selfish to think like this, but a baby would have intruded on the limited time I had with him and distracted us from each other. When he comes back to me, I won't share him with anyone. It will just be the two of us, like it used to be. That's all I am hoping and praying for, in the comfort of my home and not in some temple, making a spectacle of myself and supplying material for all those gossip-happy ghouls out there.'

'I will also pray for you and the two of you will be reunited soon.'

I didn't doubt it for a minute. Devundi stayed a little longer so that I could keep holding little Arundhati. When they left, the house once again descended into a state of sorrow and abject loneliness. But it felt more bearable. Life went on heedless of the sadness of an abandoned wife, and whisked me along, uncaring that I was unwilling. Nothing seemed to change in my routine, even though everything had changed.

Amma still visited every few days, bringing food and a bracing dose of her practicality. She insisted that we pray and sing together at home, when I refused to let her drag me to the temple or the park, asserting that being steeped in gloom and doom did no one any good.

Devundi visited too and sometimes brought her children. I played with all of them, but Arundhati was my favourite.

I was grateful for these interludes that brightened up the otherwise unchanging grey of my existence, which was reduced to pining for my absent husband. It got to be too much to bear, and I was heartily sick of myself. Over and over again, I did my best to distract myself with all the nothings that each day brought with it, but it didn't matter, because I inevitably circled back to him and the gaping hole he had left in my heart.

No thanks to Ponni and Muthu, I came to know that Madhavi was expecting a child. The general populace felt almost as discombobulated over this piece of news as I did since she was not performing, and they missed watching her dance. Instead, they contented themselves with gossip about how Kovalan was doing everything in his power to pamper her. His ships were filled with treasures meant solely to elicit a smile from her. They said he was determined to find the rarest delicacies from across the seas for her delectation. That the ships had travelled to the ends of the world and brought back rare birds and animals for her to marvel at. They said that he covered her with gold and gems every single day. The entire world seemed aware that he was fiercely committed to fulfilling her heart's every whim and no man had ever doted on his lover as much as he did.

None of this made sense to me. Sometimes I wished she would drop dead. Then I'd feel horrid and wish that I would drop dead instead. Neither of those things happened. It felt impossible to carry on like this. But carry on we all did. The two of them together, and I, all alone. The thought made me cry. And I hated it when I cried. My eyes swelled up, my nose ran, my hair became dry and stringy, making me look plainer and more unattractive than I actually was. If Kovalan saw me in this state, surely he would run away again.

Dredging up the last remnants of my energy, I would oil my hair and apply a mixture of curd, turmeric and honey on my face, in a desperate attempt to make myself prettier. Doing all these things did not make me feel any better. But it was something to do with the time I had, and I told myself it would eventually serve a purpose, when Kovalan took me in his arms and marvelled at how soft and smooth my skin was even as he caressed my unresisting body all over.

I desperately wanted to heal. To feel better. To end this limbo I was trapped in. Some days were better than others, but most days were beyond awful. I thought that time would make everything better. But it didn't. The pain of being separated from him only worsened as I realized that I would never be happy without him. I had no interests that were not aligned with his. I had no likes that mattered more than my liking for him. There was nothing I wished to do that did not include him. I hated myself for being this way, but I couldn't help it. Without Kovalan, there was no life or love in my life.

The cycle of pain and thwarted hope went on and on, even when I felt like I just couldn't go on. But I had to. Because something inside me insisted that he would return to me. Some part of me was convinced that our story was not over yet, and

I knew the insane voices in my head and heart were right, and I believed, even though it was madness to do so. I felt it in my blood and in my bones, and my heart was gladdened as the soul soared high on the wings of renewed hope.

He named the baby Manimegalai, after his family deity. I doubt that there was a lovelier child with a sweeter disposition in the three worlds. After all, she was the daughter of Kovalan and Madhavi. How could she be otherwise? Their happy little family was now complete. All the gossips swore that he was lost to me, his pitiful wife, forever. But that did not matter, did it? Because I did not believe it for a minute. We were meant to be together. It was as simple as that. But there was more.

I heard the news from Ponni and Muthu, who began each day with an account of what Kovalan had been up to, and I always listened without their knowledge, quiet as a mouse, eager to learn something, anything, about what he was doing.

'They say she is the apple of his eye,' this was Ponni, who did all the digging. 'Little Manimegalai is quite the beauty, I am told. Takes after her mother. Chitrapati has big plans for the poor mite, who will no doubt grow up to become a famed dasi and steal some other virtuous woman's husband from right under her nose. Then the idiot males out there will ogle her in public performances and cover her with gold so that she can live happily ever after with her illicit lover and ill-gotten gains. Where is the justice in that, I ask you? Perhaps I should have been a dasi. Except, I can't dance, and when I sing, even the crows are terrified!'

Muthu was equally incensed. 'It burns me up to learn that they are so happy. Every man in Puhar desires that Madhavi, and all of them would part with their entire fortunes for the pleasure of her company, but it is said that she is uncharacteristically faithful to her lover. It is customary for these dasis to string along as many men as possible to pay for their extravagant lifestyles. But Madhavi refuses to have anything to do with her army of admirers. She only has eyes for our Master, and it is said that they are never apart. What kind of witchcraft is this? Surely she cannot love him? Are these creatures even capable of a fine emotion like love? And even if I could sing and dance and chew paan daintily like those painted dolls, I would never be a dasi. Where is the decency in that?'

'What's love got to do with it?' Ponni scoffed, though it might have been in response to Muthu's avowed refusal to become a dasi. 'Master is one of the richest men in Puhar. Or at least he used to be.'

'What do you mean?' Muthu's voice was filled with dread. 'I have heard it whispered that he is almost as rich as our King!'

'He used to be! But that was a long time ago. They say he has somehow managed the impossible feat of frittering away his near inexhaustible funds and that he has eaten away his entire capital. I heard it from a good source that Chitrapati is already on the lookout for a new patron or patrons for Madhavi. Although even Kubera with his vast treasury would be unequal to the task of appeasing that woman's greed. How a mother worthy of being called one can pimp out her own daughter, I'll never know.'

'But that's impossible! Master could not have been that foolish, and the Mistress, as the only child of a merchant prince, is also fabulously wealthy. Surely even the avarice of a dasi is unequal to the task of snatching it all away?'

'It is not just her,' whispered Ponni, 'apparently Master does not have much of a head for business, and over the last few years he has done nothing but spend and squander everything without making good investments that can yield tangible returns. Every fraudster and charlatan in the country only needs to tell him a sob story and he immediately begins to support them as well as their extended families, paying all their bills without demur. Did you hear about the woman who killed the mongoose? Her husband left her because he could not afford to pay the exorbitant price for the compensatory rites and rituals. Master decided to help this wretch and paid all the expenses incurred just because this woman could not tell the difference between a mongoose and a snake and was not smart enough to stay out of the way when they were fighting! He has made a laughingstock of himself. His poor father must be so distraught! It is a good thing the Mistress does not know that he has also frittered away everything her parents gave her.'

Muthu gasped. 'Everything? But he has not set foot here in years! What about her jewellery? Surely that is intact?'

Ponni shook her head. 'You know she has never cared about jewellery and things like that. You will not find a nobler soul in this world. That evil Chitrapati sent one of her stooges to the Mistress with a message. It said that Master owed her a lot of money and she must be repaid immediately. Without a word, she gave him all her jewellery and sent me along to make sure that her jewels were used to pay off the debt. Master seldom leaves Madhavi's house, and I spotted him there. Do you know that he didn't even ask me how his wife was doing? At least he had the decency to look shamefaced when that odious woman took possession of his wife's jewellery. For shame!'

I couldn't listen anymore. I knew that Kovalan was not doing well financially. The entire world seemed to know about it. Madhavi's mother had been complaining to anyone who would listen that her daughter was forced to pay for the wild expenditure of her lover and the father of her child, and that only the most unworthy of men would put their paramour in such a position. Kovalan must surely have been at the receiving end of her demeaning mutterings and constant abuse. He was a sensitive person and a proud man who had always lacked the mean, calculating manner that seemed to be the only guarantor of success these days. It was not like in Appa's or Mama's time, when people were still honest and conducted their business honourably without seeking to cheat or swindle. I knew that his good intentions and kindness would be misread as gullibility and that people often laughed at him behind his back. The harsh words of Chitrapati and his detractors would have hurt him deeply.

Amma would think me a fool, but he was still my husband. And I wanted to help him. Money and jewellery had not helped save my marriage, which was the only thing that mattered to me. What use did I have for all these things? Kovalan was welcome to use all of it as he saw fit. Dear Devundi also helped by buying my silk saris and silver at a very good price. She has a large heart. With these funds, I was able to pay Ponni and Muthu their wages and keep the household running.

To be completely honest, my intentions were not entirely altruistic. I just wanted Kovalan to come back to me. The sooner the better. And if the loss of our fortune and the wrath of Chitrapati would hasten that process, so be it. Besides, if Ponni was to be believed, one of Madhavi's extremely wealthy admirers was most persistent and determined to make the danseuse his paramour, no matter the cost. May the Gods in their infinite wisdom grant him his desire so that I would get my husband back, penniless but penitent.

MADHAVI

Many Honeyed Moons

I ADORED BEING SO helplessly in love with him. Having been swept off my feet, I plunged heart-first into a brave new realm awash with bright bursts of many-splendoured hues. It was so unbearably glorious that I could barely stand it. But I was determined to savour this extraordinary experience with every fibre of my being and dived into the deep end of desire, unwilling to let caution stand in the way of the complete and utter enjoyment of these intoxicating new sensations.

It felt like we were one and the same person, an extension of the same heart and soul. This was everything I had ever wanted—love and lust leavened with intimacy and infinite tenderness. It was this way from the very beginning when Vasantamala brought him to me. I was waiting in a secluded pavilion on the seashore that was set up by my attendants, beneath a flowering champa tree I had chosen myself. It was one of my favourite spots because we could enjoy the sea breeze without the stench of fish and salt in our nostrils, thanks to the perfumed flowers that rained down on us, prodded by the incessant breeze, in a gentle cascade of feather-like kisses. Most importantly, we were far away from prying eyes, especially those of my mother.

Uncharacteristically shy for someone trained in the sixty-four arts of love, I could not bring myself to look at him. Chittu would have been furious had she seen the state he had reduced me to.

Kovalan seemed very sure of himself and lacked the nervousness that I was fighting with mixed results. He introduced himself and said some very sweet things about my arangetram. I stuttered my thanks and fell silent. Many people showered me with lavish praise following my arangetram and subsequent performances, but after he came into my life, it was Kovalan's compliments I treasured most of all. All he had to say was, '*Nee romba azhaga irukka*—you are so beautiful!' with that teasing smile of his, and I would be floored, smiling so hard for hours afterwards that my face would hurt.

With a casually possessive air, he took my hand in his, and we walked off into the distance, away from the attendants who were buzzing around, our wishes in accord, with only the soft sand beneath our feet, a bejewelled night sky and the sea breeze for company.

We walked on in silence, holding hands, pausing occasionally to admire the waves gambolling playfully as they reached out for the full moon and drinking in its silvery radiance. We slowly left everything that had gone into the making of our respective existences behind us, a gradual divesting of gathered baggage and gentle shedding of many skins until all that remained was our naked remains. Sometimes I am convinced that we should have kept on walking to the end of the world and beyond without ever turning back.

For two people who seemed to have forgotten our words, when we did start talking, we couldn't stop. He asked me all sorts of questions about myself, and I, too, was eager to learn everything I could about him. It was easy to talk to him, and easier still to laugh out loud at the steady stream of trivialities that poured forth with little bits and pieces of the oddities that went into the making of us.

He told me about his fondness for the deep blue sea, which had nearly claimed his life. 'I have always loved being in the water, but once I swam out a little too far, and the sea was in one of her moods and choppier than usual. Suddenly I was far away from land, with my legs cramping, sudden panic preventing me from drawing a breath, and the certain realization that I wasn't going to make it back to shore. Not without divine intervention anyway.'

I squeezed his hand. 'What happened? Surely there must have been someone around to help?'

He shook his head. 'I sank like a stone, and that would have been the end. But the waves took ahold of me and tossed me back onto the shore. My father insisted that it was our family deity Manimegalai who saved my life and gave me back to them. I am grateful to her, of course, but I must not forget the burly fisherman who pumped the water out of my lungs with iron fists that almost cracked my ribs and brought me back to the land of the living.'

Shivering a little, I drew closer to him and we settled down on a stone bench, gazing at the placid sea. The feeling of his thighs grazing against mine felt nice. 'I am grateful to Goddess Manimegalai and that fisherman too. Not to forget the friendly waves that saved you from the unforgiving depths. I fear the sea, but I am also a little in love with it.'

'I am jealous of the sea then…' he said, and I laughed at him for being so silly, but I was touched too.

'Don't be…' I said reassuringly, laying my head on his shoulder. In response, he placed his head on mine. His hair fell softly over my forehead, and I loved the way it felt. Of all the beautiful moments we shared, this one will always remain my favourite.

'I love the sea because her mercurial mood swings remind me

of my own. I love that she is besotted with the all-encompassing, unchanging vastness of the sky, and he with her reckless, relentless passion. No matter the infinite distance between them, they never stop striving to be together, and somehow, somewhere over the furthest horizon, they are united, together at last, never to be parted because they have worked too hard and sacrificed too much to make it into each other's arms. And they lie happily entwined for the rest of time, and all it took was an impossible leap across the endless distance, made possible only by the madness of true love.'

'That's a very sweet way to look at it...' he said, nuzzling the top of my head, 'and even if she doesn't make it all the way up to the sky, she still has the faithful shore, doesn't she? But what's a love story if it is not unnecessarily complicated?'

I remember thinking at the time that our love story hadn't been complicated at all. It was the easiest thing in the world simply because the two of us together made all the sense it was possible to make. Our union always felt effortless. And inevitable. And right.

'May I ask you something?' I nodded in response to his question, still cosily nestled against his shoulder.

'Why me? You could have your pick of not just all the red-blooded men in the known world, but the Gods in heaven as well. Of course I loved you the moment I set eyes on you, but I thought I might as well reach for a beautiful dream and try to hold on to it with all the strength I could muster. Imagine my surprise when I saw your friend holding the very wreath our King had presented to you, signalling for me and indicating that I must follow. Without hesitation, I did so and found that my impossible wish had been granted to me.'

'It is simple really...' I murmured in his ear. 'One look at you and I knew.'

'Knew what? You must tell me!'

'One look at you and I realized that I need not have been so afraid. There was nothing to fear, you see. For as long as I can remember, the thing I dreaded the most was ending up in the bed of a man who would love me at night and leave me in the morning, because he had no further use for me. It was the demon in my head which frightened me more than all the others. Even in my dreams, I was not safe because I would be trying hard to hold on to someone or something that had no wish to hold me, even for a little while. They would let go of me and I would fall and keep falling...'

Kovalan drew me into a tight embrace, and I breathed in his scent. It was hard to articulate what I was feeling then but I had to get the words out. 'One look at you and I knew you would never do that to me. That we would love each other and carry on being in love for the rest of our lives and beyond. For that is what I desire above all else. To love and be loved forever. Temporary relationships of convenience would kill me like nothing else would. I have had enough of the monetization of love and desire. If you left me, even if it was for just one moment...'

'I won't! This I promise you by all the things I hold sacred.' He said it simply and firmly. That was enough for me. Almost.

It was impossible not to think of her. His wife. The one who had already earned comparisons with Arundhati and the rest of the chaste women so celebrated by poets. They said it was thanks to virtuous wives like her that Chola Nadu remained prosperous, ever victorious in battle and free from the twin evils of famine and drought. They said that the Gods themselves worshipped her because she worshipped no one but her husband. *People were fools and they said the most foolish things.*

I pushed the unwelcome thoughts of her from my mind.

We sat there a little longer and talked about this and that and everything in between.

By the time we made it back to the pleasure pavilion, all was still. We were wide awake though, barely able to keep our hands off each other. With sudden eagerness, he pinned me against the wooden frame of the pavilion, and I offered no resistance as he ran his hands over my hips and thighs, exploring the contours of my body with a fervent enthusiasm that made me gasp aloud in surprise and a touch of apprehension.

'I like your curves!' he murmured against my ear, nibbling softly on the lobe, as his hands continued to roam, gripping my waist and making their way over the rest of my body, inch by inch. 'Your skin is so soft and smooth!'

He paused without warning, and I nearly cried out loud. Still holding me close, his fingers cupping my chin, he whispered, 'Are you scared?' I nodded, unable to say anything else. It was terrifying and exciting to be so intimate with a real man.

He held my face tenderly in the palm of his hands, pushing back the tendrils of hair that framed it as he lowered his lips to mine. I sighed with satisfaction when he kissed me softly, holding me by the hips, clasping my splayed fingers with sudden possessiveness and letting his delicate tongue probe the inside of my mouth. I loved the taste of him.

'Are you still scared?' he teased, breathlessly.

'No!' I whispered, tugging at his bottom lip with my teeth. 'I want you.'

Hungrily, we kissed each other. Our tongues touched and I slid my fingers into his hair, pulling him even closer, wanting us to simply melt into each other and become an indistinguishable mess of body parts. I threw my arms around his neck and moaned as the kiss deepened, making me light-headed with desire.

I tilted my head, allowing his tongue further access. Freeing his lips, which had been glued to mine, he gnawed lightly on my chin before making his way to my neck and covering it with kisses that felt like a butterfly flapping against my throat. I wanted more. Of everything he was doing. And even more. Of whatever he was going to do as well.

I liked the skin I wore so much more when he touched it. Making it prickle with pleasure. When he licked it. Nibbled on it. I liked the way my hair felt when he ran his fingers through my tresses or tugged at it. He said he loved the feel of my hair against his body. I loved that he loved it. My mouth would never feel right again if his tongue was not deep inside it. If I could just keep kissing him and be kissed by him for the rest of eternity, you would not hear a word of complaint from me.

We would have the rest of our lives to kiss. Slowly. Deeply. Passionately. But now I wanted more. So much more. I quickly discarded my jewellery and my garments, while he pulled off his own, discarding them carelessly on the sandy beach.

All the while our lips and hands sought each other, and we kept kissing, exploring our bodies, hating to be apart, even for the brief time it took us to divest ourselves of everything that stood between us.

I ran my fingers over his smooth chest, admiring how taut his body was, cupping his firm buttocks and drawing him close to me. I groaned as he lowered his mouth to my breasts, his tongue tracing my nipples in turn.

'Do you like that?' he asked. Kovalan always did that. It was sweet the way he kept checking to see if I liked what he was doing. The way he took imaginary notes to remind himself of the things that drove me wild. I moaned in response and he covered my right nipple with his mouth, latching onto it and suckling so urgently that I cried out from the pleasure and pain.

'I love your breasts...' he remarked. 'I like that they taste and feel so sweet. I love the scent of you. It drives me insane!' I think I thanked him. Or maybe I laughed. Who knows? I did not want him to talk. Or for him to admire me. I just wanted him to take me and make me his. For him to lose himself in the moment, the way I was utterly lost.

We collapsed on the mattress, which was stuffed with the down of mating swans. It was shielded with screens that I had painted myself, depicting the sea's love for the sky, so we could have our privacy and still enjoy the breeze and the starry sky above us. The dear moon was a benevolent and discreet witness to our love, lulling everyone else to sleep so we could have the night solely to ourselves.

Kovalan was keen to pleasure me. 'I want it to be memorable,' he whispered. 'I want it to last for you. I want you to scream and moan for me.' It was the loveliest thing. He knew it was my first time and he could not have been more kind or thoughtful.

He kissed me again. And again. His lips trailed kisses across the jawline and my neck. I moaned as he latched onto my nipple again, trailing soft, moist kisses across my belly, making his way further down. Slowly, he spread my legs. I ignored the instinct to cover myself with my hands. He buried his head between my legs and lapped thirstily until I was so wet I thought my head would explode and my deeply arched spine would break in two. Only then did he lower himself inside me, stopping immediately when I cried out at the sudden stabbing pain that assaulted me amidst the heady waves of pleasure.

'Am I hurting you?' he asked with deep concern, and I shook my head vigorously.

'I don't want you to stop!' He didn't.

Slowly and deeply, he thrust into me again and again, grabbing my legs behind my knees and lowering his mouth to kiss mine. I wasn't sure if I was falling or floating, but all I knew was that I never wanted to feel the ground beneath me again. His back muscles clenched with sudden tension after his release but by then I had almost melted into the mattress, purring with satisfaction.

We rested briefly, murmuring to each other about how good it felt. How well we fit into each other. Neither of us could wait to do it again. This time, when he was inside me, my arms were stretched over my head, with his fingers entwined in mine. Our cheeks were pressed together and we gasped in unison. He tilted his head and slid his tongue into my ear. I repaid the favour, and slowly we settled into a steady rhythm of pulling out and thrusting in, until he released for the second time. We collapsed in each other's arms, exhausted but smiling fit to burst. I didn't think I'd ever stop smiling while he was with me like this. Especially like this. I hadn't ever felt this good in my entire life.

We made love deep into the night. We talked. We kissed. The pleasure we experienced each time only intensified. It only hurt when he wasn't kissing me. The pain was only unbearable when he was not inside me. I could not bear it when he pulled out. Unwilling to release him, I tightened the little circlet of muscles deep inside me and held on, refusing to let him withdraw. I held him like that until his male hardness could envelop me again. We kept making love. We kept on making love. We might have dozed off. Then one of us would stir, waking the other, and before we knew it, we would be kissing again and anxious to make love. We talked a little. We kissed a lot. And we kept making love. Neither of us ever wanted to stop. And we didn't. He held me tight and refused to let go. I didn't want him to. And thus we remained, locked together in an embrace from which neither of us ever wanted to free ourselves.

⌇

We were happy together. Even after we eventually left our love nest on the beach and made it back home. Kovalan was all my unspoken desires, and every hidden longing made into flesh. There was something about his measured manner and the way he looked at me that made me so happy I needed nothing else.

After I got to know him better, I realized that the thing I loved best about him was that there was never one who loved laughter as much as he did. His eyes were always crinkled up as if he was enjoying a joke he simply could not wait to share with you, and his gleeful spirit was so infectious!

With Vasanta's help, an entire wing of the house was made over for Kovalan and me. We worked hard to make sure he had everything he would possibly need to be comfortable with us. I managed to find out the names of the man who made his clothes, the cook who prepared his meals at his parents' home, the paintings and sculptures he admired, the instruments he liked to play, the tutors who could help him improve his talent for music and singing, the scholars, storytellers, scribes and poets most likely to amuse him, and I hired them all.

This would be our private space, and I was determined to make sure it was perfect. Kovalan was all I would ever need, and our relationship was bound to thrive as long as it was just the two of us. I wanted to make sure that no one intruded on our time together and, in the early days at least, I largely succeeded. The two of us spent the days and nights making love and talking, unable and unwilling to be parted from each other.

Unobtrusive attendants sent by Vasantamala took care of all

our needs, keeping us plied with food and drink. We would eat off each other's bodies and pour the drinks over ourselves, before licking it off. These shenanigans drove us wild with passion and we would keep on coupling. Over and over again, pausing only to rest so we could refresh ourselves for further lovemaking. It was the most breathtakingly gorgeous thing in the three worlds!

Everything in my life was better now since he was in it. He made me happy. He said I made him happy. We were so happy that it scared me a little. But I was too happy to notice.

It was not long before the demands of the world invaded our privacy. But we were so full of joy, and life itself stretched out before us like a blank canvas we could sketch on as per our exact wishes. Initially, Chittu seemed determined not to express either happiness or unhappiness over my choice of a partner, but she thawed almost at once. Kovalan was always at ease with everyone, irrespective of their social rank or calling, and people in turn felt at ease with him. To my irritation, Chittu began to confide in him, sharing things from the past and her concerns for the future. They would sit together, chew the stupid paan Chittu had prepared, and just talk.

Kovalan was a wonderful listener and always paid attention to everything people spilled out to him. Soon, he was everybody's confidant. Everyone who resided with us took to seeking him out, knowing that they would find a steady friend and generous benefactor who would help them with their troubles. He loved artists and seemed to enjoy spending time with the mixed assortment of people who were always traipsing in and out of the house.

As for me, after my initial lapse, I had returned to training and dancing again with a vengeance. The dance had given me everything I had dared to dream of, and I was grateful and faithful to my muse. Ayya was pleased, and so was Chittu, when I started receiving invitations to perform at the palace for the King and his court on ceremonial occasions or for visiting dignitaries from distant lands, at temple festivals and the most prestigious sabhas in the land. I was richly compensated for my performances and for the first time in my life, there was an easing of the tension regarding our tight finances. It felt like we could all breathe easier, and we were relieved.

Kovalan loved to see me dance. He was never far from me and would remain glued to his seat, refusing to eat or drink, preferring instead to watch with all the concentration he could muster. Never an intrusive presence, he stayed on the circumference of the wonderful vistas I was exploring, content to leave me alone as I roamed the farthest frontiers of the known and unknown, wilder and freer than I had ever been before, because now I was anchored by love.

Each new piece Ayya choreographed for me was a revelation, a blessed opportunity for me to learn and grow as a lover, dancer and human being. A perfect experience in itself that I cherished deeply. Every golden chance I was given to train and perform, every stage I was given, every new song or dance was a gift from the universe. Having him by my side to share my joy and celebrate my achievements was the greatest blessing of all. I was deliriously happy.

I had a bigger say in the running of the household and with Vasanta's help, contrived to lessen wasteful expenditure. We were still committed to charitable causes, but I felt it was best not to splurge so much on things we didn't really need, like countless silks, even more pieces of jewellery and assorted odds and ends that cost the sun, moon and stars. To my surprise, not even Chittu protested. Perhaps she was mellowing with age.

Life was good. And it became even better when I got pregnant. When I told him the news, he grabbed me by the waist and spun me around until I was dizzy. 'I think it will be a girl as beautiful as you,' he insisted. 'I am going to love her so much and place the three worlds at her feet!'

I wasn't certain about the gender of my baby at the time, but it was a sweet little thing and barely gave me any trouble. Much to Chittu's intense irritation, I went on training and dancing because I wasn't yet showing, and I liked to keep busy. She didn't complain, though, about the income my dancing continued to generate. The dreaded morning sickness, nausea and dizzy spells bothered me only intermittently, and Vasantamala was always around with magical solutions for any unpleasant surprises my body sprung on me. I had no idea what I would do without her.

Kovalan was an absolute dear too. He always made me feel pampered and was the most caring lover a girl could ask for, but the prospect of becoming a father delighted him so much, he felt he had to devote every moment of his time to making me happy. With an extravagance that defied belief, he bought so many silks, jewels, sculptures wrought in gold and silver, that even Chittu was dazzled and utterly delighted by this generosity. As always with him, all these precious gifts he showered me with were practically beside the point and I kept telling him there was no need to spend so much on me. It was the little things he did that always wrung my heart.

Chittu proclaimed herself annoyed by my unwillingness to pay heed to her council on navigating the terrain of pregnancy. Like Kovalan, she also seemed convinced that I was carrying a baby girl. 'What use could we possibly have for boys? There are too many of them as it is, and most of them are useless.'

She was also full of grave misgivings and couldn't hold her

tongue about them. 'You have to be careful now,' she dragged me aside for the unavoidable lecture. 'Nothing destroys a woman's looks like a bloody pregnancy. You should have seen me before I gave birth to you. How magnificent I was...but then you came and stole my youth and looks. That was the thanks I got for giving you the gift of life after enduring more pain and intense discomfort than I could bear.'

I rolled my eyes at her. Chittu had never made a secret of the fact that she hated motherhood and was not quite cut out for it. She had only gone through it because Paati had told her she wouldn't be young forever and needed a daughter to keep the family tradition alive. 'Or you could hold off having a daughter until you are old and decrepit, with a mouth full of missing teeth, and attempt to sustain a career as a dancer while doddering in dotage. It will be amusing to see how that works out for you.' With this dire warning hanging over her head, she had grudgingly given birth to me. Now she was hoping that history would repeat itself and I too would lose my looks after giving birth to a daughter. Chittu was nothing if not spiteful.

Kovalan, on the other hand, thought I was the loveliest thing in all of creation. 'I would not have thought it possible, but you are becoming even more beautiful with every passing day. Impending motherhood has transformed you. Even your dance is practically otherworldly now. No Apsara in Indra's court will ever measure up to you!' I was pleased but swatted his arm playfully to stem the tide of hyperbole.

He was undeterred. 'Your body is blossoming! It is filling out and your breasts are bigger and heavier. They deserve all the love in the world!' He buried his face between my breasts and carried on complimenting them like the silly thing he could be at times. I loved it when he was being a silly thing.

'Oh! Stop it! You are just being a silly thing! I feel heavy and unwieldy!'

'Madhavi, you are the one who is being silly. If you get any prettier, the King is probably going to outlaw you, because the envious Indra will show up here with the sole purpose of claiming you for himself. Without your beauty and your art to keep it afloat, Puhar will sink to the bottom of the sea and...'

I burst out laughing. He said the most hilarious things. Kovalan said he loved it when I laughed. I loved him for saying it. He was kissing me, making me sinfully aroused. It had been years, but I was always surprised at how much we still needed each other. How intensely pleasurable our lovemaking still was.

Ever the cynic, Chittu was having none of it. 'Of course you are not glowing. I'll admit that you are carrying the extra weight with becoming grace, but you are still taking your youth and looks for granted. You had better use that special blend of oils and herbs I instructed Vasantamala to brew for you. Don't be lazy. Apply it religiously all over your body. Otherwise, your skin will be covered with ugly stretch marks and your breasts will also start to sag.'

Of course I was using her stupid oils. Kovalan liked to apply it himself, and he did it so patiently and skilfully, massaging every inch of me with such consummate tenderness that I swooned every time and rewarded him many times over for his caring nature by increasing my own exertions towards pleasing him on our shared bed.

Kovalan scandalized the entire household by remaining by my side when I went into labour. He was even more scared than I was, but he stayed anyway. I asked for his hand, and he placed it in mine and did not remove it once. Not even when I hurt him, when the contractions became intense. And painful.

Not once did he let go. I cried then. I don't know why. But I just loved him so much. All I wanted for myself was to keep on loving him. And to keep on being loved by him.

The midwife misunderstood my tears. She said it was almost over. Kovalan didn't get it either. He kissed me on the forehead to comfort me. And I loved him even more deeply than I did a minute ago. And then it happened. Amidst an outpouring of blood and smelly fluids, we became parents.

'It's a girl,' Vasantamala informed us, sounding relieved. She sent someone to tell Chittu the happy tidings.

'What shall we name her?' I asked Kovalan through a delirium of happiness and exhaustion.

'Her name is...' he paused for a beat. 'Manimegalai!' We said it at the same time.

Manimegalai. The daughter we had made. The child of our hearts. She would be so incredibly special. Now I truly had everything. Was that even possible? There were too many who had little or nothing. What had I done to deserve all this good fortune? I ignored the part of my brain which was bypassing the pleasure to access the hidden dread and unlock the darkest and most relentless of my demons. The one that always assured me that abandonment would be my fate. No matter how hard I tried to avert it. No matter how fiercely and uninhibitedly I loved. No matter what I did. Or didn't.

∽

I needed to believe that everything was as perfect as it could be. Therefore, I believed it. Even when the tiny tears and trifling imperfections showed up on our painstakingly put-together parchment of perfection. Especially when the tears, which were originally just tiny rips, widened and then widened some more.

I chose stubborn blindness over good sense. And why not? For the longest time, everything had been perfect. But perfection is a rare state to achieve. And even rarer still to preserve. I should have known that.

It is hard to pinpoint the precise factor which made everything unravel, and with undue haste at that. Contrary to Chittu's hopes and predictions, neither the pregnancy nor the baby was to blame. My body made such a miraculous recovery that Chittu declared it was most indecorous to be blessed with such good health.

We had a wet nurse for the baby, and Vasantamala concocted one of her miracle cures. It involved crushing jasmine flowers and other herbs and applying them to my breasts at regular intervals throughout the day and drinking a herbal potion she had brewed with very specific but mysterious ingredients to stop the production of breast milk. She is such a blessing! My body had been through a lot, and I was so relieved that it did not have to be put through further rigours demanded by motherhood.

I began to dance within days. Unlike birthing, the gruelling physical exertion dance demanded was never less than gratifying. Within months, I was performing once again at key events in Puhar. It was exhilarating. Even more so when I realized that I had secretly feared that the months of not being able to dance, combined with motherhood, would lead to a decline in my popularity and eventually be the death knell for my career. To my immense relief, people had missed me. My absence had only increased their fondness, and I was grateful for the adulation showered upon me. I had danced until I started showing, but even the few months I had spent away from dancing weighed heavily on my soul. It felt good to immerse myself in the music once again and move as one with it.

Manimegalai was as well-behaved as it was possible for a baby to be. She had the good sense to cry within reason, refrain from falling sick, submit to Vasantamala's upbringing, tolerate Chittu's interfering, and grow up with minimal fuss and muss. She was a good-looking girl with beautiful manners and a calm demeanour. I made sure to spend time with her, but I sensed that it would do her good not to see me too often. Having Chittu loom over my life like a shadow had never been good for my health or happiness and I wanted to spare her the venom of a mother's love.

Kovalan remained the best of lovers, but he took to fatherhood just as I had taken to motherhood, in that he didn't want much to do with it. A strange restlessness had taken root in him, causing him to veer alarmingly between listlessness and increasing melancholy. The laughter that had been such a huge part of him seemed to have dried up entirely.

When I tried to talk to him about it, he didn't want to say much. But Vasantamala heard him complaining to the random people who floated in and out of our residence that his best days were behind him and that he did not have much to show for his life. Whatever was that supposed to mean? He had me. He had Manimegalai. He was blessed with health and wealth. What more could he possibly want? The dissatisfaction he was starting to feel could have contributed to the cracks. I wanted to fix it, but there was so much to do and so little time.

Kovalan's reckless spending may have been a factor in fraying the finely woven fabric of our flawless love. Compared to him, Chittu herself was the model of forbearance and temperance. He was kind and generous. I loved that about him. But I did not like that he was kind and generous to a fault. He was a soft touch for anyone with a sob story. There were many among the poor and unfortunate who benefited from his munificence. I respected that. There were many more charlatans who sought to swindle him out of the large fortune he had inherited, and they were successful. It was harder to respect that. It certainly infuriated Chittu. She firmly believed that the only people who should benefit from his profligacy were us. It drove her mad to think that it did not take any special skill in the fine art of womanly manipulation to rob Kovalan of his riches.

I probably should have talked to him about it. But he hated discussing finances. And I, in turn, did not care for any kind of awkwardness between us. It always made our lovemaking feel forced and monotonous, and I couldn't stand that. Besides, it was his money. And he had the freedom to do what he pleased, didn't he?

∽

It took a while, but the Goddess of Prosperity finally deserted him. I did not mind too much. Fortunately, I was making enough for the two of us. It should be sufficient, if only he did not persist in his thriftless ways.

The loss of his fortune weighed heavily on Kovalan. Vasantamala and I bent over backwards to make sure he was treated with the respect he deserved and that he was never out of funds to pursue his interests in the manner he was accustomed to. But that was not enough. People talked. And they could be mean. His reduced circumstances made him even more susceptible to moodiness and endless brooding. Never mean-spirited, he became increasingly deflated, and I missed the buoyancy that had made it such a pleasure to be around him.

Chittu was furious. She went from being his fast friend to his worst enemy in the blink of an eye. Every time she saw me, the haranguing would begin. 'If only you had listened to me and become the King's concubine. Then we wouldn't be in the situation we are in now. This is the problem with girls who think they know better than their mothers when it comes to choosing a suitable paramour. It is not too late. Send this wastrel away and you will be flooded with offers from suitable men who would part with their entire fortunes in exchange for a smile from Madhavi.'

I ignored her. But Chittu was on a mission. She turned to directing her ire at Kovalan. I shielded him from her wrath and cold contempt as best I could. He was a sensitive soul who was no match for Chittu's calculated cruelty. But I could not protect him all the time, since I was busier than ever as the blessed offers to perform continued to pour in. I hoped that my popularity would please Chittu, but of course, there was no pleasing her. Even Vasantamala proved unequal to the task of shielding Kovalan from my mother's constant jibes, especially since her first allegiance was always to me and she was constantly by my side.

'Sometimes it is best to let these things resolve themselves,' was her advice to me, and I was happy to listen, since it did not call for action on my part. I could happily dance for days on end, but the very idea of exerting myself in the problematic areas of my life proved too much to even think about.

Kovalan, with his boyish innocence and tendency to walk around with his head in the clouds, did not often get the import of Chittu's words, which was a mercy. But he did sense her antipathy and wisely chose not to confront her. Instead, he distanced himself from her and distracted himself with new amusements in a bid to allay his enduring ennui. But nothing could lift his spirits. Conversation did not stir him. Good food and drink lost their appeal. Music and dance left him enervated. Not even Manimegalai could elicit a smile from him.

Chittu had changed tacks. She gave up her constant needling in favour of committing herself to ruining poor Kovalan fully. She sent a messenger to his residence, and they were instructed to tell his wife that Kovalan owed Chittu money. That poor woman was thus persuaded to part with all her jewellery, which my mother had long coveted. It came to my knowledge that she had given them up without the least hesitation. I was furious and insisted that Chittu return them to their rightful owner. To my surprise, she was angrier still and firmly refused to do as I demanded.

'Are you mad, Madhavi?' Her jowls were quivering, and she looked so monstrous that Manimegalai wailed in consternation. 'Of course I will not return it. And despite what you think, I did not keep any of the pieces, except for a few exceptional ones. And even those are not for me. I am saving them for poor Manimegalai, who will not inherit anything if her parents keep up with their combined foolishness. The rest was used to pay off his creditors who keep showing up at our doorstep. Had I not paid them back in full, they would have sent thugs to despoil our beautiful home. It is so humiliating!

'I did not work so hard and invest so much of my own resources in your dance only for this shameless man to throw it all away and drive us into the streets. Even a rabid dog has no respect for a man with no money. Why should I treat him any differently than he deserves?'

I trembled not only in outrage but also overwhelming fear. If Chittu kept up with this torrential outpouring of hatefulness, she would succeed in driving dear Kovalan from my arms. How cruel she was! Did she not realize that he was the best among men and his only flaw was generosity, which was a virtue?

'I didn't hear you complain when he so generously parted with his fortune to indulge your many whims,' I snarled at her, 'and you have the nerve to accuse Kovalan of shamelessness when you are the shameless one who can't see past a person's material worth. This is precisely what is wrong with all of us. We discard men callously after we have relieved them of their funds, and then we weep and wail when we ourselves are cast aside when our looks fade. Embracing a lifestyle like this is tantamount to selling your soul. Don't think for a minute that I will do that. If you drive Kovalan away from me, I will kill...'

'Grow up Madhavi,' she said, brushing aside the insults and threats like they were nothing, which was hardly surprising, for she was far more adept at their usage. 'He is going to leave you and return to his silly wife, who I am told still worships only him every single day. She will have use for him, even if all he has is a soiled loincloth to his name. Can't you see that he is not impervious to the insults being heaped on him by all of Puhar for burning through a fortune as vast as his? Don't you realize that your dazzling success and the accolades you enjoy makes him bitter and resentful, especially in comparison to his own abysmal failure and state of penury? This love story you swear by is over. But I give you my word... I won't let him ruin you before he leaves you.'

I burst into tears. 'Don't you drive him away from me!' I screamed at her. 'I will never dance again if you keep insulting him like this. Mark my words.'

'Of course you will...' she said. 'If you don't want him to leave you, we must remedy our financial situation immediately. As things stand now, he is spending your money faster than you can earn it. Why, only yesterday he adopted a woman whose imbecile son accused a woman of adultery because she refused his advances. When this abomination of a man's falseness was revealed, he was deservedly sentenced to death because the woman in question had a cast-iron alibi. Kovalan not only volunteered to take his place to appease the rascal's mother, who was wailing and beating her chest like a demented woman, but also brought her back here and promised to take care of all her needs for the rest of her life. The man can barely scrape together two coins, but he dares to bring these wretched people under my roof without so much as a by-your-leave.'

'He doesn't need your permission,' I bit out, 'this is my house now.'

'What pretty airs you give yourself, Mistress,' she retorted sarcastically, 'but you need me to help you replenish our rapidly dwindling resources thanks to Kovalan's assorted stupidities.'

'Just leave him alone,' I said tiredly. 'If you promise to do that, I will remedy our financial situation. I give you my word.'

'I promise not to say a word to him if you do exactly as I say from now on. You will dance where I tell you to, and I will hear nothing of your fine airs and scruples. Do you hear me?'

Dispiritedly, I nodded. I simply could not lose Kovalan. Soon I was giving private dance performances in the homes of disreputable men. Something I had sworn never to do. For the men who demanded this of me had next to no interest in the merits of music, dance, art, or culture. All they wanted to do was leer at me like the lecherous swine they were and make their wretched advances after trapping me alone. I had to fend off these monsters by myself. It was soul-crushing and so debasing, I wanted to kill myself. Every such encounter left me feeling soiled and defiled. I hated Chittu for doing this to me. But even Vasantamala said we didn't have much of a choice.

'I know what you are going through,' she said sympathetically, after she had rescued me from a fat man who tried to grope me, 'and I will do what I can to make this easier for you. But from a practical point of view, perhaps it is best if you leave feelings out of this. It is just a job that needs to be done in exchange for payment. And these men may feel otherwise, but they can't make you do something you don't want to, can they? I don't think you should inflict so much hurt on yourself over their actions. You are being harder on yourself and crueller to yourself than they are. Please stop doing that.'

I suppose she was right, but it was impossible not to feel conflicted about the direction my life had taken. The worst part was that seeing Kovalan's plight made me realize that I did not want the same thing to happen to me. All my life there had been the overriding fear that we would lose everything, despite the heavy price we had paid for it, and the thought of being left with nothing terrified me. Vasantamala was right. A dancing girl could not afford to have too many fine scruples lest she be undervalued and forcibly relegated to the status of a vesha and deprived of choice altogether.

But at least Chittu and Kovalan were fast friends again, singing songs and chewing *vetrilai paaku* together, as if things hadn't changed at all in our once happy household.

∽

Things were puttering along ruinously when Vasantamala, bursting with excitement, managed to arrange a rendezvous between Senapati Seyon and me, at his request. He was the valiant commander-in-chief of the Chola army.

'And he is so handsome!' Vasantamala gushed.

My initial response was fear. These military men felt compelled to constantly prove their masculinity and sexual prowess. Nothing good ever came of all this posturing and violent pelvic thrusting. The prospect of being alone with him made me shudder. But as Vasanta pointed out, the requests from powerful men were commands and to flout them was to imperil ourselves. I wondered if choice was a damnable illusion, and submitted to what was expected of me with all the grace I could muster.

I entered his palatial home with grave misgivings. It was a pleasant surprise. Seyon was not like the others of his ilk. He did not demand that I dance for him, nor did he attempt to ingratiate himself with me. All he wanted was for us to have a meal together. I was suspicious at first, but gradually I warmed to him. The Senapati was a remarkably good-looking man who radiated raw power and charisma. He did not brag about his many achievements or seek to impress me. Neither did he ply me with insincere praise in the hope that it would somehow convince me to spread my legs for him. He just told me amusing anecdotes from his travels, none of which featured spilled blood, guts, glory, or sexual bravado. After what felt like forever, I laughed out loud. It felt good to feel good after ages, and that immediately ruined the mood and made me question everything.

'Why am I here?' I asked him, unable to leave well enough alone. If he wanted to ravish me, it was best that I disabused him of his presumptuous notions. With a start, I realized that the mere thought had made me wet, and my cheeks burned in response. What a hypocrite I was becoming!

'I thought it was obvious...' His smile was wry. 'Beautiful women are plentiful, so it was not your beauty alone which drew me to you. It was simply the fact that you are without guile or coquettish wiles. It is not particularly hard to defeat an enemy on the battlefield. It is harder to deal with people who have ulterior motives and seek to use or defraud you to advance their ambition or whatever piddling motive they have. You are different.

'And you do not want anything to do with my power or fortune. It is refreshing. I sent for you because you have haunted my dreams for the longest time, and I wanted to meet you in person. To see if there is anything special to explore, provided you are willing, of course.'

'Well, you have met me in person,' I said hesitantly.

He took my hands in his with so much affection that I shivered with anticipation. Did he know that I was spoken for? I got the feeling that it wouldn't matter to him. That this was a man who could not be bothered with conventional rules and regulations. That he would adhere solely to the principles of his own making.

Seyon was still holding my hands, and he was so masterful that I did not pull away. I could not have, even if I had wanted to. 'All I want from you is a kiss, that is, if you will permit me the pleasure and privilege of tasting your lips.'

I did not even hesitate. Neither did he. He kissed me. And we went on kissing. It felt nice to be kissed like this. Properly. By a man who knew how to. We became breathless, but we could not stop kissing. I reached for his manhood because I could not wait any longer. I wanted him so much that I could barely stand it. To my immense satisfaction, he wanted me even more. Entire armies would not have been able to keep us apart after that. The urges that drove us were too powerful. It was exciting, intoxicating and inescapable. There was nothing to do but to surrender, without fear or compunction. And we did! Oh, how we did!

Good sense had abandoned me. Every time I left him, I swore I would never return, but it was hopeless. There was no escaping the highs of illicit sex. He was a busy man, but the Senapati always made a little time for me. So that we could be together. I was flattered and more than a little touched. It did not make sense, but it felt right to be with him. Denying him alone felt wrong. I never denied him. I could not. Was I falling in love with him? What about Kovalan? I did not want to think.

All I wanted to do was surrender to whatever this was. Again and again. Like the men Seyon had overpowered on the battlefield. And enslaved.

But he was a very busy man. And there were too many demands on his time. Which made the moments we managed to snatch for ourselves feel even more special. I liked being in his arms. He was a powerful man who could have crushed me, but I loved the restraint he exercised, even though he was insatiable. I nearly wept when the Senapati broke free of a passionate embrace to tell me the bad news. 'Duty calls, my love! I must leave for the battlefield. I will continue to dream of you. Remember me in your prayers and dreams. If I come back, we will meet again.'

When the Senapati left, I was in a state of absolute turmoil. It was my expectation that guilt and shame would tear me apart. But they were absent. It had felt good to be loved like that. By a man like the Senapati. He haunted my dreams now. But I still cared deeply about Kovalan. None of it made sense to me. Then or now.

∽

I went back on my word to Chittu. After my impassioned affair with the Senapati, which left me craving for more and beset by endless yearning, I refused to dance in people's homes. To my surprise, Chittu did not protest. Vasanta told me that this was because Senapati Seyon had been most generous and indicated to Chittu that he hoped to become my permanent patron. I had no idea how to respond. Part of my heart leapt with joy, another part contracted with misery at the thought of breaking Kovalan's heart or leaving him in his time of need. Mercifully, I didn't have time to dwell on it.

Frenetic preparations for the Indravizha celebration, which would go on for twenty-eight days, were already underway. This was the most important event in Puhar. If the myths the old timers are forever talking about are to be believed, it was an ancient king of the Chola clan with the tongue-twisting name—Tunjaivilerinda Toditthota Sembiyan—who was the first to introduce this festival in praise of Indra, the King of the Devas and mighty wielder of the thunderbolt. His own ancestor Mucukunda had once assisted Indra in his war against the Asuras, and following their joint triumph, Puhar had enjoyed the goodwill and protection of the God of Thunder.

Succeeding monarchs had carried on this ritual because it was believed that if the Indravizha was not celebrated with pomp and splendour in a manner befitting the most irascible and egoistic of the Gods, a fierce *bhutam*, enforcer of Indra's will, would rain destruction on Puhar and cause it to be swallowed by the sea. As if that could ever happen! But having been told this tale for generations, people believed in the implicit wisdom of not provoking Indra and celebrated Indravizha annually to appease him.

King Manarkilli had declared at court that, as the pride and jewel of the Chola Kingdom, my skills as a dancer would be suitably showcased over the course of the festival. This honour had been accorded to me many times before, but I always breathed a sigh of relief and murmured a prayer of gratitude to Indra, who blessed me with these wonderful opportunities each time.

Rehearsals were most strenuous, and the process consumed me as always. I had little time to think or ponder over my actions and ruminate endlessly on their ramifications. Kovalan, who formerly chose to be constantly by my side, had for a while now taken to wandering off by himself lost in his thoughts. And that suited me perfectly.

The days passed in a blur. When the festival rolled around, I felt better than I had in a long time. The punishing schedule had taken a lot out of me, but I was exuberant. Diving deep into the demands of the dance left me feeling cleansed. I sought out the quiet places away from the chaos that had taken control of my life. Slowly but surely, I found them, and away from the swirling madness I found comfort, peace and spiritual healing. If only I didn't have to return to the complications of life.

My performance was a triumph, and both King Manarkilli as well as the visiting dignitaries showered me with praise and gold. Chittu was thrilled. I was euphoric too, but knew from long experience that the elation would wear off. Before that happened, I wished to return to Kovalan and repair the suddenly fragile bond between us. I owed him that for the years of love and happiness we had shared together.

In an inspired moment, I asked Vasantamala to set up a pavilion on the beach at the same spot where our romantic odyssey had begun. Kovalan was unenthusiastic as ever, but he relented when I cajoled him. I was hoping we could talk a little over a delicious meal and later make love under the stars again. *It was too soon to give up on us.* Or so I thought.

Kovalan picked listlessly at his food, and my heart quailed. 'What's troubling you? Won't you tell me?'

He smiled sadly at me. 'I wish I knew... All I know is that it is time for me to break my promise to you.'

'What do you mean? I don't understand.' But of course I did. Dread coursed through my insides and suddenly, I could not breathe.

'Don't make me spell it out for you, Madhavi!' His voice was more distressed than angry, and it broke my heart. 'I was not a faithful husband but as a lover, I did not break faith. Can you say the same?'

'I have not betrayed you…' I began, but stopped, unable to lie to him even if it meant sparing him a world of grief. I really had no intention of betraying him. Belatedly, I realized that I had just wanted to feel loved again.

'Don't, Madhavi!' There was sadness in his eyes, which shone with unshed tears. 'I loved you and I will go on loving you, but love is never ever going to be enough. Our time together was magical, but it is time now for both of us to go our separate ways.'

He rose to go, with an air of finality that left me petrified. I clutched his hand in desperation. 'You cannot leave me!' I pleaded, all dignity, self-respect and thoughts of Seyon forgotten.

Gently, he pried my fingers loose. Shaking his head with the same infinite sorrow that was clutching at my heart, he turned on his heel and walked away. I lay alone on our bed, staring up at the stars through a blur of tears. It was hard to believe that he was gone. Never to return. It was even harder to realize that he was right. Love would never ever be enough. And yet it was all I wanted. All I would ever want. Having become addicted to love, I could never go back to a life where there was none. But that was the wretched wasteland I was doomed to return to. Turning my face away from the stars, I wept until I could weep no more.

KANNAGI

Paradise Regained

I NEVER DOUBTED THAT he would come back to me. It was always just a matter of time. Every second spent apart from him felt like an eternity, but if that was the price I had to pay so that we could be reunited for all time, I would gladly pay it with interest. Everyone admired my patience and resilience, or so said Muthu and Ponni every time they whispered about what they had discovered about Kovalan and Madhavi while I listened intently. But I was an impatient wife who had no choice but to be patient and do whatever it took to maintain some semblance of mental equanimity. My mother thought of everything, and if it had not been for her support I would have collapsed in an ungainly heap and never recovered. Aware of our reduced circumstances, even the poor had stopped visiting my home and asking for alms. It was a painful blow.

Amma also retained Muthu and Ponni, whom I could no longer afford to pay. I was grateful to her for employing them. They wanted to spend a few hours helping me out every day, telling me that it was what Amma had instructed them to do, but I politely and firmly declined. I think they understood. I did all the cooking and cleaning myself. It gave me something to do and made me tired enough that I was able to get a little sleep every few days or so.

The day Kovalan returned to me, I remember talking to

Devundi in the evening. She had come by after I had finished my duties for the day and was sitting in the dark, with only my increasingly bitter thoughts for company. Very thoughtfully, she had brought some *prasadam—sambhar saadham* and sweet *pongal*. I didn't have much of an appetite, but I appreciated the gesture.

'You must eat, Kannagi! I prayed especially for you and gave the Gods a piece of my mind for putting you through all this misery. But you must not be aggrieved. Something tells me that your suffering has come to an end. Believe me when I say that future generations will grow up hearing stories of your courage and grace in the face of insupportable torment and will love you just as much as we all love and admire Arundhati, whose virtue and chastity we have been taught to emulate...or else!'

She giggled a little at that, and I managed a small smile. I knew Devundi had little patience with the saintly Arundhati and the impossible standards she had set for women. In fact, I think she named her daughter Arundhati just so she could yell at her and compare her to monkeys and donkeys every time she got into mischief.

Devundi leaned closer and whispered, 'Did you know that Madhavi is having an affair with the Senapati? It is the worst-kept secret in Puhar. The man has long been determined to make her his paramour and it is said that she was his most challenging and stubborn adversary, but in the end she succumbed, as they all do. Can you believe that? Despite her airs, she is no different from the others in her profession.'

I did not feel like responding to that. Devundi did not say it, but I knew she felt Kovalan had received his comeuppance, and that just made me sad. Despite what everyone who didn't know him at all said, he never intended to hurt me, and I never wanted him to be hurt, on my or anybody else's account. As for the rumours about Madhavi, I doubted they were true. She seemed like a refined person. It was certain that she was not like the other dancing girls who had little use for a man unless he had the means to fund their exorbitant way of life.

'Didn't little Arundhati accompany you to the temple?' I asked Devundi, to change the subject as tactfully as I could.

'She is unwell, and you know I can't handle my children when they are not in the best of health. The maid or my mother-in-law or one of the husband's sisters, I am not sure which, is taking care of her, I think. I went to the temple mainly to get away from all the fussing. It is too bad! The child finds it impossible to be silent and sleep until she is fully recovered. She keeps complaining about the bitter potions she must swallow, and I just couldn't take it anymore.'

'Oh, the poor little thing! I hope she recovers soon.'

'Let's not talk about sick children. It bores me to tears. Why don't you just tell me what's on your mind instead? Something is clearly bothering you, and you might as well tell me before you explode.' She was looking at me intently, and there was no hiding from my dear friend.

I shook my head to clear it, trying to find the words. 'Last night, I had a dream. Kovalan came back to me. But I didn't want him to. Can you imagine that? It jolted me even in my sleep, and I wanted to wake up to stop this feeling, but I couldn't. We held hands and were walking through some strange land. Suddenly I snatched my hand back and begged him to leave me. To run away as fast as he could. To go back the way we had come. In fact, I screamed and wailed like a demented person urging him to run. Can you imagine me creating a scene like that? The terror and dread that engulfed me...it was so...it felt like being stung by a thousand scorpions. I am so scared, Devundi! I can't shake the feeling that something evil is about to happen and there is nothing I can do to make it go away.'

Devundi hugged me and stroked my head. 'You poor thing! Dreams don't mean anything real, do they? It is probably because you have been so unhappy and anxious about the future. Why don't we go to the temple together? I will take you there tomorrow. The pujari says there is a special ritual he can perform which will ensure lasting marital happiness. It will make you feel better. I can take care of all the arrangements. I am sure your mother will approve too!'

I shook my head wearily. I could not afford to pay for a special puja, nor did I want Amma or Devundi to bear the cost. Both had been more than generous. I couldn't repay them for all the help rendered in this lifetime. How could I accept any more aid from them? Besides, I might be as naive as everyone swore I was, but even I knew that the solution to life's problems would never be as simple as hiring a pujari to perform some elaborate ritual.

Devundi was not done trying to make me feel better. 'I have these disturbing dreams too! I am always in the middle of a sexual act. It is always something unspeakable and utterly taboo. Worst of all, there is never a stitch on me. If that were not awful enough, my depraved conduct is witnessed by all of Puhar. It is mortifying and I want to stop and disappear. But I carry on doing it. And suddenly the mob is out for my blood, and I am running, naked as the day I was born, breasts jiggling, and they catch up with me and I have nowhere to go but manage to jump on the roof. Then, I find myself...'

Ponni charged into the house. 'Master is on his way home. All your prayers and good deeds were not in vain. He is walking towards us from the Merchants Square. They say he used the last of his funds to pay off all standing debts and is returning to you!'

I could not think of a single thing to say. Nor did I know how to react. So many competing feelings were warring for my attention that I could not process them in the least. One particularly urgent thought crowded out the rest and I cried out in consternation. In the old days, Muthu and Ponni would prepare me to receive Kovalan in the evenings and I would pretend to be reluctant, but I loved how his eyes lit up when they landed on my face. He would shower me with the prettiest compliments. They would make me blush and I felt uncomfortable. How much I had missed that. But that had been many moons ago. Now I must look an absolute fright.

I had not oiled or washed my hair or even combed it in ages. For all I knew, there was a family of rats nesting in the greasy, tangled mess this very minute. My eyes were puffy and encircled by dark patches from all the self-pity-induced crying and sleeplessness. It probably made me look like a demoness or a sad old hag. Having not eaten well in a long time, I was little more than a bag of bones, and my breasts were sunken pouches. He had always liked my breasts more than the other parts of me, or so I gathered, but there was not much that was left of them! If he had left me when I was as pretty as I was ever going to be, what would he do now when he saw me in this hideous state? Besides, he was returning from Madhavi's plump, well-rounded arms. And she couldn't look ugly even if she tried. What was I supposed to do?

'He can't see me like this,' I wailed in misery. 'Why! I look simply awful!'

Devundi and Ponni sprang into action. They quickly drew up a bath for me and scrubbed and polished the ruinous apparition

The Wife and the Dancing Girl

between them as best they could. There were no aromatic oils or even a single decent sari in the house, but we used some of the leftover cooking oil that my skin drank up thirstily since it had been reduced to an arid desert. And we used some curd and turmeric on my face in a vain bid to give my countenance some lustre.

But there was still the question of a sari. The only one I now owned was worn out and, though I was usually neat and tidy, there was a small stain on it. That was enough to drive me to tears. If only I hadn't sold all my saris! What was I going to do?

Muthu barged in just then. She came in bearing the gift of a sari that Amma had sent, and my heart was so filled with joy at this small miracle my mother had wrought, anticipating my needs long before I even knew there was a need, that I felt like I had been given a fresh lease of life. In auspicious shades of turmeric yellow and kungumam red, the blessed sari was soft to the touch and too beautiful for words. Holding it in my hands, with tears in my eyes, I knew that I was finally going to be happy. So very happy at long last!

'Here Kannagi! You can wear my chain,' Devundi offered kindly but I shook my head.

'He always said I did not need any ornaments to enhance my looks,' I said, feeling a little shy. 'He insisted that my simplicity and modesty were the only adornments I would ever need.'

Ponni nodded vigorously. 'Master would scold Muthu and I when we bedecked her in rich silks and fine jewellery. He would say that our Mistress was so delicate, we were being cruel to her by weighing her down with so many heavy ornaments. Remember how he used to twirl you around and say that you were the most beautiful girl in all the land?'

'He would say that she was lighter than air,' Muthu chimed

in, 'that he had married not a delicate flower but the prettiest of petals!'

We giggled together at the memory. I could hardly keep still while they fussed over me. Muthu used some lampblack to define my eyes, and Devundi found some kungumam the temple priest had given her to make the auspicious mark of the pottu on my forehead, and suddenly I felt as if I had emerged from the ashes of my grief, a brand-new person.

Kovalan would soon be here, and I could scarce contain my eagerness. With immense thoughtfulness, my friends melted away in an instant. Suddenly alone, I barely had a moment to gather my thoughts when I heard Kovalan open the front door. As he walked in with that familiar stride that I knew so well despite the uncharacteristic hesitation, the years simply melted away. It was like he had never been gone. I wanted to rush into his arms, but I was rooted to the spot, unable to move or string together a coherent sentence.

'Dearest Kannagi! How wonderful it is to see that beautiful, sweet face which is incapable of mustering a stern expression even for one who has earned it… I never did deserve you!' Gently, he took my hands in his own. 'Can you forgive this fool?'

'There is nothing to forgive,' I told him simply, relieved that my voice did not squeak, 'and you shouldn't talk about my husband like that. I won't stand for it.'

He smiled at my pathetic attempt to make a joke, but there was so much sadness in his eyes that tore at my heart. Despite my efforts to look nice for him and his gallant compliment, I knew he noticed the difference in my appearance. My bones were sticking out from my body in the most unflattering way, and I cursed myself for not eating better. Although he was stroking my wrist affectionately, I could tell that the absence of bangles or rings bothered him no end. He was thinking of the jewels that I had given away and was surely berating himself for it. I wished I could tell him that I had been happy to help him and that all the ornaments in the world held little value to me. He was the only thing that mattered.

Making him sit down, I fussed over him, the way I had in the past. Doing little things to make him comfortable gave me immense pleasure. I had missed this. I had missed him so much. I fed him some of the prasadam that Devundi had brought and relished the feel of his tongue on my fingers. It was the most beautiful feeling in the world. I wished I could feed him with my own hands, every single day for the rest of our lives.

Kovalan seemed relieved that I was not angry with him and ate with a good appetite. Occasionally, his eyes would dart around the house, noting that of all the fine things we had once owned, nothing remained. I tried to think of something to say to distract him. Inspiration struck and I told him about Devundi's dream, feeling very daring as I did so. This made him smile, which in turn made me smile. He had always enjoyed listening to the more shocking things Amma and Devundi said, going so far as to agree with them. It was nice to talk and smile like this. But it was a temporary respite.

'I can't believe I have done this to you, Kannagi!' He looked so sad and defeated that it broke my heart. 'So much has been lost, and it is my stupidity that's to blame. If only that woman hadn't made you give up your jewellery, perhaps we could have gone away from this accursed place and made a fresh start elsewhere. How will I show my face to your parents or mine? I have made life impossible not just for you, but for me as well, and even if you can forgive me, I can never forgive myself.'

I could not bear to hear him lament. He was too distraught

to see it, but I knew that now that we were together, everything was going to be perfect. We were going to be better than fine. As his wife, it fell to me to make him see the obvious. In a flash, it came to me. Scrambling to my feet, I ran to my almirah to fetch the one priceless possession that remained to us. Amma, in her infinite wisdom, had not only saved me, but also my husband. For that alone, I wished that the Gods would bless her with every happiness across eternity.

Kovalan looked at me questioningly as I placed the box wrapped in cloth with its precious contents in his hand.

'You mustn't give up hope,' I was surprised at how steady I sounded, 'we still have my anklets. Amma always said they were the most valuable pieces in the collection she put together for our wedding. With these, we can make all your dreams come true. Take them! I want you to have them.'

Overcome with emotion, he threw his arms around me. My flesh trembled in response. 'When I came to you, I was a broken man with not a thing to my name. I barely had the will to keep on going, but you have made me whole again. For a long time now, I have been feeling lost. It felt like my life was bereft of meaning and purpose. But now I can finally see a path ahead of me. I will use the money from the sale of one of your anklets to start over. We will regain everything we have lost, but that is not my goal. My purpose now is to spend every moment I have left making you happy and finally becoming worthy of a girl like you.'

I hugged him back tightly. Fighting back tears. How could he still not know that he would never have to try to make me happy now that he had come back to me?

He held my face in his hands and his eyes were alight with determination. 'Kannagi! I must make a clean break with my past. There is nothing for us here in Puhar. Or even in Chola Nadu.

Let us depart to a better place. Madurai, the capital city of the Pandyas, ruled by the famous King Nedunjeliyan, would be ideal. They say he is a just man, and hardworking people can make a wonderful life for themselves in his capital city. I can't wait for the rest of our life to begin, but you must tell me how you feel about it. The journey to Madurai will be arduous for someone as frail as you, and I have already put you through enough. If you wish to stay here, I will accede to your wishes and perhaps...'

For the first time in our entire married life, I interrupted my husband. 'Let us leave immediately!' Once again, I was surprised at how determined I sounded. 'You are right. There is nothing for us here in Puhar. And don't worry about my ability to make this journey to Madurai. I have no wish to remain a bird in a cage, who has no choice but to accept what happens to her. Let us embark on this new adventure and I am sure that the Goddess of Fortune will favour us.'

I meant every word I said and was thrilled by the newfound recklessness coursing through my veins. But what I left unsaid also motivated me just as much. At the back of my mind, I could still feel her overreaching presence. The spectre that had proved to be the bane of my existence all these years. The ethereal dancing girl that no man could resist. Not even a good man who loved his wife with all his heart. If we stayed here, he might be lured back into her web of enchantment. I'd rather plummet down an unknown road that was most certainly filled with hidden terrors, but also fresh hope, new adventures and a rekindled romance. Leaving Puhar was the right thing to do. I had never been more certain about anything in my life, apart from my love for Kovalan. My resolve was frightening. And thrilling.

Kovalan seemed as taken aback by my intensity as I was but delighted as well. It emboldened me to speak further. 'We must leave now. Immediately. Your parents, mine, and all our well-wishers will attempt to dissuade us from leaving. Having made up our minds, why should we stay on? The path to our new life awaits. Let us go this very minute.'

The thought of embarking on an exciting journey filled us to the brim with a heady exuberance that propelled us into prompt action. We had nothing of value save the anklets. There was nothing else to pack. It felt like a good omen. To leave everything behind us. Even the grief, resentment, bitterness, recriminations… instead of carrying them in our blood, where they would taint new beginnings.

With long hours to go before the first light of dawn, Kovalan and I left our home. There was no hesitation from either of us. A long time ago I had loved our beautiful house with its many treasures, but it had witnessed the agony of my soul when my marriage disintegrated. It had seen my endless pain and was a constant reminder of the terrible loneliness I endured, rendering it unsuitable for habitation. I did not look back.

It was a cold and windy night. No one ventured into the streets, which were dark and empty. Everything was quiet. No one bore witness to our stealthy departure. Feeling very much like an intrepid explorer venturing into the unknown, there was a spring in my step. Never in my entire life had I ventured out after dark, and this was most exciting. How pretty everything looked, bathed in silver and cloaked in shimmering shadows. Even the dust and dirt glinted in the sheen of the luminescent moonlight.

We walked past familiar landmarks, the Pasupata and Vishnu temples, the Buddhist viharas, the Jain Dilwaras, the parks, gardens, statues, and ponds, without stopping. I murmured silent prayers to all the Gods, Goddesses, enlightened beings, as well as the unknown forces that governed our fate, to bless us. I fervently begged them all to give us fair winds on this new journey and to keep us safe from harm. With a twinge of guilt, I thought of Amma, Appa and Devundi. But something told me that they would be proud of my decision. Not necessarily of the fact that I had departed without a word to them, but of my choice to stop being afraid all the time, and to follow my heart wherever it led me.

I had not set foot outside our house for years now. It had seemed inconceivable to me to go anywhere without my husband. The world outside my home was so scary. No one talked about it openly, but we heard all sorts of things. Of people being robbed, having their throats slit, of women being violated in their own homes by soldiers who enjoyed the King's protection. There were hateful people whose words could cut you in half as surely as a drawn sword. Disreputable men who groped ladies when they thought no one was looking. And even if people saw this kind of misbehaviour, they pretended not to see it, or they blamed the women for conducting themselves in an indecorous manner. The thought of being shamed as a loose woman who deserved the bad things that happened to her always terrified me.

Devundi was always telling me shocking stories about how difficult it was to be a woman in this world. Women accused of lewd and lascivious conduct were paraded around Puhar after being whipped and made to carry seven rocks on their head. Devundi wasn't sure if the rocks had any symbolic meaning and felt it was more of an invitation to pelt these women with stones and dirt. If they were convicted of more serious crimes, they faced the death penalty.

That was why the importance of being a good girl was drilled into us, even if it meant burying every natural instinct and impulse to live or breathe a little.

People were cruel. They would have whispered that not having a husband to warm my bed anymore, I was seeking someone else to take his place. Even a horrid accusation like that without the least veracity could ruin a woman. I shuddered at the thought of being paraded around like a harlot, with people spitting at my feet or making the mark to ward off the evil eye from themselves so that they were spared a similar fate.

This is why I had been too petrified to even go to the temple without Kovalan's protection. That was why my beloved home had become an iron cage, shrinking a little each day, and I found myself without the will or the means to escape the confinement.

With Kovalan's return, all these shackles crumbled to dust, and I felt liberated and free. I could hardly wait to see new temples, meet interesting people, and visit scenic spots. There were those who swore that Madurai was more beautiful than Puhar, and I was eager to ascertain the truth of it for myself. We would build ourselves a small and comfortable home there, on the banks of the Vaigai River, perhaps with a little garden…we would be so happy. Instead of being a quiet little mouse, I would make friends with the ladies and invite them home in the evenings to sing *bhajan*s. My new home would be filled with love, laughter, good food and songs. Kovalan would never want to leave again.

Kovalan did not want to leave through any of the main city gates, as there would be security guards posted there who would ask us endless questions. Instead, we scaled a wall to make it to the other side. I thought back to that long-ago day when Kovalan had found me perched on a tree, and the memory made me smile.

He remembered that day too. 'I am glad your climbing skills are intact,' he teased, with a familiar glint in his eye.

We skirted the perimeter till we found the parapet that would lead us across the deep moat. It was said that bloodthirsty crocodiles were always lurking in the water. Every few months there would be a scandal when some unfortunate visitor to Puhar, or worse, a child, fell in and was devoured by the crocodiles.

On that night, I was not afraid of crocodiles, snakes, scorpions or guards. Not a soul stirred as we made our way stealthily out of Puhar. Kovalan led us westward. We walked on in silence. I was leaving the city of my birth and my beloved parents, but I could not have been happier. Kovalan had come back to me. I had known he would. It felt good to be right. Simply being by his side had ensured that all was well in my world again. Every time he took me by the hand or waist to steer me safely past thorny or rough terrain, my heart would do a little dance, and a tiny smile would flit across my face. He was all I ever wanted. I would give up everything else in my life for the pleasure of being with him. It was that simple.

∽

Kovalan need not have worried about my ability to make the journey to Madurai, skinny and frail though I was. My energy was boundless, and I felt I could travel across the length and breadth of the three worlds without breaking a sweat. Of course, it took some getting used to, but I was too busy having the time of my life to take note of the inconveniences and discomforts of travelling by foot, especially the perils and precariousness of using the great outdoors for private ablutions as well as performing inconvenient and unavoidable bodily functions. For the first few days I was a little abashed and simply couldn't go, but soon I got used to it. Mostly out of extreme necessity.

There were other trials and tribulations for us to cope with, but these were minor and hardly worthy of note. More importantly, there was so much to see, think and feel that my sense organs could scarcely cope. We were walking along the north bank of the Kaveri, but I might as well have been exploring the moon, for it was all unknown territory for one who had travelled no further than her father's and husband's homes, with a brief sojourn in her in-laws' house. Who knew that the world out there was so exciting? The land was fertile and beautiful, the people were friendly. There was an abundance of fresh water and food. Kovalan and I were enchanted by the newness and beauty of it all.

Despite our circumstances, we found so many reasons to smile. Naturally, I was afraid to be this happy. The last time I had experienced joy so profound was when I married Kovalan. So much had gone wrong since then. But perhaps the sadness of the past few years had been the price exacted for a happier future, I reasoned to myself, to quiet the unease. It worked, and I allowed myself to relax and not think too far ahead of the moment I was in. Besides, there was still so much to see, and do and experience.

There were so many species of birds, fish, small animals and reptiles that I had never seen before. Kovalan and I amused ourselves by trying to identify them. The overabundance of snakes was a matter of concern to Kovalan, who felt he should stay up at night to keep an eye out for them. I would have been terrified too, except I remembered that we had my anklets with the blessed Nagamani gems in them and they would ward off not just snakes but other poisonous creatures too. When I told Kovalan about this, he was relieved, and we slept peacefully at night.

We made our way as best as could be managed, often stopping to ask fellow travellers for directions.

'There are troubled times ahead,' said a holy man who travelled with us part of the way with a slight frown, 'especially since our King Manarkilli's health is failing. Already the power-hungry are circling around the throne, and who knows how much blood will be spilled before the succession issue is resolved? You must visit the hermitage of Sadhvi Kavundi Adigal before you proceed to Madurai. It will do you both good. Surely you must have heard of that renowned renunciant whose goodness is a bright light in a dark world, warming the souls of all who are fortunate enough to be in her presence?'

Kovalan nodded in recognition, but I hadn't heard of this female renunciant. How very extraordinary. The holy man was still speaking. 'From what I have heard, Kavundi Adigal is also headed to the capital city of the Pandyas. She is a wise soul and kindly. It is my belief that she will take the two of you under her wing and make sure you make it to your journey's end safely.'

He was staring at me as he spoke, and the clear, penetrating gaze was disconcerting. I edged closer to Kovalan, and the sage took note. 'Don't be afraid,' he said gently, 'you are braver than you think. Fully fit to fulfil the will of the Gods as decreed by fate. Remember that we are never given more than our ability to withstand. And you can carry the weight of the three worlds on those frail shoulders.'

With these cryptic words, he blessed us, gave Kovalan detailed directions to find the hermitage of Kavundi Adigal, and went on his way. Kovalan shook his head in wonder. 'How wrong I have been about my wife. That wise man spoke of your strength and bravery, and here I was worried that I would have to carry you to Madurai on my shoulders and that you would scream and faint every time a little rat scurried across the path. Now I can rest easy, secure in the protection of the Goddess, born to fulfil the will of the Gods.'

I shook my head. 'I don't mean to be unkind, but I really wish that Sage had not spoken the way he did.' All I wanted was a peaceful life with my husband. Why did he talk about how I could carry the weight of the world on my shoulders? I had absolutely no desire to do anything of that sort.

The Sage's words had put Kovalan in high spirits, however, and he insisted on carrying me on his shoulders for a little while. 'Now, all you must do is keep an eye out for lions and tigers and bears. And dacoits. Why, I am sure you can reduce them all to ashes with all the merit you have accrued from being the best of women.'

In the old days, I would have made him set me down immediately, feeling he was being too childish and acting without dignity. But now I loved it. And I did not care if anyone was watching or judging us. It felt lovely to be so carefree and enjoy myself.

Progress was slow, but we were too busy having a wonderful time to care. We were no longer Kovalan and Kannagi. None of the people we met along the way knew us, and we didn't know them either. Therefore, we could be whoever we wanted to be. It felt like the past had been scrubbed clean and this made Kovalan happy. The days settled into a hazy pattern. We walked until we could walk no more. There was never any certainty about where our next meal would come from, but we never went hungry. Or lacked a roof over our heads. Everyone was so nice and went out of their way to help us. People we had never met before fussed over the two of us, opening their homes and hearts to us.

Kovalan and I did not want to talk about our real identities, and nobody seemed inclined to pry or probe. They insisted on feeding us, however, and often wouldn't let us depart until we had rested for the night. The womenfolk would present me with saris, taking note of the wear and tear mine had been subjected to, and tie sacred threads around my wrists to ward off the evil eye. They also did their very best to fatten me up.

Kovalan and I were grateful for their hospitality, and we repaid them as best we could. I would help with the cooking and cleaning. Kovalan would sing for our hosts and tell them stories about Gods and Goddesses. But we never stayed long. We had to find Kavundi Adigal, who would then lead the way to Madurai, where our new life awaited.

While I enjoyed meeting new people, I treasured our time together. For entire stretches, it felt like we were the only people left in this world. During the hottest parts of the day, we would rest in shady groves or on the bank of the river, trailing our feet in the water. Kovalan would place my head on his lap and gently massage my neck and shoulders, before tenderly rocking me to sleep. Sometimes he would sing, and I never tired of hearing his voice. He picked up flowers and wove them into my hair, or made floral necklaces to adorn my neck. We would snuggle together during the long nights, and I would fall asleep with my head buried in his chest. He would always tend to my feet before we settled down for the night, checking for cuts or bruises.

We bathed in the river on the rare occasions when we could be assured of complete privacy. We would wash our clothes and while waiting for them to dry, we made love with frantic abandon. Kovalan had been hesitant. It was I who initiated the physical intimacy. It was so much better than I remembered. I was hungry for his touch, and he was so thoughtful, gazing into my eyes to check if I was moaning in pleasure or pain. Afterwards, we would both feel so good that whatever wounds had been inflicted on us over the period of separation were healed. The fact that we could not make love whenever and wherever we pleased only increased our desire. It was frustrating that we could not indulge our need, but we had a lifetime ahead of us. We knew we had to be patient.

⸜

Kovalan and I had little difficulty finding Kavundi Adigal's ashram, although we had to leave the beaten path. By his reckoning we were about 30 *kavuthams* from Madurai. The ashram was in a remote location, past rocky terrain. The renunciant had made her home in a cave, which for all its bareness was nevertheless warm and welcoming in the shimmering hues of a particularly hot morning. Kavundi herself seemed to have blended in with the rocks and boulders, so grey and gaunt was she. Even her face, sari and shaven head were ashen. We prostrated ourselves before the renunciant and waited patiently for her to address us, though she was as still and silent as a stone.

'I have been waiting for you…' Kavundi said abruptly, her eyes still closed, 'you will find some fruits and fresh water on that ledge over there. Refresh yourselves and rest for a bit. We will leave this very evening, for we still have a long way to go. You have only chosen the hottest time of the year to travel. The road to Madurai will be rougher from here. We must make our way across the wilderness, but we will find the best way. It is a good thing you came to me, children.'

I suppose we should have been struck dumb or rendered awestruck by her yogic vision or whatever it was that made her so omniscient, but there was a matter-of-factness to her that demanded the same from us. We tried to pay obeisance but she laughed throatily, urging us to get on with it, and we just did as we were told.

Having waited out the heat, we were on our way. Kavundi had grabbed her water pot, begging bowl and the peacock feathers without which Jaina monks never travelled. This was to gently sweep the path ahead of them to avoid stepping on insects or other small, helpless creatures. She didn't ask us any questions nor evince any interest in us. Instead, she murmured prayers constantly and picked the route with unerring care, even though her eyes were usually half-closed and unfocused. I was certain that she knew everything about our past too. But she was sympathetic and sweet, if a little strange, so I didn't mind too much.

We travelled at a steady clip after that, still making our way past the Kaveri, where we were not too far from riverine settlements, ubiquitous shrines and tiny hamlets. There were paddy and sugarcane fields. Sometimes Kavundi would be stopped by crowds of people who had gathered to hear her and she would preach a bit about the eternal truth. Her efforts would be rewarded with food, flowers and other humble offerings.

Kovalan and I enjoyed listening to her sermons, especially since she adopted a very soothing tone. Mostly Kavundi talked about karma and how no man or woman would ever be exempt from the sum of their deeds both good and bad, since every action and reaction would reap a harvest and there was no escaping the cycle of life, death and rebirth. Kavundi constantly said that desire was the root cause of all evil and it must be rooted out to achieve salvation. I thought that it was a pity because I had just learned not to be afraid of desire and to enjoy it without guilt.

'Does she mean that we should abstain from all kinds of desire?' I asked Kovalan. 'Even the good ones?' I meant sex, of course, but I could not say it out loud and wondered if I would ever be rid of my prudish ways.

He shrugged. 'You can have all the sex you want just so long as it is not a desire that has enslaved you. Or something like that, I think. Sensual indulgence if balanced by spiritual growth is not a sin.' A shadow flickered across his face momentarily, and I knew he was thinking of her. It was not something to get unduly upset about, I decided firmly. Of course, he was bound to think of her now and then.

The three of us partook of a meal kindly served by Kavundi's followers, and we walked on into the night. With the moon to guide us, we tended to carry on with our travels to avoid the heat of the day. I enjoyed the peace and quiet. We would stop only when fatigue crept up on us or if we found a likely place to rest. Kavundi usually preferred to stay in small shrines belonging to local deities or raised in honour of fallen heroes who were believed to serve as the guardians of the villages from which they hailed.

During the journey, I spoke to Kavundi at length to clarify some of the doubts that had arisen in my mind after listening to her moral discourses. Kovalan still seemed a little moody and I thought it best to give him some time to sift through his thoughts. He had wandered off by himself and I watched him go, mild anxiety stirring in my heart.

Meanwhile, Kavundi was saying something which I could not begin to comprehend in its entirety. 'You are young, child, and it wouldn't hurt to remember that denying your natural impulses only makes them stronger. Repression leads to resentment, which in turn leads to rage and regret. Life is too fleeting to be lived like that. None of this will help you break free from the coils of desire. We are but lamps whose flames burn only as long as the wick and the oil last, if the fierce winds and rains don't snuff us out first. It is best to spread light and warmth for as long as life is allotted to us, doing whatever it takes to do that most effectively.' Whenever Kavundi said these things, all I had were endless questions, which she would be happy enough to answer. Which in turn would lead to more questions. I usually gave up.

The Wife and the Dancing Girl

We sat in silence afterwards. I can't be sure what was on Kavundi Adigal's mind, but I was feeling a little disturbed. My temples throbbed suddenly, and I did my best to clear my head.

Kavundi retired to say her prayers and meditate. Kovalan hadn't returned yet and I set off to look for him, panic beating an uneven rhythm in my chest. He crept up behind me and grabbed me by the waist, pulling me into a grove, where the wind rustled among the trees. If he expected me to scream or struggle, he was sadly disappointed because I turned around and embraced him fiercely. He hugged me back and held me close.

'I was late coming back, because I wanted to find something for you to eat or drink. There are not many people hereabouts but there was a small farm. Their cow has just given birth, so I waited for the good wife to prepare the *seempaal*, which I know you love.'

We fed each other the delicacy and it tasted heavenly. Leaning over, I kissed him hungrily and, unable to restrain myself, I got on top of him. I had never wanted him more, nor him me. I nibbled his nipple, clawed at his back, and tugged at his hair. My antics drove him wild and he made love to me many times that night. Exhausted and happy, we slowly crept back to the shrine where we had left Kavundi and tried to rest. In each other's arms, we finally dozed off. I didn't know it then, but it was the last time we would make love.

∽

Led by Kavundi, we made our way past temple towns like Srirangam and Uraiyur, the old Chola capital. The Arivan temple at Uraiyur was famous and it was pleasant to receive *darshan* there. At every holy spot we passed, I begged the Gods for their blessings. I pleaded with them to keep us safe from harm.

I appealed for their help to preserve our love for the rest of time. Even if there were no shrines or monasteries, I still prayed and beseeched the Gods with all my might.

Fortified by prayer, we were making steady progress on our journey southwards. We were no longer within the boundaries of Chola Nadu. Feeling intensely patriotic, Kovalan and I discussed the valour of our late King Karikalan and the great Kings before him. From stray bits of conversation, we had ascertained that civil war was brewing between rival factions in court now that King Manarkilli's health was failing. Perhaps it was best that we were leaving before violent conflict broke out. Talk of war made us apprehensive and we walked in silence, conserving our strength.

A passing pilgrim helped us with directions. Scratching the tuft of matted louse-ridden hair he wore in a messy topknot, he took his time answering our question about the quickest and safest route to Madurai:

'I don't think there is an easy road to Madurai, especially for this young lady here who should never have left home. Why, she is so fragile, the wind could snatch her up in seconds. And this is the worst time of the year to travel with the weather being unbearably hot, but let me think... I suggest you follow the straight path that leads to Lake Kodumbai. It gets tricky from there. There is a road to Madurai on the right, but it is not safe. Fierce, warlike tribes lurk in those parts and making your way across the Sirumalai Hills is no easy feat.

'If you are inclined to be adventurous, you could take the underground passage to the left of Kodumbai. It is somewhat circuitous but filled with marvels. You see, there are three lakes thither. If you were to risk a dip in these, one would bless you with divine knowledge, the second would open your eyes to past lives, and the third would grant you the wishes of your heart.'

Kavundi was polite but firm. 'We thank you for your help, kind Sir, but the path we must take is clear to me.'

The man bowed and went on his way.

Kavundi told us that we would make our way to Lake Kodumbai and take the middle path from there. 'Unless you have a hankering to bathe in miraculous lakes which offer everything for the price of nothing?' There was a twinkle in her eyes that told us we were being tested.

Kovalan shook his head. 'I have a deep suspicion of all things that glitter. And I am even more suspicious of things that sound a little too good to be true.' When he talked like this, he sounded very much like a boy who had only very reluctantly grown into a boyish man. Even when his newfound cynicism was evident, I still found his views endearing.

Regarding the path we must take, I found myself in agreement with Kavundi and Kovalan. If divine knowledge was anything like those things Kavundi preached about in her sermons, I felt ignorance might be more blissful. Even preferable to the purported delights of salvation. And what was the point of knowing about our past lives? The present was all that mattered. Besides the yet-to-be-determined future, of course. As for having my heart's desires fulfilled, I already had Kovalan. Asking for more would be pure greed.

As the pilgrim with the roving eye had predicted, it was rough going from there. The heat baked our heads, brought our blood to boiling point, threatened to melt the flesh off our bones, and sapped the strength from our limbs. Thirst was our constant companion.

Kovalan often left the main road to find us something to drink. I struggled miserably with the conflicting impulses of wanting to hold on to him with all my strength and letting him go. He would be gone a long time, and my anxiety would build to a fever pitch. Then he would return with precious water that he had gathered in lotus leaves, neatly folded into cups or coconut husks. Kavundi would take her cup and choose a shady spot to sip her water slowly. Kovalan would moisten my cracked lips with his tongue before feeding me the water one small mouthful at a time to prevent my choking and spitting out the water. The water mixed with his saliva tasted like the nectar of immortality, bringing me back from the dead instantly.

But the thirst returned with mean-spirited vengeance every time it was quenched. My feet were tormented by the thorns and sharp stones, leaving them covered in cuts, bruises and painful blisters. The pain was welcome since it distracted me from the thirst. The unrelenting discomfort was a dampener on our increasingly beleaguered but ever-willing spirits. However, Kovalan and I were determined to endure.

Despite the will to go on, our weakened bodies occasionally rebelled; putting one bleeding foot in front of the other took every ounce of strength I possessed and more. And just when I could not move an inch without blacking out, Kovalan carried me in his arms, though he was barely in better shape than I was, and we walked on, halting only when we found a strange shrine that sprang up amidst the starkness of the surrounding wilderness.

It was cool inside, and I was pleased to rest my aching feet for a minute. My eyelids were on the verge of drooping from extreme exhaustion, when the quiet was shattered by the sudden appearance of a band of fierce tribals. Their clothes were unlike anything I had seen and clearly revealed more than they concealed. But I was too tired to be embarrassed. Instead, I watched them with mounting curiosity.

The men wore their hair long and had unruly beards. Nearly

all of them were armed to the teeth and those who didn't carry weapons carried drums on which they pounded out a savage beat. The women also let their hair loose and some carried knives. They all had bloodshot eyes and appeared to be intoxicated.

Sensing my apprehension, Kavundi hastened to reassure me. 'This is a sacred space, and they are only here to worship their beloved Goddess. It may be a little different from what you are accustomed to, but there is no need to be scared. Get some rest, child. You have earned it, for there is none as resilient as you! Even hardened warriors making this journey for the very first time would have given up long ago. May you ever be blessed! As for me, I will repair to a quieter spot and meditate for a while.'

Kovalan seemed fascinated by the sight of these people. 'They are the Aynar,' he said. 'From what I have heard, they are a hardy people and excellent fighters. Depending on their inclinations, they ally themselves with the Cholas, Cheras or Pandyas and acquit themselves well on the battlefield. They live by their own rules and refuse to be subjugated and folded into the Kingdoms that surround them.'

At first they ignored us, devoting their entire attention towards Aiyai, the Patron Goddess of the Hunters. She was far more terrifying than her devotees. Her hair was thick and tangled, with snakeskins and a boar's tusk woven into it. A necklace made of teeth—I couldn't make out whether they belonged to humans or wild animals—was fastened across her throat. The sole garment she wore was a tiger skin gathered around her waist. She held a bow in one hand and a sword in the other, seated on a majestic stag with recurved antlers. Her bared breasts stood proud and tall, glistening with the merest hint of perspiration. The Goddess was a sight to behold, inducing awe and terror in equal measure.

The Aynar placed their offerings in front of her. These included horns and antlers of the beasts they had hunted, live game birds whose necks were severed, and the blood, which was carefully collected in dishes and placed before Aiyai. Some offered ornaments and locks of their hair. Then they began to sing and dance themselves into a trance while the drummers pounded out the harsh beats.

A young woman dressed to resemble Aiyai, sporting the same tiger skin and uncovered breasts, took the lead. She swayed slowly at first, gradually working herself into a frenzy, her eyeballs retracting into her forehead, leaving the whites of her eyes exposed. The possessed woman opened her mouth to render raucous tunes that were both incoherent and incomprehensible but undeniably deep and meaningful. She exhorted her followers between shrieks and shrill cries to fight for their rights, remember their roots, and please the Goddess.

'The Aynar must never settle for peace like peasants when power and prosperity are within their grasp. This land is your birthright! Reclaim this land, not just for yourselves but for your children and theirs. Fight for as long as your manhood prevails, for that is the only way you can please the Goddess!'

Hysterical laughter rang out, resounding to the high heavens as she continued to spin and weave, keening and wailing in turn. My skin prickled at the sight of her, but I was suddenly wide awake and mesmerized by the intensity of her movements.

Anxious to prove themselves, the men screamed and shouted themselves hoarse. Some led in a buffalo, which they proceeded to sacrifice to the Goddess. Blood spurted out of the slaughtered creature and once more, it was gathered in dishes. The first offering was made to Aiyai and the rest were quaffed liberally by the men and women. I remember thinking that I would rather die of thirst than drink some poor creature's blood. It was terrifying but I could not look away.

The possessed woman suddenly turned her attention to me and raised a lone finger.

'The Goddess walks among us,' she shrieked. Suddenly all eyes turned to me, and I wished fervently that I could shrink myself into insignificance. 'This is a jewel among women. The peerless Queen of Tamilagam who hails from Chola Nadu. Worship her, you blind fools, and she may spare you from the flames of her wrath.'

As one they prostrated themselves before me, and I prayed that the ground beneath my feet would open up and swallow me whole. I tried to hide behind Kovalan, but they wouldn't let me. The women gathered around me. Some touched my hair, others ran their fingers over my face, murmuring bemusedly about what a soft little thing I was. They tsked over my feet before proceeding to apply cooling salves and binding these with strips of cloth they tore off their own garments.

They insisted on sharing their food with us. There was much feasting and roasted buffalo meat to be consumed with generous quantities of toddy. We were offered choice cuts of the meat but declined since we had started consuming only vegetarian food, out of respect to Kavundi Adigal. But we did accept the cooked rice and fresh buffalo milk we were offered. It was delicious. When nothing remained and the carcass had been stripped to bare bones, they faded away into the gathering dusk. There was no sign of the possessed lady.

With full stomachs, Kovalan and I curled up against each other, more comfortable than we had been in a while. His eyes were shining. I could tell that he was pleased with all the attention his wife was getting. I wasn't.

'I know they were kind and meant well but I really wish that girl had not said all those things. It was disturbing and made me feel bad.'

'How can you say that, Kannagi?' Kovalan was shocked. 'You are a goddess and the best among women. It was nice of them to recognize your true worth.'

I said nothing. But I wanted to be a goddess exactly as much as I wanted to be a whore. There was no point in upsetting Kovalan though. Having refreshed ourselves, Kovalan and I woke up in the morning, performed our ablutions, and went to find Kavundi so we could resume our journey.

'The hardest part of the journey is behind us, children,' Kavundi said with a smile. 'We have entered Pandya Nadu and need not worry about dacoits and wild beasts since the paths are well patrolled by King Nedunjeliyan's soldiers. In fact, it will be perfectly safe to travel at night. You can rest and relax here for a little while longer. We will leave in the evening when it is cooler.'

Pleased to avoid the scorching sun, we obliged. The going was relatively easy after that. Even our eyes grew accustomed to the darkness. The kindness of the Aynar women stood me in good stead as it was easier to protect my feet from sharp stones and thorns now that they were properly bound.

We had halted in a small village when a man approached Kovalan. I heard him introduce himself. His name was Kausikan and he came from Puhar. He took Kovalan aside for a word in private. I could see the scroll he carried with the ornamental seal and knew that he was an emissary from Madhavi. It did not bother me. The past might be behind you, but it was not going to recede completely and go elsewhere, was it? Kovalan appeared ill at ease, but he heard the man out and spoke a few words to him before asking him to leave with a few murmured instructions. He handed the scroll back to him and returned to me, his face serene and set in cheerful lines.

It occurred to me that Kovalan seemed relieved to have made a clean break from the past. Besides, it was obvious that he had no inclination of walking all the way back to Puhar and Madhavi. That eased my mind somewhat.

'That man will inform your parents and mine that we are in good health and plan to settle down in Madurai. It will set their minds at ease, I hope.' This was all the information he volunteered, and I didn't probe further.

Later that evening, Kovalan, who was in high spirits, borrowed a yaal from one of the villagers and entertained us with music and song. Even Kavundi was delighted, clapping and dancing with the others. I didn't feel like joining in though. Dancing was for dancing girls. Instead, I sat down with some of the women and tried to strike up a conversation.

'Is Madurai far from here?' they smiled sympathetically when they heard the anxiety in my voice.

'You have come a long way, haven't you? Don't worry, Madurai is close. It is only a day's journey from here.'

Following their suggestion, I took a deep breath and got the heady whiff of jasmine borne by the southern breeze. How unlike the salty tang of Puhar. Kovalan and I were filled with delight as we walked towards the capital of Pandya Nadu.

'The food is supposed to be delicious,' Kovalan told me. 'Provided you can handle the spice!'

His hand was resting lightly on my shoulder, and I could sense his excitement. We could hear the Vaigai before we could feast our eyes on her resplendent beauty! Unlike the tempestuous splendour of the Kaveri, this river had a sedate kind of gorgeousness, undulating gracefully, her sparkling surface shimmering beneath the sun, speckled with blooms from the trees hugging her voluptuous curves. It was a spectacular sight.

On the southern bank, we could see the city walls and the famed arched entrances, of which there were four, but we could see just the one. The flags carrying the Pandyan insignia, which was the fish, flew tall and proud. The city itself bore a festive air and we felt like we were being warmly welcomed.

The people seemed nice too and appeared pleased that Kovalan and I were charmed by the beauty of their beloved city. 'Once you have set foot on the soil of Madurai, a lifelong love affair begins, and you will never be happy anywhere else,' they assured us with sublime confidence.

Kavundi smiled. 'The love the Pandyas have for their capital city is unrivalled. In fact, if they travel too far from the banks of the Vaigai, they feel like the proverbial fish out of water. I have seen them fall sick pining away for their beloved Madurai, refusing to eat because they miss the food from their homeland, which they swear is unrivalled. And no medicine can cure them of this mysterious malady. But once the Vaigai is within their sights, the recovery is instantaneous, and they are full of vitality again.'

Kovalan and I laughed at this. There was no doubt that this place was beautiful. We could not wait to try the food and begin our lives here. Once again, I beseeched all the Gods in the pantheon. It was crucial that they lend Kovalan their protection and help him sell the anklets at a good price. Everything depended on that. But it was a simple matter of business... What could possibly go wrong?

MADHAVI

Desolation

There are only two kinds of men to love. The bad ones, who break your heart even though you are wary from the start and have your shield and sword up, on full alert. Then there are the good men who give you their word that they will never leave you. Or hurt you. Or make you cry. Or stop loving you. They mean every word, of course. And fully intend to love you to death and beyond. But they break your heart just the same, except with them you ignored reason and good sense to tear down all defences and give them everything you possessed unreservedly. To love with the full capacity of your heart. With every atom of your being. Without fear. Or restraint. Because you took a leap of faith uncaring that you could be smashed to death against the rocks of your folly below. Impaled through the heart that was given away.

An utter fool in love, I firmly believed that Kovalan would come back. If not for me, then at least for the daughter we made together. For the promise he made to me. But of course, he did not come back. In fact, he took to his heels to put as much distance as possible between himself and his former paramour, lest he be tempted to get entrapped within the web of enchantment and deceit woven by her wiles and manipulations. All of Puhar was agog over the news. Kovalan and his saintly wife had left Puhar in the dead of the night without even telling their parents.

The uncharitable said that Kovalan had snuck away like a thief because he could not repay his debts. I knew this wasn't true. He would never do such a thing. At his worst, he was a good man, after all. Anyone who knew him even a little would know that he'd rather suffer than let another suffer on his account. Unless it came to matters of the heart. In that case, he was not above inflicting hurt on one who had loved him and who would never dream of hurting him.

Many opined that they wouldn't last a day and had become a tragedy waiting to happen. It was whispered that they would be murdered by dacoits or set upon by wild animals if they didn't get lost and die of thirst or starvation first. For the rest, they already served as a cautionary tale to be told and retold to impressionable young men and foolish older men who were led by their loins about the hideous dangers posed by dancing girls and their ilk.

The most vicious creatures gathered all their outrage over the loss of a considerable fortune by a prominent merchant prince of Puhar which had driven him to such desperate straits, so that it could be weaponized against one dancing girl in particular who had supposedly seduced him, stripped him bare of every measly coin he had ever possessed, before throwing out the empty husk of a man like so much garbage. Much was made of the fact that he had been deprived of even his wife's jewellery. Naturally, all the blame was laid at the door of this very embodiment of evil and receptacle of vice.

What right did any of them have to judge me? I seethed inwardly. How dare Kovalan condemn and leave me when I would never dream of thinking less of him for the choices he had made, under duress or otherwise? Yet, try as I might, I could not be angry with him. I could not stop longing to be in his arms again.

To have him kiss me, till I was breathless and dizzy with desire. I could not stop thinking about him. I lay awake at nights, sifting through tantalizing memories wishing I could figure out a way to turn back time, so we could somehow return to that first night on the beach when we had been so impossibly happy. I could hardly wait for him to come back to me someday. He would come back, wouldn't he? How could he stay away from me?

I could have cried my eyes out in the quiet comfort of the home we had made together, awash with the remnants of our ill-fated love, and pined the years away with sorrowful fortitude like his much revered and ever-righteous wife. But I chose not to cower in tears under the covers. Instead, I spent my days dancing and dancing some more, until I could dance no more. My life would always be what I made of it. No man shall have the power to make or break it, I told myself firmly. Not Kovalan and certainly not Seyon.

People hissed and booed at my dance performances, which they nevertheless attended in droves, if only to express their fury. Ironically, my unpopularity had made me popular, and I received more invitations to dance than I could handle. I accepted them all, and in the days that followed I was so tired I could barely think, which was a relief.

Dance was helping me heal. But sometimes, disaster arrives in droves. The invitations to dance I had been flooded with dried up without warning. War was brewing and people were preparing for hard times. Dance, music and celebration were the last thing on people's minds. This constant ebb and flow of fortune was nothing new, but it was harder on me this time for obvious reasons. Still, I was determined not to make a spectacle of myself for the benefit of my detractors by collapsing in a heap of misery, the way I was inclined to. Instead, I gathered my resolve and sought out quiet places and kind people who would help me past the chaos and towards peace.

Peace was more elusive than ever, especially in those troubled times. Our King Manarkilli had passed away. We knew he had been ailing for some time, but we all hoped and prayed that he would recover quickly. People compared him unfavourably to his legendary father, but they were doing him an injustice. He had preserved nearly everything that Karikalan had stood for—maintaining peace, securing the boundaries of his kingdom, and providing his invaluable patronage for artists. I was one among many who had been a beneficiary of his boundless kindness. With him gone, Chittu and I were deprived of royal patronage in the power vacuum his absence created, leaving us vulnerable to the endless scheming of those who sought to see us brought low. But our troubles were insignificant compared to the conflict that was coming to a boil, threatening the very fabric of Chola Nadu.

Nedumkilli, Manarkilli's son, was next in line to the throne. He was the heir apparent but there were challengers to his rule. Killivallavan and his younger brother Illamkilli, relatives of Manarkilli, were determined to oust the crown prince, and they had formed a confederacy with the Killis based in Uraiyur, the former capital of the Chola Kingdom, who were supposed to be loyal to the King and his natural heirs. Determined to defend and secure his birthright, Nedumkilli had sent his father's Senapati, Seyon, as his emissary to Senguttuvan, the King of the Cheras at Vanji, who was his nephew, to seek his aid. A war for the Tiger Throne seemed imminent, and we braced for it.

In this political landscape, the demand for dasis had not entirely waned. Some would accompany the soldiers to war and perform ritual dances to please and placate their Gods in the hope of securing a victory. But if the stories were to be believed, they were shamelessly passed around and shared among high-ranking military officials who were predators in armour. It took a brave dasi or one who desperately needed the money to agree to travel with the army. I was neither.

Seyon succeeded in his effort to win Cheran Senguttuvan's support and in return for his loyalty, was given the hand of Nedumkilli's daughter. I heard that the Commander was smitten with his new wife, especially since it was the politically expedient move to consolidate his burgeoning power. He certainly could not afford to be seen with the likes of a dancer who had just driven one of the leading lights of Puhar to poverty, and to compound her crime, driven him and his delicate flower of a wife to leave their home behind for distant, inhospitable lands. Besides, he was busy mustering the forces and gathering an army to join Cheran Senguttuvan's so that they could wipe out the Confederacy of rebel Killis and secure the throne for Nedumkilli.

Chittu was as uncaring about civil wars as she was about Kovalan's departure, though she did fret about Nedumkilli's complete lack of interest in the wellbeing of our family. She had tried to secure an audience with him but was turned away sternly and firmly. Chittu was furious and scathing in her condemnation of him.

'If he gets his head chopped off and his body stuffed with straw when the rebel Killis defeat him in battle, it will serve him right,' she said viciously, before turning her attention to me and sighing loudly to convey her despair about the difficulty of having a daughter who did not treat her will as God's edict.

She firmly believed that sadness and tears eroded a woman's looks even more quickly and efficiently than childbirth and was most concerned that I was doing nothing to remedy the situation to improve my market value.

'Will you stop being so melodramatic? There is no need to cry over spilt milk every single night. That is how foolish wives who are unable to keep their husbands in their beds behave. People flock to see your eyes sparkling with laughter and mischief. Nobody wants to see sadness and defeat underscored by puffy eyes with dark bags beneath. It is a revolting sight!'

I was more amused than angry. It was just like Chittu to see only the professional and cosmetic ramifications of heartbreak.

'You were naive to love him so much,' she informed me brusquely. 'If you must be so foolish as to love, at least have the sense to love one of the Gods, fiercely and passionately. Then the people will elevate you to sainthood and build temples in your honour instead of comparing you unfavourably to chaste wives who have no choice but to remain chaste because no man desires them. Not even their husbands.'

I supposed it was her own way of trying to make me feel better, but as always, I wished she would keep her unsolicited opinions to herself. Used as I was to her ways, her unrivalled capacity for aggravation was proving harder and harder to ignore.

'Don't you fret about our Senapati Seyon either,' Chittu continued. 'He has been undefeated in battle, and they say the same about Senguttuvan. Between the two of them, they will crush those irksome Killis and restore peace. The victory will be celebrated with dance and music. Seyon, having proved his loyalty to the King, will send for you.'

She went on and on about the odds of Seyon securing a win for Nedumkilli when she had formerly been hoping for a grisly end to the King-in-waiting who had not cared to accede to her demand to see him. My mother was nothing if not inconstant.

'Madhavi! Pay attention! It is not good for my lungs to scream like this just because you are too foolish to listen to your mother.

We must start thinking about Manimegalai's future. A suitable guru must be found so that her training can commence. You were a lot younger when we began to train you. Manimegalai is a beautiful girl, and under my tutelage she will become the greatest dasi of all time. You must talk to the head priest of the Pasupata Temple about her pottu kattuthal. We must not make the mistakes we made with you. Are you listening to me? I know you wish you hadn't had her because she reminds you of her father, but you can't wish away motherhood. At least try to be a good mother and do the right thing for your daughter, the way I did.'

That shook me right out of the stupor I had sunk into. I should have seen this coming. Of course Chittu would want Manimegalai to follow in her footsteps. When I was pregnant with the dear child, she had spent so much on pujas to ensure that I was blessed with a baby girl. When Manimegalai was born, she was overjoyed, fully convinced that like her female ancestors, she would grow up to be a danseuse par excellence. I, on the other hand, would see her become a dancer only over my dead and burnt corpse.

'Listen to me carefully, Chittu. I will not repeat myself. Manimegalai will not be trained. Not as a dancer. And definitely not as a dasi. Not while there is life left in me. You are too short-sighted to see it. But there is no future for our profession. There is so much hatred and contempt for what we do. All people want is to drag us down from our increasingly flimsy pedestals so that we can rot in a sewer of shame. This fear of the inevitable poisons our very lives. My daughter will have no part of any of it.

'Our so-called way of life, which is so dear to you, was devised by men to satisfy their own lusts. Marriage is yet another institution erected for the benefit of men. Manimegalai need not be a whore or a wife. I want her to make something of her life, which will not entail her being enslaved by the demeaning demands of men. As her mother, this is my gift to her, and I will not let anyone thwart my will.'

Mother was too taken aback for a moment. When she let fly with all the invectives her embittered heart could bring to bear, I had left the room, leaving her to rave and rant as loudly and for as long as possible. She could do her worst, for all the good it would do her. My mind was made up on this matter.

Vasantamala agreed with my views. She had always been more of a mother to Manimegalai than I had, and her opinion mattered to me.

'That little girl is special,' she insisted. 'Wise beyond her years, her powers of comprehension are second to none. And for all her reserve and gentle ways, she is filled with courage and strength. Mark my word, she will forge her own path and make us all proud.'

It was a relief to note that her views regarding Manimegalai's future were allied with my own. I now had an ally against Chittu. Vasantamala had always been more adept in the art of dealing with my mother, particularly when she was on the warpath.

My friend had been sympathetic and supportive in the dark days following the abrupt abandonment that was inflicted on me. She let me lean on her when Kovalan did the unthinkable. She kept me company when I sat daydreaming on the terrace or lay awake at night thinking of nothing, trying in vain to keep the painful memories from dragging me down under. She would lay my head on her lap and massage my forehead until I fell asleep. When there were no dance programmes to prepare for, she kept the music alive in my heart by singing my favourite songs and strumming her yaal. How fortunate I was to have a friend like her who stayed by my side in good times and bad.

'I sent Kausikan with a scroll bearing your seal to find Kovalan and deliver it to him. It was a sketch I made of you. If that doesn't melt his heart, I don't know what will.' That was so typical of her. Always acting in my best interests.

'That was nice of you Vasanta, but I don't think he will be moved by the artificial entreaties of a dancing girl.' I heard the self-pity in my voice and hated myself for it.

'You must not give up hope,' she said bracingly. 'And so what if he is gone? Kovalan is a good man, but he ought not to have done this to you. It was thoughtless of him to put you in such a precarious position. Everything you did for him was with love. How could he not see that? But no matter. There will be light, love and laughter in your life again. Your heart is full of joy that you have generously shared with so many people. All of it will be returned to you with interest.

'Your mother is right about some things. She says the best way to deal with lost love is to replace it. Immediately. If not sooner. The Senapati will send for you as soon as he returns in triumph from the battlefield.'

I shook my head. 'There is no room for love or desire in my life anymore. Even dance has lost its charm for me. It is time to move on. The restlessness I have been fighting all my life is getting the better of me. I must do something about it. We must leave this place together. It is too full of him.'

She nodded in agreement. Dearest Vasanta! For a moment, she was lost in thought, then she finally spoke up. 'There is this Bhikshu, a Buddhist monk named Atisha. He cannot be summoned to us, but he conducts classes every single day, educating people on the Threefold Path of Buddhism under a banyan tree in a beautiful hermitage, like the Buddha did. People from all walks of life can be found there. I chanced upon this place while returning from the marketplace, and there was something about him that caught my attention. Listening to him, I felt more at peace yet energized. Why don't we go?'

I perked up at once. Unlike Chittu, it was usually a good idea to listen to Vasanta and follow her advice. 'Yes! Let's go today itself. And we will take Manimegalai with us. It will do her good to listen to wise men and prepare herself to deal with overbearing grandmothers determined to lead her astray.'

'Your mother is going to kill us! But something tells me this is the right thing for us to do.'

'I don't care about Chittu! And I have a good feeling about this Bhikshu. Manimegalai is such a quiet child. Sometimes I forget about her very existence because she has faded into the background and seems so far away from here. Perhaps she is ruminating on the mysteries of the universe. Who knows, maybe one day she will be one of the enlightened souls and history will venerate her as a saint. Maybe our Manimegalai will even become famous. Chittu will get her wish, just not in the manner she has envisioned, if I have anything to do with it.'

As we walked towards the hermitage where peace supposedly awaited, my restless thoughts resurfaced. Even now, despite everything, a part of me stubbornly held on to the belief that we would somehow find our way back to each other against all odds. If not in this lifetime, maybe the next. I would gladly submit to the endless rigours of the cycle of birth and rebirth if it meant I could be with him again. Even if I risked losing him all over again. Just as long as we could rekindle our love. Endlessly across the aeons.

KANNAGI

Paradise Lost

Kovalan and I were determined to love Madurai, put aside our fears and make a fresh start. Kavundi, whose kindness towards us was inexhaustible, led us to a commune on the outskirts of Madurai, where holy men and women of different faiths who had renounced all ties to the material world congregated over the course of their wandering ways. Since Kovalan and I were on the brink of exhaustion, she arranged for us to spend the night there until we could find accommodation elsewhere.

We ate a light meal served to us by kind-hearted strangers and retired to the quarters allotted to us. That first night in Madurai was miserable. Kovalan fell asleep at once. He was almost as weighed down by anxiety as I was, but that seldom interfered with his sleep. I, on the other hand, lay wide awake and agitated, feeling very homesick. I sorely missed my parents, Devundi, little Arundhati, Ponni, Muthu and my in-laws. It occurred to me, not for the first time since our departure from Puhar, that I didn't have a home of my own. The sari I wore was the only one in my possession and it seemed to me that strength of will was the only thing keeping it from falling to pieces and leaving me naked. Over the past few months, we had subsisted solely on meals offered to us by benevolent strangers, *anna dhanam* served in temples, and fruits, nuts and berries we managed to forage.

From being the daughter and son of the foremost merchant

princes of Chola Nadu, we were now little more than beggars in the Pandya territory. The enormity of our loss struck me anew and cold panic settled in my heart. For the minutest of moments, I wished I was safe and sound in my own home in Puhar, even if that meant Kovalan remained firmly ensconced in Madhavi's embrace. *Why was I feeling like this?* Kovalan was all I had ever wanted and though the journey to Madurai had been tough, being with him had made me the happiest I had been in ages. It made no sense that on the eve of our new life together, I was trapped in the throes of crippling apprehension and hopelessness.

It would never do to think like this. I urged myself to be strong enough for us. Glancing at the sleeping form of Kovalan, I realized something was wrong. He was not enjoying a restful slumber and seemed to be writhing in pain. I was already feeling uneasy, but his obvious discomfort made it a thousand times worse, and I started shivering though it was a warm, muggy night.

Sick at heart, I realized that my husband was a changed man. Afflictions of the head, heart and mind had reduced him to a flickering shadow of his former self. He was no longer the man I had fallen in love with. The realization left me dangerously close to tears. But I was also no longer the innocent girl who had lived only to love Kovalan and be loved by him. Now that I was an old hand at dealing with pain, I knew I would have to be tougher and more resilient than ever to make something of our new life together. It would take arduous effort, but I was confident that the dying embers of our love could be rekindled, if not into a blazing conflagration, then perhaps to a gentle flame that I could cup between my palms to protect it from hostile elements. If I could manage this much, the years ahead would be filled with peace, quiet and companionship.

∽

The Wife and the Dancing Girl

In the morning, Kovalan woke me up with a gentle kiss on my forehead. I loved his soft kisses. But I wanted more. It had not been possible to indulge our mutual desire for a while now and I missed having him inside me. As soon as we had our own roof over our heads, we would make love to our hearts' content, I promised myself.

'Rise and shine, sleepyhead! We have a big day ahead of us.' He had brought us water for refreshing ourselves and some food. He seemed determined to be cheery and enthusiastic, but it was obvious he was tense and nervous about starting over. Not for the first time, I wished I could instill some confidence in him. Some women were so capable when it came to moulding their men to bring out the best in them. I simply did not know how. Instead, doing my best to be supportive, I let him talk and listened quietly as we ate.

'I have been talking to Kavundi...' he said hesitantly.

Clearing his throat, Kovalan continued, 'The Sadhvi has been such a blessing. She suggested I make enquiries at the Merchants' Guild about how best to secure some capital and set up my own business in Madurai. According to her, many of them are sure to know our fathers well and would have certainly done a lot of business transactions with them and would be more than happy to lend a helping hand, and offer guidance and sage counsel.'

I nodded in agreement as I bit into the softest and fluffiest *idli* that had ever been steamed outside my mother's kitchen. The sambhar and chutney had been prepared without onions, garlic or spices, but it was quite flavoursome, and I savoured every mouthful as I mulled things over. Kavundi was right. Kovalan needed all the help he could get, and if a mutual acquaintance of our fathers could be tracked down, we would have a benefactor who would steer us through the rocky new beginnings and help us settle down. Thinking it made me feel guilty, but Kovalan did not quite have what it took to be an entrepreneur. It was best for him to put himself under the tutelage of someone who did.

Kovalan was eating too but he seemed too preoccupied to do justice to the meal. 'Kavundi means well, but I don't want to visit the Merchants' Guild like a beggar seeking alms.'

He paused again, looking stricken. I knew he felt he had damaged his father's name by his conduct, and he did not want to be judged harshly by the members of the Merchants' Guild in Madurai. If they were anything like their counterparts in Puhar, they would not look too kindly on a man who had frittered away a fortune worthy of a king. I wanted to tell him that he must forgive himself for his mistakes and move on. But, as usual, the words would not materialize in my head, and I did not utter a single word.

Kovalan was gnawing on a fingernail, an atypical gesture. 'It would be more prudent for me to find a respectable jeweller and sell one of your anklets without delay. Once I have the capital, it will be easier to set up some small business that will serve our interests. But before that, I will head into the city today to get my bearings. Tomorrow I shall make the sale. We will use the money to find a house and set up shop here.'

I sighed to myself. If only he would do as Kavundi Adigal had advised him. She had brought us here safely, and her counsel was sound. I said nothing about my reservations. However, it was important that I showed him my unwavering support.

With a smile I hoped he found encouraging, I said, 'That is a good plan. Why don't we go into the city together? We could take in the sights and if possible, visit a temple and seek the blessings of the Gods to protect us. Kavundi has done enough for us. If I were to stay on here, I would feel like I am taking advantage of her kindness.'

'Who are you and what have you done with my wife?' he teased, but his heart was not in it. 'Seriously, I'd like us to go and see Madurai together, but there's plenty of time for that in the future. Right now, you need to rest, and it is not right for a lady of your standing to be seen on the mean streets or exposed to the pleasure dens of the courtesans. A sage told me that unlike our Puhar, the people of this land have rather libertine ideas. King Nedunjeliyan travels openly with his concubines in horse-drawn carriages, where they embrace him in full view of the public.'

Kovalan sounded somewhat disapproving. Recently, he had adopted a sterner stand on moral and ethical issues, viewing breaches in decorum with mounting disdain. 'The sage told me that every single day the King sends covered carts and loaded palanquins with expensive gifts like jewelled couches, fans made of yaks' tails, ornaments wrought with precious stones and the highest grade of gold, bejewelled betel boxes, and fine silks to his favourites among the dasis and courtesans, much to the chagrin of his Queen Kopperundevi.'

At the mention of the dancing girls, I had to strain to suppress the flare of irritation. *Why were all men so obsessed with that lot?* And none of what he was saying was new to me. No matter what corner of the known world we went to, it was always the same. Dasis and their sisters-in-vice, the veshas, were always revered, pampered, and amply rewarded for catering to the debauched whims of humanity, while wives were expected to suffer in silence, committed to virtue with no hope of reward.

Undeterred by my mood, Kovalan prattled on. 'The veshas ply their trade openly and live in the finest establishments in the city, built with baked bricks and engraved tiles. Speaking of tiles, they do not have to wear them on their heads as a mark of shame. In Madurai, such practices are considered barbaric and outdated. Hard to believe, isn't it?'

'Shall we find some temporary lodgings where we might stay, till we can afford a house of our own?' I was determined to change the subject.

'Oh, I forgot to tell you... Kavundi Adigal took care of this problem. She said that a cowherdess named Madari, who is well known to her, will be coming shortly with her daily offering of milk and curds for the inhabitants here. Kavundi said she will ask Madari to let us stay with her. I was told that she is a kind woman who will take good care of you while I am in the city. Come, let us ask Kavundi's blessing before we leave.'

It was hard to say goodbye to her. She had looked after us like a mother and I knew it would be impossible to repay her for all she had done for us. I touched her feet with all the reverence in my heart. As I bent down, the tears that had pooled in my eyes tumbled onto her feet and she immediately put her hands on my shoulders and raised me to my feet.

'Your faith is not misplaced,' she whispered, looking deep into my eyes. 'It takes courage to believe in love, even if there is no good reason for it. The path you have chosen has not brought you much by way of pleasure, but I am proud of your persistence, for all that you have endured will be rewarded with lasting peace.'

∫

Having taken leave of Kavundi, Kovalan and I ventured forth with Madari, who had arrived like a breath of invigorating air and was delivering her dairy goods, effusively exchanging pleasantries with all in the vicinity. Kavundi's words had filled me with blessed comfort, as had the sight of Madari, the cowherdess who had generously offered us the use of her home. Madari, a cheerful older woman who had probably looked the same in her youth as she did now and would look the same decades from now, had the weathered look of someone who lived as one with Mother Nature in the great outdoors. Although she was a little corpulent, her arms and back were well muscled from the hard labour of milking cows and carrying pots of milk, butter and curd to sell at market. She was talkative, warm-hearted and seemed to be a very caring person. I took to her immediately.

She chattered on endlessly as she led us to her home. 'It's a simple life for me. My cows are all that matter. Animals are nicer than people, don't you think? Don't get me wrong. You both seem like perfectly nice people, but I feel it is hard to trust most of our kind. Why, I had to plant a thorn hedge around my humble hut to protect my pots from thieves, and I have a dog to warn me when someone is after my cows. The King is supposed to protect us, but all he cares about are his own interests and those who are rich enough to align their interests with his own.'

Kovalan seemed disturbed to hear that. 'I was told that King Nedunjeliyan has a spotless reputation. The bards have composed beautiful verses praising his righteous sceptre, the *sengkol* which remains unbent. That all his subjects benefit from his protection, which is like the cool shade beneath his white umbrella borne aloft by those who serve him. They say he is the very embodiment of virtue and lives solely to see justice served.'

Madari chuckled softly. I saw her glance at us for a moment and then look away. Kavundi must have told her a little about us. That we were of noble birth and had fallen on hard times. That fleeting glance told me that she thought we were naive and clueless about the ways of the world.

'When you pay people with gold coins to compose verses in

your honour, they do so,' she said instead. 'I don't concern myself with the politics of the royal court. The bovine are simpler to comprehend, even if they demand your undivided devotion in exchange for their many bounties. But from what I hear, King Nedunjeliyan is more devoted to dancing girls than his duty and there is going to be trouble if he keeps it up. Why, he had a public falling out with his Queen Kopperundevi because of his inordinate fondness for beautiful women, and the entire Kingdom can talk of little else. Every time these royals have their spats, the reverberations are felt all the way from the palace to the humblest hovel in the land. It is a pity.'

Kovalan looked uncomfortable, and I was not exactly pleased to hear of the Pandya King's passion for the pretty dasis in his kingdom. We had travelled a long way to escape these temptresses, only to be reminded constantly that they were everywhere and there was no escaping their blandishments.

Oblivious to the roiling emotions in our hearts, Madari went on cheerfully, 'Don't worry about a thing though. It takes time for these things to come to a boil. We must be careful to go about our work and not get in the way when the powerful fight each other over the petty things they are always fighting over, lest we become collateral damage. Another piece of good news: we are almost home! You both look like you could do with a nice bath, some refreshment and rest, which you will find in abundance under my roof.'

We could smell the enclosures of the cowherds long before we got there. The scent of dung, freshly mown hay, milk and the powerful odour unique to cattle and goats was overpowering. The goatherds and cowherds were bustling about as they readied the herds to take them out to graze and I could barely hear my thoughts over the sounds of lowing and bleating. Some carried staves and sickles. The women carried pots on their heads, while some of the men had tied them to the ends of sticks, which they then slung over their shoulders.

Madari knew them all, of course, and kept stopping to chat. About this and that. She introduced us to all her friends. I tried to be friendly and cheerful. Madari seemed very proud of what must have been an onerous responsibility. I knew that our presence was an inconvenience for her, as she had to take care of us first at the beginning of a busy day before tending to the cattle, but if she felt the same way, she showed no signs of it. Instead, she seemed most enthusiastic about hosting us in her home. It was a charming little hut with red earthen walls festooned with drying dung cakes, a thatched roof and the well-tended hedge she had told us about.

A striking young woman was standing to one side, looking at us appraisingly. She had the longest and thickest hair I had ever seen, which she wore in a severe plait into which she had woven strands of jasmine flowers. The effect was exquisite. Her complexion was dusky, making me think of Krishna with the inky complexion and those indefinable features that made him so utterly irresistible.

Madari performed the introductions. We were told that this was Aiyai, her daughter. This girl must have been named after the Goddess so revered by the Aynar. I was reminded of our experience at her shrine and shifted uncomfortably, trying not to dwell on it.

Aiyai seemed amused at the sight of us and, at first, I could not understand why. But a quick glimpse of Madari's courtyard revealed an ancient dog that was blind in one eye, a bird with an injured wing that twittered bleakly from a woven basket, and a large collection of broken pots that served no discernible purpose.

Clearly, Madari had a penchant for bringing home things that were in dire need of repair. And her daughter was used to her mother's ways.

She had a sweet if somewhat cynical smile and seemed to have her mother's friendly disposition. 'Don't stand there gawping, Aiyai! I know our noble guests look exactly like Krishna and Nappinai but that is hardly reason enough for you to dawdle, instead of helping me take care of them.'

Nappinai? If memory served, Pinnai, as she was also known, was Krishna's wife from his time at Brindavan among the cowherds. Most people remembered Rukmini as Krishna's beloved wife. A few would know about Satyabhama, Jambavati or the others. And all knew about his Radha. But Nappinai had been forgotten, except among the cowherds who still worshipped her as their Patron Goddess. I did not wish to be compared to her or have Kovalan equated to Krishna, who supposedly loved Radha more than his other wives and mistresses. But in the end, he had left her too. I glanced at my husband, whose thoughts seemed to be elsewhere. Madari, meanwhile, was still calling out instructions to her daughter.

'Fetch some water for our guests. They have travelled a long way and desperately need a bath. Why don't you give Kannagi one of your saris? And you must run to our neighbour's and borrow a *veshti sattai* for the young master here.'

These people had so little and yet they gave so generously. Tears pricked my eyelids again and I wished that I could repay them. I promised myself that once we had remedied our financial situation, I would visit Madari and the attractive Aiyai who was scrambling around to keep up with her mother's orders, bearing gifts of saris, new pots, and cooking utensils. Perhaps even a good little guard dog with both eyes intact and a cow or two.

How good it felt to take a proper bath. The warm water felt divine. I scrubbed off layers and layers of dust and dirt that seemed to have taken up permanent residence on my person. When I emerged, neatly attired in a freshly laundered sari, I felt better. Aiyai oiled my hair and plaited it with flower strands, as she did for herself, and darkened the ends of my eyes with kohl. That was very sweet of her and made me feel very pretty.

Kovalan looked resplendent too after his bath. Madari had sent for a masseuse to knead the sore, aching muscles in his neck, shoulders, back and legs. I heard him groan with relief and hoped that all the stress and uncertainty he had been nursing had melted away. Our benevolent hostess urged him to rest and go into the city on the morrow, but he was in a hurry to get started. He thanked Madari profusely for the hospitality and partook of a little fruit and milk that she had laid out for him. The dear lady knew the lay of the land like the back of her hand and gave Kovalan detailed directions about the shortest route through the city gates and beyond.

'And don't you worry about your beautiful wife. I will stay here and look after her. Aiyai and I will make sure that she lacks for nothing.'

With a relieved smile, Kovalan bid us farewell and left the enclosure. My heart lurched as he walked away. How I wished it was acceptable for a wife to accompany her husband wherever he went, even if it was for business.

Madari insisted I rest for a while. She laid out a reed mat and, assisted by Aiyai, insisted on massaging my feet and throbbing head with a balm that felt like the touch of God. After days of hard travel and nights haunted by nightmares, it was a relief to sleep the sleep of the dead. For the first and only time in my life, I slept through a good part of the morning, and woke up feeling more refreshed than I had in a long time.

Scrambling to my feet, I realized that Madari was dozing at the head of the mat, while fanning my face gently. Aiyai was preparing the midday meal silently. The one-eyed dog was on guard duty, and he stood dutifully at the threshold, staring at me with a glassy gaze. Determined to make myself useful, I rose to help Aiyai, who motioned for me to sit, while Madari continued to nap, swaying gently and muttering in her sleep.

'I am almost done...' Aiyai said conversationally. 'You must be hungry. Here, have some buttermilk. It is a very hot day.'

I accepted the drink gratefully, while Aiyai carried on with her work, humming a little. It had been mildly spiced and was delicious. Without waiting for me to ask, Aiyai poured me some more. That was very nice of her, and I found myself warming to this girl whom I had just met.

Aiyai told me a little bit about herself. 'My mother is all I have in the world,' she said. 'Appa left her when she was pregnant with me. He ran away with a flower seller. Amma said that it was the nicest thing he ever did for her. She did most of the work around here anyway, while he idled around when he wasn't getting drunk. At least he had enough sense to leave us a roof over our heads and the cows.'

Her tone was noncommittal, and I knew she didn't want pity, but I felt sorry for her anyway. Poor Madari. It was impossible for me to comprehend how she had managed to survive her pregnancy and raise Aiyai all by herself. Surely it must have been monumentally difficult. And all this time I had been feeling sorry for myself about the troubles we had weathered.

'You are different, aren't you?' her smile was sardonic. 'You talk too little and think too much. Amma says that you are the most virtuous of women. A rare treasure who loves her

The Wife and the Dancing Girl

husband and has faithfully remained by his side through good times and bad.'

How could I possibly respond to a statement like that? I drank a little more buttermilk and watched her as she stirred the contents of the vessel on the stove. 'I loved my husband too,' she said, her eyes far away now. 'He lived next door, and we knew each other all our lives. We have a custom here in the cowherd community, where little girls are encouraged to select bulls from the common herds when they are still calves. The raising, grooming and feeding of the bull is our responsibility. When of marriageable age, the bull is let loose in a contest that is open to all interested suitors and the young man who can tame it wins the hand of the girl.'

'What a charming custom!' I said. 'Your husband must be a very good bull fighter. And a brave man!'

'He was...' she affirmed.

Madari, who had just woken, joined us, yawning loudly. Setting the fan aside, she began laying out plantain leaves for our midday meal, which was ready. They served me first before helping themselves. It felt lovely to be taken care of like this. There was hot rice, vegetables, curds and the most delicious milk sweets I had ever eaten. It was a simple, nourishing meal and I enjoyed every bite as well as the company I found myself in. Too bad Kovalan was off in the city and could not join us. But without a man in our midst, the conversation flowed easily.

Madari continued the story Aiyai had been telling. 'Veeran was a good boy, and I remember how delighted he was over his triumph. Eventually, he became quite famous, with many considering him the finest bull tamer in the land. He participated in and won many contests as well as prizes. Once, he even won pouches of gold coins which were attached to the horns of the fierce bulls from the royal stables.'

'I was so proud of him,' Aiyai said with a sad smile. 'He didn't care for the prizes, and he was careless with them, buying me the most extravagant jewellery with his winnings. Why! I was the envy of every girl in Madurai. My man was not only wildly successful, he was also the very best of lovers.'

Her voice trailed off and her eyes reflected the bittersweet memories that buffeted her. I almost did not want to know what had become of him.

'After all these years, I still can't believe he is gone...' she said almost to herself. 'While returning home, after yet another bull-taming contest where he had emerged triumphant, dacoits attacked him as well as the men who had accompanied him. They need not have. He would have gladly given his winnings away because he was that sort of man. They need not have killed him for it either. But they did.'

Aiyai was dry-eyed but Madari and I cried when we heard her story. She looked at us dispassionately before returning to her food with a shrug. I hated it when a love story ended in a tragedy. Why had the Gods seen fit to take away the man she loved? What had Madari done to deserve a man who would abandon her while she was pregnant with his daughter? It was impossible to understand these things.

Chewing her food slowly, Aiyai said, 'Like my father, he too left me the hut and the cattle at least. Amma and I take care of each other. We have managed on our own for many years now. Men come and go from our lives. Some help. Most are brutes, but that is just how it is. And there is no way to remove them from your life entirely. Perhaps it is for the best. Men do have their uses after all.'

'Stop it, Aiyai!' Madari said sternly. 'Kannagi does not have to listen to your strange views.'

'If she minds, she will tell me so herself,' was Aiyai's saucy rejoinder.

I smiled by way of reply and couldn't help but think that in a way tragedy had liberated these two women. They seemed so free of the burden of convention. I envied them a little, while being secretly glad that I had been spared the same fate. Neither of them seemed inclined to complain or feel sorry for themselves. Instead, they worked hard and took care of their own needs. I helped Aiyai clear away the remnants of our meal, scrub the pots and pans, and sweep the floor till the place was neat and tidy.

Madari was enjoying the vetrilai paaku she had folded for herself. The red juice dribbled from the corner of her mouth, but she didn't seem to care because she was humming again with her eyes closed, her well-fed body jiggling and swaying to the rhythm.

I waited for Madari to finish her vetrilai paaku before asking if I could prepare the evening meal for Kovalan. It had been ages since I cooked for him, and it had always been something I enjoyed doing. During our long journey here, I had missed doing that for him. Kovalan was someone who took good cooking and delicious meals for granted. The humble fare we had subsisted on had melted the fat off his bones, and this was the thinnest I had seen him, though he had always been lean and wiry. It would be nice to put in some effort to fatten him up.

'Of course, you may,' Madari touched my cheek with her hand. 'What a sweet thing you are! Why, the prettiest dasi in Madurai is worth less than your toenails, for a loving heart like yours is priceless. I tell you, if people only knew the true value of things, the world will be a better place. I am going to check on the cows now and I might take another siesta. But when I return, you shall have fresh milk and everything else you require to cook for your husband. He is a fortunate man, to have a wife like you. Aiyai will keep you company. And don't mind her if she says wicked things. She is a good girl who talks a little too much for her own good.'

Madari left, singing my praises to all who would listen, much to my chagrin. Afterwards, women dropped in to chat with Aiyai and also to see me. Most came bearing small gifts of food or clothing. It was lovely of them to go out of their way to make me feel so comfortable and welcome. Suddenly I had no wish to leave this place. Perhaps Kovalan and I could have a simple life right here. We could build our own little hut and perhaps buy a few goats and cows. With time, I would stop being so scared of their horns and learn to care for them.

The chaos of a big city was fast losing its charm. Especially one where everybody had too much money to indulge their vices. Although from the little I had gathered from Aiyai, too little money was no deterrent to engaging in sin either. My head hurt when I thought about all this. Aiyai was looking at me again. Clearly, she found me to be something of an oddity.

'May I ask you something?' I began hesitantly. Aiyai nodded and leaned forward. 'How did you go on without him? Kovalan left me for a little while. And I simply couldn't bear it. In my darkest moments, I almost wished that he was an evil man who had killed me instead. Being dead seemed preferable to being without him.'

'I wanted to be dead too. But I didn't have much of a choice, and now, I don't mind being alive so much,' Aiyai said simply. 'Our love was the most perfect thing, just until it was all gone. It is futile to love one who is never coming back, though for the longest time I could not stop. The business of living is too demanding in the end, and I did not have the luxury of grieving for too long. There is always so much that needs to be done hereabouts, and I could not neglect my chores or give up on life.'

I was dangerously close to tears again. What was the matter with me?

'You may not want to hear this,' Aiyai said, and it was clear that she would speak her mind anyway, 'but I am not always alone and unloved either. Many men have sought my company and still do. Some claim to love me. Others just want me. A few are nice. But most are not. In the beginning, I was very much in love with a man who had left this realm, and it was my wish to remain faithful to him, even though he was no more. I fought off my suitors, or at least tried to. Unlike bulls, it's not easy to train or tame men when they wish to have their way with you. Now I no longer resist those who seek me out. Especially those who can and do make my life easier. Why, just today, one of them took the cattle out to graze and promised to milk them too, because I wanted to spend a quiet day at my mother's house with her charming guest. There are also others who fix my roof, mend the fence, clean out the sheds, and tend to the garden. Men are not entirely worthless if you learn how to deal with them.'

I had no idea what to make of the shocking things Aiyai was saying in that matter-of-fact manner of hers, without the faintest trace of guilt or regret. We had been taught that a virtuous woman should remain devoted to her husband alone. Even after death. Merely thinking of any man other than her husband was a grievous sin. Naturally, I did not say any of these things aloud, but I didn't have to.

Aiyai smiled at me. 'A widow's lot is not an easy one, Kannagi. We are taught that death is preferable to dishonour but try telling that to yourself when you are hungry or when you still have some zest for life, even if it doesn't have much to recommend it. Try telling that to yourself when you are lonely at night and want nothing more than the comfort of a warm body by your side for the duration of a few hours of pure pleasure. I have had enough of tears and loneliness. Now, I would rather help myself to pleasure, which is in scarce supply anyway, and use whatever means I can to make the days and nights easier to endure. You may not approve of my choices, but I stopped seeking the approval of others a long time ago.'

It was a lot to take in, but I could not bring myself to judge her actions either. Not entirely anyway. 'I don't have the right to approve or disapprove of anyone,' I told her instead. Hadn't I secretly been happy when Kovalan lost all his money because dancing girls had little use for men without means? Hadn't I in a way deprived Madhavi of her lover and an innocent child of her father? And here I had been pitying Aiyai, whose father had abandoned her and husband had died, while also believing myself to be better than her though I knew nothing of suffering on such a scale, while benefitting from her hospitality. I could no longer understand myself. Perhaps I never did. It would have been a relief to talk to her openly about all this, but it felt like I would be betraying Kovalan if I did so.

'All my life, I have loved only him,' I said, sounding piteous to my own ears. 'Even when we lost everything, I didn't care because I was certain it would bring him back to me. But now that I have him, I am terrified that I will lose him again. I won't be able to go on without him.' And suddenly, I burst into tears like the fool I had always been and was always going to be.

'Amma is going to kill me for upsetting you,' she said, throwing her arms around me and soothing me, the way Amma or Devundi would.

'I am not upset,' I blubbered between sobs, 'it is just that I...'

'Don't worry about it,' she said kindly, 'you don't have to

revisit your past just because I did. May the Gods grant you and your husband a lifetime of happiness. It is the very least they can do after everything you have been through. Dry your eyes, Kannagi!'

I composed myself quickly and Aiyai fixed the smeared kohl she herself had applied. She was the nicest person in the three worlds. Just like her mother. May the Gods grant them a lifetime of happiness too. They certainly deserved it.

'Oh look! Amma is back!' She cried out. 'And she has brought everything you need to prepare a meal fit for a King. I have asked her to stay with me tonight so you will have the place to yourself. Do call if you need anything. And even if you don't, I will check in on you to make sure you are comfortable and are not too distressed by the events from my past or yours!'

Madari gave me the provisions she had brought home and enquired about my wellbeing. She threw a sharp glance at Aiyai but seemed pleased that I looked well-rested and prettier than I had when she left me, as she put it. Then, with cheery waves, mother and daughter left me to my own devices.

∫

Kovalan came home in good spirits and couldn't stop talking about all the things he had seen and done while washing his hands and feet with the water I had kept aside for the purpose in a small clay pot. It was one of the gifts I had received from Madari's neighbour, a cross-eyed woman who examined my face minutely, holding my chin with her hand, to my acute discomfort, and commenting at length on my pearl-like teeth, which fascinated her.

He carried on talking as he settled down on the woven mat I had placed for him to sit on. I listened closely while laying out the plantain leaf and serving him the food I had prepared specially for him. He ate with relish, and I was happy.

Among Madari's provisions I had found some *chenai kizhangu*, the elephant-footed yam, which was one of Kovalan's favourite dishes, especially when stir-fried in coconut oil with spices till it was crisp and clattered around the pan most satisfyingly. He bit into it with every sign of enjoyment, and I was glad.

'Did you know that Madurai is derived from *Mathuram*—which means "sweetness"? Lord Shiva supposedly consecrated the city built by Kulasekhara Pandya after a Swayambhu lingam was discovered in the very heart of a forest known as Kadambavanam. Drops of nectar from his matted locks fell on the city, hence its name. Isn't that something?'

Between bites, he briefly mentioned the pleasure gardens on the banks of the Vaigai, before moving on a little too quickly and going on at length about the heavily fortified palace and towers or some such thing with a lot more enthusiasm than a topic like that warranted.

I served him some more food, which he eagerly accepted before telling me about Madurai's famed Sangams for art and literature where poets, musicians and scholars declaimed their best work. The temples were of surpassing beauty, he enthused, and promised to take me as soon as possible. I hoped it wasn't on a day when some other dazzling danseuse was having her arangetram. According to Kovalan, there was an energy and upbeat vibe to the place, which made Madurai's reputation as a centre for beauty, fine art, architecture and scholarship well deserved.

He had visited the market and seen the merchandise on display. There were sacks of grain, paddy, millets, sorghum, ragi and spices. Textile merchants had also displayed their wares, and Kovalan was taken with the quality of the silks, cottons and the brilliant use of dyes, which gave the fabrics a bright colour and sheen which was unique. The jewellers' street had been his destination all along and he had taken the time to look at all the stalls where precious and semi-precious stones from diamonds, rubies, sapphires, emeralds and pearls to lapis lazuli, onyx, rose quartz, topaz, corals, jade and opals dazzled the eye. For a while, he fell silent and concentrated on chewing and swallowing his food.

Suddenly he looked up and said with great warmth, 'I have missed your cooking. Everything tastes divine! When I set out this morning, I was wracked by doubt but then I visited the section where the goldsmiths showcased some of their best work. Believe me, there is nothing there to match the magnificence of your anklets, which are worthy of a Queen. We will get an excellent price for it. Now, more than ever, I am confident that it was the right decision to come here.'

He leaned in closer and whispered, 'You know I never entertain common gossip, but everybody is talking about it, and I could not help but listen. Queen Kopperundevi has been feuding with the King for a while now. To placate her and win back her affection, he commissioned the making of a pair of anklets, but shortly after these were presented to her, one went missing. The Queen insisted that the culprit be found and brought to justice, but so far they have had no luck. Be that as it may, word on the street is that because of this drama, every lady of means in Madurai wishes to own a pair of exquisite anklets like yours but very few goldsmiths have the otherworldly skills required to manage the intricate design and tracery. Our luck has finally turned, Kannagi! Because of the demand, your anklet will command a King's ransom, and we will have the requisite sum to establish ourselves here.'

Still smiling, he beckoned for me to sit next to him and insisted on feeding me, as was his wont. 'Dearest Kannagi! I don't know what I would have done without you. Even now, I am unable to comprehend why I did some of the things I did. No woman would have found it in her heart to forgive me my trespasses. But not only did you do just that, you also enthusiastically agreed to leave everything you have ever known to embark on a perilous journey to a strange new land at my request. I worried that you might not be strong enough to make the trip, but I need not have. For it was your strength that replenished my own courage and confidence every time either dwindled.'

He took my hands in his and kissed them before placing them over his eyes in a loving gesture that still melted my heart.

Slowly, I placed my head on his lap, and he began to stroke my hair gently. 'Your hair is so soft and fine! I love these flowers you have woven into them. Soon, you shall also have strings of pearls to adorn them.'

'I'll be happy if we were to remain here and milk cows for a living. You don't owe me anything. I want you to know that. Aiyai and Madari told me about the difficulties they themselves have weathered and it got me thinking. We are not always responsible for the things that befall us. The important thing is to try and make the best of it. I do wish that things had gone differently for us but there is no point in dwelling on the past. Going forward, I am just happy that we are together again. Everything else is immaterial.'

Leaning forward, he kissed me softly on the lips. 'You have always asked for so little, Kannagi! It is why you deserve to have everything. I shall place the three worlds at your feet! You will see…' He did not finish the sentence. Instead, he yawned so loudly, we were both startled.

I was on my feet in an instant. Clearing away the dinner things, I rolled out Madari's reed mat and prepared it for him to

The Wife and the Dancing Girl

rest. Aiyai had left some oil for my use as well, and I used it to massage some of the tiredness from his knotted limbs. He was asleep in an instant. I sat by his side, fanning him and taking in the sight of that dear face, which I loved better than anything else in the world.

Soon, I was yawning too. Setting aside the fan, I curled up next to him, loving the feel of his body against mine. He was just so perfect exactly the way he was. But if Kovalan wished to make something of himself so that his father and mother would be proud of him, then he had every right to try and make it happen. I would stand by his side and treat his dreams as if they were my own and help them come true! For both our sakes.

∽

I woke up early. Gathering my hair and tying it into a messy *kondai*, I glanced at the sleeping form of my husband. He would want an early start since he was heading into the capital again. Until the sale of my anklet was successfully concluded, he would know no peace of mind.

There was a well not too far from the hut that served the entire community. Aiyai joined me and we fetched some water together. 'I'll come and look in on you later. It is going to be a very busy day for us, since it is our turn to supply the palace with milk, curd and freshly churned butter. You can join us if you want to and come with us to the palace.'

'Of course, I would love to help.'

Returning to the hut, I tried to boil some milk for Kovalan, but it had curdled and split. Amma would have said that it was a terrible omen, but I decided not to dwell on such superstitious beliefs and tried to maintain a positive mindset. It had probably gone a little bad from the suffocating heat, for it was the height of summer, but it was an unusual occurrence among cowherds who always had fresh milk. Despite vague misgivings, I determinedly shrugged it aside and laid out some fruits instead for Kovalan to break his fast.

Taking out my anklets to set one aside for the sale, I examined them minutely for a minute. I had forgotten how heavy they were. For some reason, I had never liked them much and wore them only on my wedding day, at my mother's insistence. My fingers lingered on the elaborate grooves, the heavy but smooth clasp along with the rubies and diamonds that glittered even in the faint light of dawn. The pattern of the blooms was exquisitely done and the workmanship so fine, it clearly bespoke of genius.

The little gems the hollow anklets were filled with tinkled a little though I hadn't even shaken them. I remembered the story Appa told me about how the precious Nagamani gems, potent and venomous in their great power, had been procured and the lives lost in the process. It could have been a fancy or a trick of the light but suddenly the anklets seemed splattered with blood. Shivering a little and scolding myself for being silly, I wrapped one up in the white cloth it had come with. It was Amma and Appa's gift to me, filled with all the love in their hearts for their only daughter. They would be our salvation and our hope for a good life.

I heard Kovalan stirring and turned quickly to attend to his needs. He was more subdued than he had been last night. Quietly, he readied himself for the day ahead. Aiyai beckoned to me discreetly from outside the hut. She held two garlands of flowers, which she had lovingly strung together for us. Her long, graceful fingers were so deft, and she had done a wonderful job. I smiled in gratitude and took them from her. How thoughtful of her to do this though she had a busy day ahead of her. It was too bad Kovalan no longer had the fine, gold chains he had worn earlier, but this garland would do just as well and bring out the elegant persona he had been born with. The goldsmiths would be impressed by his appearance and welcome him to their shops and give him the very best price for my anklet.

Kovalan smiled as I placed the garland on his shoulders, and he placed the other one on mine. I leaned in for a kiss, but he was too absent-minded to notice and merely nodded in farewell. Taking the wrapped anklet, he strode out with a resolute air. Madari was coming towards the hut with a lively gait despite her advanced years and slightly hunched back. I could hear her assuring Kovalan repeatedly, that she would take good care of me. Thanking her profusely and touching her feet with respect, Kovalan went on his way. That was the last time I saw my husband alive.

∫

The day took a turn for the worse, almost immediately after Kovalan's departure. Aiyai came running towards us and I could tell something was terribly wrong, even from a distance. 'Amma! Come quickly,' she cried out, 'we are in trouble! The milk we set aside to be churned to make fresh butter has gone bad. It hasn't curdled at all. Imagine that! Such a thing has happened only once before.'

Although she was upset, Aiyai did not complete the sentence, even though her eyes were aflame with anguish. I remembered her dead husband, who was attacked and killed by dacoits for his prize money. Hurriedly, she went on, 'We could have used yesterday's butter to make ghee, but it has gone rancid too and refuses to melt. And have you been to the shed yet? The animals are behaving very strangely. I have never seen anything like it!'

'Oh no! There is more?' Madari threw up her hands in frustration. 'And this could not have happened at a worse time.

Why today of all days? Only the mischievous Gods know! Why must they send calamity in droves?'

We hurriedly made our way to the cowshed, and I will never forget the sight that met our eyes. The huge eyes of the bulls and cows were glistening with unshed tears as they lay huddled and shivering together, having miraculously escaped their ropes. The bells that usually hung from their necks lay scattered on the floor, rolling amidst the scattered straw, striking a dolorous requiem. The lambs were not frisking as was their wont and lay in abject silence. Following Aiyai's horrified gaze, I saw that the dung heaps were riddled with hundreds of fat, wriggling maggots, each one the size of my thumb. It was a sight to strike terror in our hearts and melt the innards.

Aiyai and Madari were looking so distressed that it seemed clear that they thought the ill omens portended an impending catastrophe. Madari was the one who was moving and speaking briskly, though her voice shook. She called out to one of the young girls, 'Vinda! You must run and tell your mother about the mishap that has occurred in our shed. Ask her to take butter and ghee to the palace on my behalf. When it is her turn, I will take up the task. Hurry!'

Then she shook an already shaken Aiyai by the shoulder. 'It is nothing! Something has frightened the animals. Perhaps they caught a whiff of the wolves from the hills that are always preying on them. We must calm them as best as we can. Let us summon the neighbours and together we shall perform the Kuravai for Kannagi, our special guest. The ancient dance ritual that was put in practice when Lord Krishna walked on this *punya* Bhoomi always gladdens the soul and never fails to please the Gods. Perhaps they can be persuaded to part with a blessing and scatter the malevolent forces. Send for some of your male friends as well. We can use their help. The shed must be cleaned out thoroughly.'

The unmarried girls who were tending the bulls in keeping with custom emerged, in answer to Madari's summons. They looked very pleased indeed to be called upon to perform the Kuravai. Each one prettier than the one before, they arrived with a spring in their step and a smile on their faces. Interlocking their hands, they formed a circle, singing and dancing as one to a lively beat with practised grace. They enacted well-known stories from Krishna's life, particularly the most joyous days he had spent as a cowherd with Balarama and pretty Pinnai by his side. Tale after tale was performed about the butter thief who stole hearts with equal felicity, the slayer of demons, the architect of a war that annihilated an age to usher in another, the avatar of mighty Vishnu, the divine protector.

Aiyai sat by my side, refusing to let go of my hand, which she clasped tightly, and I held on gratefully. I knew she understood the state I was in. The Kuravai seemed to go on and on, evoking a spectrum of sublime emotions. But I could not savour it though they danced with impassioned ardour. Without cease, my eyes scanned the horizon, hoping to see him walking towards me with outstretched arms seeking to clasp me against his chest. There was no sign of him though, as time marched on implacable and unheeding as ever.

With mounting disquiet, I looked out into the distance, staring as one entranced, willing the universe to make my husband materialize in front of me at the earliest.

Fear bubbled up from deep within my gut, flooding every pore with pulsing panic that spilled over and sloshed against my insides. *Something bad had happened. To Kovalan. If only I could go to him. Where was he?* I plunged into the abyss of my terror. I fell. Hard and fast, trapped in a nightmare realm from which I couldn't claw my way out, despite the desperate strength employed. In that surreal space of endless suffering, Kovalan was falling faster, slipping and sliding further and further beyond my reach, plunging into the eternal darkness, shoved down a slippery slope of blood and guts. And try as I might, it was impossible to grab him by the hand and hold on.

All at once, I realized I was living the nightmare that had plagued me all this time. My heart was torn asunder by grief and pain as every fragment of fear, every stray tendril of anxiety, every expectation of dread was realized, coalesced into those moments, and the realness of it was a thousand times worse than my worst presupposition of impending peril.

A young milkmaid who had just returned from the city, where she had been selling her wares, ran into our midst just then, calling out loudly for my hostess. 'Madari! Madari! Alas! A terrible fate has overtaken the poor young man who was your honoured guest! I saw it with my...' She stopped dead in her tracks when she laid eyes on me. Her chest was heaving with agitation and there were tears streaming down her cheeks.

'Calm yourself, girl, and speak up! What's wrong?' Madari asked her.

The girl shook her head, unable to say another word. She could not stop staring at me. Or crying.

Aiyai tightened her grip on me as I wailed. Long and loud. Years and years of silence and unspoken words surged out of me in an unstoppable frenzy. I did not recognize my voice. It was hoarse, discordant, and boomed louder than the *rishabha* note struck on a battle horn. 'What happened to my husband? Tell me the truth! I must know everything.' Worry and fury were gnawing at my very sanity, and I tried to brace myself against the unspeakable evil that had overtaken me.

The girl was sobbing piteously. Aiyai grabbed her by the shoulder and shook her hard. 'It was the anklet!' she said, the words tumbling out at last. 'They accused him of stealing the Queen's anklet. The goldsmith he had tried to sell an anklet to, took it to the King at once and named her husband a thief. The royal decree was issued, and the Guards carried it out immediately. They killed him! With their swords! He is dead. I saw his…it is lying near a small shrine beside the goldsmith's shop where he had been waiting.'

My senses were swimming. If only the sword that had killed my husband had pierced my heart too! I collapsed in a dead faint then. And lay sprawled on the floor for long moments that felt like an eternity. But no, I would not let the darkness claim me. Not yet.

Aiyai was holding me. Brushing her aside, I got to my feet.

'Your King is the filthy thief!' Once again, I did not recognize my own voice or the wrath that spiked every syllable I uttered, as I hurled the truth in my words like projectiles at the gathering crowd. 'Nedunjeliyan, in addition to being a depraved womanizer, is the unworthiest of Kings! How dare he listen to false accusations and deliver an incorrect verdict without even bothering with a proper trial? My husband was innocent and a victim of a blundering tyrant who will answer to me for his crimes! I will prove the falseness of his accusations! See if I don't!'

Aiyai stood by my side and galvanized by my voice, she cried out, 'This noble lady speaks the truth! My mother and I will bear witness. They came to Madurai all the way from distant Puhar merely a couple of days ago and it was only yesterday that Kannagi's husband entered the gates of Madurai for the very first time. The Queen's anklet has been missing for over a month now.

How could blameless Kovalan be guilty of theft? He was only trying to sell Kannagi's anklet.'

'A proper enquiry should have been conducted before judgement was pronounced.' I roared at the crowd who had no choice but to nod in agreement. 'Your King has shamed and dishonoured not only himself but all of Pandya Nadu! History will remember his infamy, which must be cleansed with fire and blood! But for now, take me to my husband.'

Dozens had gathered and they murmured their assent. 'Nedunjeliyan must pay! All he cares about is carousing with different dasis every day and every night. Now he has gone too far by taking the life of an innocent young man who was only trying to make a living.'

'This virtuous wife forced into widowhood deserves justice!'

'Her wrath is justified! She must have her vengeance!'

The young girl who had brought us the bitter tidings, took the lead and I followed in her wake, pausing only to gather the evidence I would need to establish Kovalan's innocence, the force of my rage brushing aside the overwhelming sorrow which threatened to lay me prostate. That damned anklet!

∽

Kovalan was dead. My husband was dead. He was gone forever this time. Never to return. What was I to do with all the love I bore him? What was I to do with the life that was still left to me? And all this because of a fool of a King who cared only for pleasure and was not worthy of the dust beneath Kovalan's feet, let alone a crown, sceptre, throne and Kingdom.

If they thought I would shed useless tears over his dead body and wordlessly join him on the funeral pyre, they were mistaken. All my life, I had been dutiful, humble, meek and accepting of every hardship in the time-honoured practices prescribed for good women, for all the good it had done me. Not this time.

I had finally won his love. Now he lay dead and drowned at the bottom of a puddle of blood. But this time, I would not suffer in silence. Did they think I would perform his last rites, don the widow's whites, and disappear into the shadows, travelling from one *punya teertha* to the next, searching for the peace that was lost to me in this lifetime? Did they think I would hold my tongue and let them spread their calumny and lies about my beloved husband?

It was a surreal experience seeing and hearing the avenging fury I had become as though from a great distance, through a gauzy veil of implacable fury. There I was, raving and ranting and roaring dire imprecations against the Pandya who would face the wrath of a wronged woman. I charged forward, towards where my deceased husband lay unmoving, inciting the crowd to follow me in my quest for retribution, swearing to unleash the fury and flames of Yama's thousand hells. With one hand, I unloosed my hair, the same tresses he had caressed only the day before. The other one I held upraised, bearing the anklet that was to have been my salvation, but which had spelt my husband's and my doom instead. If it was unlimited blood the accursed ornament demanded, it shall have it! By sundown, it shall have its fill of royal scoundrels and every one of their subjects.

'Death to the King who killed an innocent man! Death to the Queen! Death to the damned!' Aiyai took up the chant and the crowd behind me, which had transformed into a mob, roared their fury and the very heavens resounded with the straining voices shrieking for violence.

The milkmaid pointed to the villainous goldsmith's shop where Kovalan had tried to sell my anklet, and the little shrine beside it, where he had spent his last moments, waiting patiently as instructed by that accursed goldsmith, unsuspecting of the terrible fate that loomed ahead of him.

I saw him as if in a trance, taking in the mangled remains that were all that was left of him. At the very spot where he had drawn his last, anguished breath. Many in the milling crowd began lamenting, loud and long, beating their chests in abject horror, so ghastly was the sight that confronted us. His eyes! They were wide open and staring. His formerly handsome face had stiffened in shock, his graceful limbs were askew, and his dhoti had come undone. My resplendent husband lay in the dirt and blood, where passersby could gawk at him and condemn him for a crime he had not committed. How dignified he had been. How dare they do this to him? I know he could not bear for me to see him like this, and I would have gladly torn out my eyes to erase the image from memory.

None of them had the decency to cover his remains even. I ran to his side, pressing my palms against the gaping wound in his side, where the sword had penetrated his unresisting flesh, even though it was a futile gesture that would not stem the flow of blood that had already ebbed out of him and ended his life. Rocking his body in my arms, I held him close and kissed him repeatedly all over his face, pressing my lips against his, knowing they would never respond again, running my hands across the formerly soft hair that was stiff and matted with grime and blood. I murmured endearments that he would never hear and did my best to comfort one who was past needing it.

I raised my voice to try and reach him across the yawning chasm that gaped open between us. 'They have torn us apart and I promise on your blood that every single one of them will pay for this heinous crime. Not one of them shall be spared for what they did to you. And when it is all over, I will find my way back to your side, no matter what it takes! All the obstacles in the world, entire oceans of blood and all of eternity shall not deter me. For we were meant to be together forever, and we will be! This is my promise to you.'

Kissing his lips one last time, I closed his eyes, easing the horror and pain they held. Ripping off my upper garment, uncaring about modesty, I covered his remains so that he would feel my embrace and be comforted by the scent of his faithful wife who would love him always as his soul journeyed to the dark realms ruled by Yama.

Then I rose to my feet, half-naked and covered in his blood. 'If there are decent, virtuous and righteous people among you, join me as I march towards the palace and your King to see justice upheld! I will not waste another moment mourning the passing of my Lord with useless tears and lamentations. Neither will I lose precious time performing the final rites. Instead, I will honour his life and memory by making sure that he is cleared of all wrongdoing. Then, the wrongdoers will be brought to their knees and pay for their crime with their own lives!'

Every single person gathered before me roared their agreement. Men and women, the old and young, shook their fists in the direction of the palace, their faces contorted with bestial anger, as they howled for blood. Savage as a pack of wolves, they swarmed over the shop of the goldsmith who had accused Kovalan, ransacked the place and smashed everything in sight before setting it on fire.

Aiyai and Madari had not left my side. At the former's signal, a group of cowherds stepped forward. They held the resisting goldsmith between them, who thrashed about wildly in their grip, defiant and unrepentant. When he saw his shop, the man looked horrified, for the precious gold jewellery he had so carefully amassed had been stolen and his workshop reduced to an enormous ball of fire that seared his eyes and scorched his skin. Prodding him with their pointed staves and cattle goads, they forced the thieving goldsmith to his knees at my feet.

He looked up and snarled, 'Your husband did not steal the anklet. I did. And if I had to do it all over again, I would. All my life, I have made beautiful things for people who did not deserve my creations. How is it possible that I can make ornaments of surpassing splendour but never afford to own them? What is another pair of anklets to the Queen who already has dozens? I decided to keep one. Art belongs to its creator, not the mindless consumers. And you shall never have it either. I have already melted it down, rather than lose it.'

Spittle flew from his mouth along with the venomous words. Aiyai struck him across the face so hard his neck snapped back, and he fell silent in shock.

'Thief!' she pointed an accusing finger at him.

'Thief! Thief! Thief!' the crowd took up the chant.

'Did you hear that?' I roared at the crowd. 'This is the man whose false accusations led to the murder of my innocent husband. I don't know how things are done here in Pandya Nadu, but in Puhar, the bastion of Chola power and centre of justice, from where I hail, do you know what the punishment for a false accusation is?'

'Death! Death! Death!' the crowd howled back, stomping their feet. Women stepped forward and spat directly on his face, raining blows on him. Men started kicking him and hitting every exposed part of him. The coward wailed piteously and begged for mercy. He would have it, when death came calling.

His assistants were brought forward by the vigilante cowherds.

They were shivering with mortal terror and held between them the steaming cauldron with the thick cloths that were sopping wet, in which the goldsmith had melted the Queen's anklet, and brought it to me for inspection. I stared at the swirling mess of molten gold, evidence of a man's greed that had destroyed my entire life. Without a word, I snatched it up and emptied the contents onto the blackguard's upturned face before bringing it down on his worthless head. He was not defiant then, when the molten metal ate through his face, neck and chest. Shrieking with agony, he writhed in the dust until an upstanding member of the mob dealt the killing blow with a recurved blade, severing his head from his convulsing body and flinging him towards me. I kicked his head to the side. The furious onlookers trampled over his dead body, crushing it into a pulpy mess and smashing his bones to splinters.

Drawing a deep breath, I issued my next command. 'Take me to Nedunjeliyan! It is his turn next!'

'Death to the King who killed an innocent man! Death to the Queen! Death to the damned!' Thousands of voices added their voices to mine. Thousands more joined them. As one we surged towards the palace gates. The mighty bell of justice at the entrance to the palace boomed, its clanging reverberating across the length and breadth of the city as we made our way to the palace gates.

Dozens of the King's guards tasked with maintaining law and order arrived on the scene, aiming to disperse the multitudes. To cow us into submission with their swords and spears. 'Go back now and escape with your lives!' the Captain of this patrol called out in a bull voice. 'Anyone who lingers will face the King's justice!' He was a burly man, with a bristling beard and a stern demeanour.

'The King's justice? That does not exist! Nedunjeliyan is a thief and murderer! He must answer for his crimes to the wife of the honest man he killed. Even a so-called King is not above the laws of Dharma,' I shrieked at him, refusing to back down.

'The word of a condemned thief's wife has even less value than that worthless scoundrel. Especially since she is a whore! Is this the sort of woman you would follow in defiance of your King? Is there not a man among you who can resist her vile blandishments?'

'Let us teach this King's cur a lesson. An evil man who dishonours a good woman seeking justice because he is too used to being the loyal lapdog of the rich and powerful,' Aiyai snarled at our followers, who were already hissing to register their contempt for the boorish Captain.

A lone stone was hurled at him with such force, it split his eyebrow open, and blood gushed into his open eye. Others followed. His men drew their swords and raised their shields. Furious, he issued his command, 'Kill them all and bring the bitch to me in chains. Since she is already naked, we will not have to strip her and parade her across the city. Tie her spreadeagled in the square and leave her to rot.'

I raised my anklet in response and watched numbly as the hordes charged into the ranks of the guards, unimpeded by their weapons and armour, tearing them to pieces and flinging various body parts in all directions without breaking my stride. Aiyai and I made our way past the thronging bodies caught up in the middle of a pitched battle. Blood and guts seemed to pour out like a river in spate. The King's guards fought their way towards me. Time and again they were beaten back. But every time one fell, another took its place. Meaty paws grabbed at my body or got a handful of my hair. I fought them off with whatever came to hand. My defenders were legion, and they intervened, sacrificing their lives for mine. 'My life is yours, Goddess!' they sang in exultation, consumed by battle lust and feverish fanaticism. I barely acknowledged the sacrifice and kept moving with Aiyai at my side, knee-deep in blood and corpses.

More guards poured in from all directions and they surrounded me. Madari interspersed herself between my body and the pitiless guards, her hands folded in supplication. 'Please! She only seeks to…' One of them brought his club down on her skull, smashing it like an overripe melon, casting her body aside like it was no more than a broken pot.

Aiyai howled and charged towards them, fighting like a demoness to reach her mother's killer. A sword slashed across her face. She fell in a heap and lay unmoving even when the guards aimed savage kicks at her like the maddened beasts they were. I rushed at them and within moments, they were upon me, tearing at what remained of my garments, rough hands pawing, groping, slapping, beating, pushing me to the ground. I lay in shock, choking and sputtering on the fumes of blood, sweat, liquor and urine. On any other day, I would have died of shame and humiliation. But not on that day.

For long moments that seemed to stretch out across the course of eternity, I lay stiff and still as an unprotesting corpse, ignoring the evil men swarming over my body. Then the rage took over. Snatching the protruding hilt of the dagger from the sheath attached to the waist of the man who was trying to pry my legs apart, I plunged it into his throat and watched imperviously as he died with a copious outpouring of blood from his mouth, his lips wide open, locked in a rictus of agony, right on top of me.

The dirty defiler's partners in crime lunged at me, hoping to finish what he started and avenge their fallen comrade in arms. Pushing the repulsive creature aside, with the dagger still in hand,

I plunged it in quick deadly strikes into the fleshy thighs of two who were almost upon me. They fell back screaming fit to burst, geysers of their blood gushing forth and drenching me as I forced myself to stand, though not a rag remained on my body. The heartless monsters who had murdered a kind, old cowherdess, mutilated her daughter, and sought to violate and kill a recently widowed woman who asked for nothing but justice, took a step back when they caught a glimpse of death in my eyes. When they saw the avenging destroyer I had become.

'Is this what you wanted?' my voice boomed into their cowardly faces rigid with fright, and they took a few paces back. Hefting the dagger in my right hand, I slashed at my left breast repeatedly with increasingly violent strokes, immune to everything but blinding fury. With superstitious dread, they continued to do their utmost to get away from me, raw panic and terror writ large across their ugly features. Gone a long way beyond suffering, I hacked at my breast in a relentless rhythm till it came free. Then I lobbed it in a vicious arc towards the retreating guards.

'Take it, you filthy beasts! Isn't it what you wanted? For every lifetime you are cursed to roam this sinful world, you will be denied a mother's breasts! Run for your lives, because in your next one, you will answer for every one of your sins and suffer the doom you deserve without the protection of mother's milk and the pleasure of a woman's body! Run as fast as you can and be damned unto eternity!'

With bitter satisfaction, I watched them flee from my sight, weeping with fear, trying in vain to dodge the blows of cudgels and spears that dogged them every step of the way. My legion of loyal followers who had accompanied me all the way from the cowherds' establishment as well as the others who had joined us along the way pursued them, calling down the wrath of the Gods, pelting them with stones, slicing their bodies open with whatever weapon came to hand, leaving them to die, ripped to shreds, spat and stomped upon, abhorred like the detestable beasts they were.

Aiyai had somehow made her way back to my side, bleeding from her many wounds and near naked as I was, holding a sword in one hand. In the other, she held my anklet, which had nearly gotten lost in the melee. Gratefully, I took it from her. 'I can't thank you enough for this and more, Aiyai. Hopefully I will not be needing it much longer.'

'Let us end this! Don't hesitate to kill all who obstruct your path, Kannagi,' she said through clenched teeth, cold determination to avenge poor Madari imbuing her with superhuman strength and endurance.

'Death to the tyrant! Death to all the tyrants in his employ! Death to all the tyrants who have despoiled Madurai!'

Every woman in the crowd picked up her chant. There were so many of them. Where had they come from? Their brightly coloured saris were stained with mud and blood. They seemed to have emerged from nowhere and were everywhere, chanting Aiyai's refrain like a prayer.

'Death to all tyrants!'

'Death to the rapists!'

'Death to the murderers!'

'Death to the thieves and liars and scoundrels!'

'Death to all men! Death to them all!'

'Kill them all! Burn them all! Burn them all!'

More and more women converged upon us, covered with wounds, bleeding copiously and in varied stages of undress. They formed a circle around us, bolstered by their wrath and my own, wary and watchful, in case the tyrant unloosed more of his assailants into our midst. Right there in the middle of the city square, which had become a battle ground with a heaving, straining throng of bloodied bodies, Aiyai and I were made to sit.

Still more women made their way towards us, braving death and, worse, bearing pots of turmeric water and milk, honey and curds, butter and ghee, which they proceeded to pour over our embattled bodies, touching our feet as they did so—their *havi*s, humble offerings for us, whom they clearly considered to be divine entities rather than two wronged women who had lost the ones they loved most in the world.

Singing devotional hymns, they tended to our wounds with touching devotion. They formed a human chain to shield and give us some privacy in the middle of a raging battle. The bleeding in my chest which had been deprived of a breast was stanched. The wound was cauterized with a ladle heated on the pyres that seemed to be blazing everywhere as I bit down on a piece of wood that had been placed in my mouth, and a poultice applied. Maybe they expected me to scream or at least faint, but I did not feel anything anymore. Hurt like this was insignificant after what I had been through. The singing, chanting and praying intensified around me.

Finally, they bound up the gaping gash that remained in place of my left breast with a clean cloth. Another attended to Aiyai's grievous injuries as she sat there with her eyes closed, a picture of stoic resilience. Still others had brought saris and draped our naked bodies with them. When we stood up again, garlands were placed around our necks. The gathered women clapped their hands and ululated in unison as we began to walk.

Once again, anklet in hand, I strode towards the palace with

Aiyai by my side. Thousands followed us. This time, no one dared to stand in my way.

⌇

At the palace, the gates were thrown open for me. The *Apathuvadigal*, the King's personal guard, led by their captain stood before me, barring passage. They were regarded as the foremost of warriors who had distinguished themselves in battle and been handpicked by the old guard to protect the King. They had sworn a dread oath to protect him at all costs. Or die trying. The respect they commanded in the Pandyan Kingdom was second only to the King himself.

The Captain held himself erect and proud. His voice was stern but to my surprise, sympathy lurked in their depths. 'State your business, noble lady. I am sworn to protect the King, and I cannot let such an unruly assemblage enter.'

'Great warrior, sworn to protect the unworthy, I am here to prove that your King has failed in his duty not just as a ruler but as a human being. I am here to accuse your King of theft! And your Queen of being in possession of stolen goods. Nedunjeliyan is guilty of the murder of an innocent man, and he must be punished for his grievous wrongdoing. It was one among the proud Apathuvadigal who struck the blow that killed my faultless husband. It was some among you who left him to bleed to death in this accursed land. All the accused must pay for their wrongdoing. You can try to stop me from seeking them out and making sure that justice is upheld. But you are doomed to fail!'

Some of the Apathuvadigal shifted uneasily. The Captain remained unperturbed. Setting aside his weapons, he bowed before me. 'I swear to secure an audience with the King for you, dear lady. If your husband's innocence is proved beyond doubt, and those among the Apathuvadigal, who have sworn to obey and enforce all orders of our King, are implicated in the death of a good man, they shall die by my hand, and I will lay their heads at your feet. This I swear by everything I hold sacred and by my own life. You shall have your say in the Pandyan court. If what you say is true, and I fear it is, this is a dark day indeed for Madurai. But I cannot let your followers in.'

A good man. It was too bad that he was doomed to die protecting a shameless tyrant. Exchanging a quick glance with Aiyai, who nodded wordlessly, I alone of my many companions made my way to the audience hall, accompanied by the Apathuvadigal, who bore themselves with grave dignity, the weight of my accusation hanging dolorously above their heads.

Word had reached Nedunjeliyan. Imperious and arrogant, he sat on his grand throne, surrounded by his ministers. The assembly hall reeked of luxury and opulence. These people had more than they knew what to do with and still they wanted more. They were so base, they would kill rather than pay the price for a golden anklet. The Pandyan Queen was seated beside him, gorgeously made up and defiantly flaunting my anklet, which adorned her feet. The entire court had gathered to watch the unfolding spectacle, eager for entertainment. The Apathuvadigal flanking the King stood at attention, all of them armed to the teeth. How smug they all looked.

Nedunjeliyan stared at me with barely concealed distaste, taking note of my unbound tresses, running his gaze insolently across my mutilated form revealed by the hastily draped sari, which was still wet with turmeric water, milk, dried blood and dirt.

'What is your complaint, woman? I will give you a fair hearing despite the ruckus and breakdown in law and order you have caused with your raving and ranting over the passing of a thief.

You have been granted clemency because grief has clearly robbed you of your senses. And it must be said that your devotion to your husband, criminal though he might have been, does you credit. But beware, my mercy is not limitless. No insolence and falsehoods will be tolerated in this court.'

I cleared my throat and spat at his feet. Pointing an insolent finger at him with calculated disrespect, I raised my voice over the loud gasps of shock from the courtiers and the stomping of feet by the angered Apathuvadigal. 'My husband was no thief. But I wish I could say the same about the Queen and her Lord husband. You have stolen not just our rightful property but a blameless life as well. All because you had no wish to pay the full price for a priceless ornament. You are a murderer! And I will prove it to you.'

The courtiers, as could be expected from lickspittle, started clamouring, furious that a bereaved woman who ought not to be seen let alone heard, in their opinion, was shouting accusations at their King. Nedunjeliyan silenced them with a raised hand.

As for me, their disapprobation meant less than nothing, and I would have my say. 'My husband and I arrived in this godforsaken land only a couple of days ago. We came all the way from Puhar, ruled by just Kings like Sibi, who offered to give his life to save a poor dove that sought his protection, and Manu Needhi Cholan, who had his own son crushed beneath the wheels of a chariot because the royal scion's vehicle had claimed the life of a blameless calf in similar fashion and its mother rang the bell of justice with her horns.

'There are many witnesses who will attest to the timing of our arrival. Kavundi Adigal, the virtuous Jaina renunciant, will vouch for us. So will the entire establishment of the cowherds. One among them was Madari, who gave us shelter. She was murdered by your cruel guards who kill and defile defenceless women instead of safeguarding them. Her daughter, Aiyai, stands at the gates of your palace, seeking justice for her slain mother and she too will vouch for the veracity of my words. How then could my husband have committed the theft of the Queen's anklet of which he was falsely accused?'

Nedunjeliyan glared at me, though he was starting to look queasy as if his last meal was not sitting well with him. 'You try my patience, woman! I cannot claim to know the methods employed by master thieves or their seeming ability to be in many places at once. But irrefutable evidence was offered as to his thievery. Pay heed to my warning! I have nothing but compassion for the demented widow of a slain thief, but you must not push me too far!'

'You shall have irrefutable evidence, oh King! Evidence that was lacking when you issued the death sentence that took the life of an innocent man.' I raised my anklet for all to see and pointed to its pair on Kopperundevi's foot. 'As anybody with eyes can see, they are a perfect match, unlike the flimsy replica on her other foot. You know the truth, Queen of the Pandyas, and still you dissemble, blinded by your greed and love for beautiful baubles. If you insist on further proof, I am happy to offer it. My anklets are hollow inside and filled with the precious and rare Nagamani gems.'

A murmur ran through the crowded court. All were craning their necks to look at the anklets in question and some were shaking their heads in great agitation.

'She is right!'

'The one in her hand is identical to the one on the Queen's foot.'

'There has been a miscarriage of justice!'

'That is impossible!' Kopperundevi cried out. 'No man can get his hands on the fabled Nagamani gems.'

The Wife and the Dancing Girl

'Then the matter is easily resolved,' Nedunjeliyan's cruel face split open in a jeer. 'The Queen's anklets are filled with flawless pearls from across the sea. Let her see the proof for herself, my Queen. Anything to stop her tedious tirade!'

With trembling hands, Kopperundevi undid the clasp and removing it from her foot, held it in her hand. Striding forward, I yanked it from her hand.

'Wait!' Kopperundevi cried out, looking pointedly at my shabby appearance. 'As a woman, I understand your grief over your husband's misdeeds. But I can't help but wonder, and I am sure every dignitary present in the court today is thinking the same thing, how you came to be in possession of those priceless anklets. As you claim, you travelled all the way here from Puhar on foot, living off the charity of the monks and finding shelter with cowherds. How could someone like you afford a pair of these priceless anklets? It is obvious that you stole the anklets from a lady of high standing in Puhar and fled in the night like the thieves you clearly are! Justice has caught up with your husband and you have the temerity to stand here after inciting the mob to riot, levelling accusations at us. As if that was not bad enough, you also want to break my anklet, which is a token of love from my husband! How dare you? It seems to me that you deserve the same fate as that common criminal.'

She looked to the King for acquiescence, but this time he hesitated. Not one member of the court spoke up in support of Kopperundevi. For when I held both the anklets in my hand, it was plain for all to see, that they were a perfect match. Every groove, the precise placement of rubies and diamonds, the delicacy of the floral pattern, even the heavy clasp was identical.

This time I did not raise my voice. There was no need. They waited in breathless silence to hear what I had to say. 'My husband

Kovalan was the son of the merchant prince Masattuvan.' The members of the Merchants' Guild present in Court looked up, nodding in recognition of the name. 'Theirs is a proud lineage of untainted honour. My husband lost his fortune, thanks to his ill-fated love for the dancing girl, Madhavi. But he did not spend it all on carousing or debauchery. He gave away his wealth to help the less fortunate. Having recognized the error of his ways, he returned to me. I gave him my anklets, so that he could sell them, and we could start over in a new land. I am not ashamed of our poverty. We have never been covetous people, unlike the lot of you, especially your Queen, who cares for nothing but gold. This is the truth, and you know it too.'

'She dares to insult your Queen,' Kopperundevi's voice was shrill, and she did not look very pretty when she sulked and spat like a cat, 'and yet, you keep quiet. All these years, I have put up with your philandering ways and the time has come for you to repay me. Have her put in chains and her tongue torn out. She must then be stripped and paraded all over Madurai, so that people learn a lesson about what happens to liars, thieves and whores who have been deprived of their breast as a mark of their shame and infamy.'

The King was looking indecisive. A few had the grace to look shamefaced. Most refused to meet my gaze. None of them could. They were staring at the floor or fixedly at my missing breast.

The Captain of the Apathuvadigal stepped forward. He had positioned himself next to the King. A silent command from him and four among his men did the same. They went down on their knees in front of me and touched my feet one by one. Only one spoke to me. 'He did not look like a thief. It felt wrong even then. Forgive me!'

The Captain had unsheathed his sword. Raising it high in the air, he struck off their heads and laid them at my feet, as promised. Quietly, his men removed the still thrashing bodies from our presence. Immediately there was an uproar. Nedunjeliyan was furious. 'Enough is enough! Guards! Arrest the Captain! He will pay for his treachery with his head. Arrest this woman immediately. The Queen's orders will be carried out. That is my royal command!'

I closed my eyes for a moment. They had been given the chance to do the right thing and clear my husband of wrongdoing. But their selfishness and petty spite would always get in the way of what remained of their sense of dharma. The good Captain was the sole exception. As for the rest of them, not one would be spared. Not one. The words of my father spoken a long time ago sounded in my ears and my eyes filled with tears on hearing that beloved voice...

Endowed with the power of Lord Shiva, the Nagamani gems are highly potent. They will bestow fame as well as fortune on the owner and protect against baleful influences and the venom of enemies. They can cause harm as well to those who have harmed the owner, which is nothing less than can be expected from a gift imbued with the essence of the Destroyer. My daughter is the best among women, and she shall have nothing but the best.

He would have asked me to show mercy. Kovalan would have too. But I knew better. Without a word, I raised my anklet. The one I had snatched from the Queen. Before she could utter a word, I snapped it in two. The gleaming Nagamani gems, bright as blood, spilled forth and scattered across the floor, bouncing off the freshly decapitated heads, hurtling across the court in all directions. Some struck the King and Queen across the face. The assemblage stared at the gems slithering around in silent horror. Then it happened.

Nedunjeliyan was the first. He was convulsing on his golden throne emblazoned with the flashing fish insignia of the Pandyas, very much like a fish out of water, facial muscles and limbs twitching violently. He was trying to speak but his words slurred, and he slumped as he fell forward on his face. We could hear his jaw break and the teeth shatter. Clearly, he was in so much pain he could barely move as he writhed in agony at the foot of the throne, foaming from the mouth.

Kopperundevi was convulsing too. She no longer looked haughtily beautiful and resplendent in her silks and jewels. Frothing from the mouth, she was looking in my direction at the unbroken anklet I still held in my hand. Her breath came in short, laboured gasps and she swayed dizzily, her face swelling to grotesque proportions. Her entire body was twitching, and blood spurted out from her ears and nose.

Other members of the court were displaying the same array of symptoms. The gems appeared to weave and writhe and twist their way across the assembly hall, glittering eerily, their crimson hearts seemingly aflame. All around there were cries of pain as men and women clutched their chests or stomachs, their faces and bodies swelling, some turning a putrid shade of green. Many lay twitching and thrashing on the floor, having lost control of their bodies. Specks of saliva and blood floated through space like ugly butterflies.

The bodies of the late King Nedunjeliyan and his Queen Kopperundevi lay inert beneath their grand thrones, which had somehow lost their lustre from the blood, froth, bodily fluids, and their life essence, which had been forcibly expelled from them.

Guards poured in from outside and they charged at me. They called me a witch and a whore and all things in between, but I was past hurt. Their words, like their sticks and stones and spears, were immaterial to me and would cause me no lasting harm. I had nothing to fear. They, on the other hand, could not have said the same. And with good reason. I'll say one thing for them though. They were brave men. Death did not scare them.

They did not flinch when I broke the other anklet in half and scattered the rest of the Nagamani gems every which way I could. Like the others before them, they died. In extreme, excruciating agony. Some quicker and cleaner than the others. But they all fell with their bodies convulsing in paroxysms of pure pain. Their tormented screams and howls of wretched despair rang out for the longest time. I revelled in it. The macabre dance of death alleviated my own misery, even if it was only momentarily.

When it was all over, the Captain of the Apathuvadigal alone remained unscathed. Sadness so profound suffused his features that even I felt sorry for him. He had watched the carnage and chaos in the killing cascade of crimson. He had failed in his oath to protect the King and Queen of the Pandyas with his life, though there had been absolutely nothing he could do to save them. He had killed the guilty among his men with his own hand, lived to be accused of treachery, seen the rest of the court die in droves, and watched the death throes of those under his command. He had not sounded the charge against me, nor had he unsheathed his weapons. The man knew they would do him no good.

Having aged a billion lifetimes over the course of the slaughter, he came towards me. There would be no angry recriminations from him. 'You have suffered, and it has made you an avenging goddess. I am sorry for everything you have lost. I apologize for the tragedy and trauma and shoddy treatment that has been meted out to you during your brief sojourn in beautiful Madurai! Forgive us, have mercy on us all.'

'It will be over soon...' I told him. 'I have avenged my husband with fire, venom, and blood. You are free to go.'

He shook his head resignedly. 'Madurai will burn, my lady! Already the rioters have gained the upper hand. Law and order have broken down entirely. There is fighting in the streets. Looters and dacoits are having a field day. Fires have been started everywhere. When news of our King's passing spreads, it will get worse. The worst of fiends are released when there is a void where power had been. Death does not discriminate. Everyone dies. Even the innocent. But you know that. It is only a matter of time before the City of Nectar will be reduced to a smouldering pile of ashes. Go in peace, Kannagi of the unbound tresses and the lone breast, bravest of warriors and fiercest of avengers. We will all be gone but the land has a long memory, and your deeds will not be forgotten. Think more kindly of us, who lacked your strength and unswerving commitment to do the right thing.'

'Don't mourn for your Madurai. It will be rebuilt and remain standing long after we are gone. I wish you peace too! Wherever you go, I hope you will be chosen to lead, for you are worthier than the one you chose to serve.'

He smiled at me, the sadness in his face wrenching at my heart. 'I failed my King and death beckons to me, so I can make amends in the afterlife. Fare thee well!'

Drawing his sword, he bowed to me, before lopping off his own head with a swift, clean stroke.

I walked out before his body joined his head on the river of death. There was no one to stop me. The grand palace and every one of the inhabitants were in Yama's domain. There was evidence of his handiwork everywhere. The Captain had been right. The lord of death did not discriminate. I did not linger and carried on walking.

Aiyai materialized by my side, a wraith who had taken shape from the gathering shadows. We walked the way we had come, past the great conflagration. She was crying. For her mother. And her beloved Madurai. There were no tears or feelings left in me. And I had no comfort to offer her. I had become a wretched instrument of fate—the weapon wielded by the powers that govern the universe to tear down a city where the rot had set in past redemption. Fire and blood alone could cleanse the land so it would have a fresh lease of life. Puhar wasn't too different. It would only be a matter of time before the sea swallowed it whole. For such was the design of cruel fate. If I were face to face with fate, I would have spat in her face too.

We kept walking. All through the long hours of the endless night. Madurai burned. Fires blazed in the dwellings of the righteous as well as the unrighteous. Palatial mansions of the rich and the hovels of the poor burned. Agni and Yama, the lords of fire and death, made merry claiming lives everywhere they went. Cows and calves, dogs and donkeys, trumpeting elephants, neighing horses, wailing humans and crying children, good and bad, men and women, everyone died. By fire, weapons wielded by rioters, rape, suffocation, shock, fright and horror that stilled their hearts, or a mere unwillingness to go on. But they all died just the same.

Some ran. A few escaped. Many were engaged in the sport of killing. None of these creatures dared approach me. On that night there was none in the three worlds more dangerous than I.

It was my hope that I would be consumed by the flames too. Then it would be truly over. But that did not happen. Instead, I walked on with only my grief, which blazed more fiercely than Agni, and Aiyai for company.

MADHAVI

Loss, Longing and Lasting Peace

You NEVER KNOW when it is the last time. I had hoped with all the desperation of a hollowed-out heart that Kovalan would return to me. Even though he had taken care to put as much distance as possible between us. But now, he would never return. To his wife, who had loved him with fanatical albeit doomed devotion. Or the dancing girl, who had loved him more than it was humanly possible to love someone and would go on loving him no matter how much it hurt or how hopeless it was.

Kovalan was beyond our reach now. He was dead. And all the love in the three worlds would not be enough to bring him back. He was gone for good.

Bad news travels fast. I was familiar with every miserable detail of the terrible tragedy that had claimed his life. He had been accused of thievery while trying to sell his wife's anklet and was executed. When I heard of his passing, I dropped to my knees, before folding over in a dead swoon.

I remembered those blasted anklets. Chittu had been obsessed with them. I distinctly remember her saying that she had never seen anything like them. She had been determined to somehow obtain them (for me, she said). Chittu was bitterly disappointed when she could not find them among Kannagi's jewels, which she had gone too far to obtain. I wished now that she had robbed Kovalan's wife of that pair too. Perhaps then they would not have

The Wife and the Dancing Girl   233

claimed the life of one who was far more precious and priceless than they were.

Vasanta gave me all the information she could gather from wherever it was that she managed to scrounge up all and sundry facts. I insisted on hearing it all, though listening to her accounts of Kovalan's fate proved so devastating, I wept hysterically, wailing and moaning on the floor, till my body ached all over and I could not breathe. And just when I thought there were no more tears left to shed, I wept some more. I simply could not stop.

Vasanta's voice was hushed. 'They say she orchestrated a bloodbath on an unprecedented scale. A lone woman armed with an anklet brought the mighty Pandyan to his knees and single-handedly reduced Madurai, that proud bastion of power since time immemorial, to ashes! It defies belief! And to think that Kannagi was always so quiet, timid, and frightened to death of just about anything and everything!'

'Tell me everything again!' I heard myself say, though I did not want to think about it or talk about it or even cry about it.

'People are saying the strangest things, and it is impossible to believe some of it, but it is certain that she proved that the ruling against Kovalan was a grave miscarriage of justice.' Vasanta was looking a little emotional too. Kovalan had been nice to her. In fact, he had been incapable of being anything but nice to all who crossed his path. 'The Brahmin Kausikan was in Madurai when it happened. He says that Kannagi transformed into a vengeful force of nature and rallied the mob, who marched with her to the palace, where she demanded justice from King Nedunjeliyan. She was able to prove that the anklet which had been taken from Kovalan was indeed hers. On hearing this and unable to bear the dishonour that would now tarnish his name across the annals of eternity, King Nedunjeliyan clutched his chest and simply dropped dead. His Queen, Kopperundevi, died too. I am assuming she joined him on the funeral pyre. Be that as it may, Kannagi was not appeased by their deaths. She insisted that Madurai itself would be the funeral pyre upon which Kovalan's remains would be cremated.'

Unlike everyone else in the kingdoms of the Cholas, Pandyas and Cheras, Chittu had no wish to discuss this subject though she was not happy about Kovalan's passing either. She acted as though he had gone and gotten himself killed simply to spite her. 'What are the odds that he would go and end up dead like this! As if his ill-advised departure from Puhar in the dead of the night was not bad enough, now we will be blamed for this calamity as well. The respect and goodwill earned by many generations of our family has evaporated in the blink of an eye, all thanks to a merchant prince's heir who couldn't manage the simple task of not losing a gargantuan fortune, and the even simpler task of selling an anklet.'

Her compassion and sensitivity as always warmed the heart, and I was too distraught to argue with her. But Kovalan's passing had been hard on her too. People did blame us in general, and her in particular, especially when word got out that she had managed to relieve Kannagi of her jewels. She could hardly step out of the house without risking getting stoned to death. It galled her no end. Chittu was convinced that Kannagi's mother and a friend of hers had been responsible for this private transaction becoming public news.

Vasanta did not think so. 'Kannagi's mother is a very dignified woman and not one given to recriminations or loose talk. They say she has been a rock of resilience and has not shed a single tear in the presence of her guests who have been flooding the house to offer condolences. Instead, she has used a considerable portion of their fortune and started a charity to help widowed women so that they may have a comfortable place to live, develop their talents, or receive funds to travel and visit holy temples. Otherwise, they will have to deal with relatives who ill-treat them or cast them out. It is most decent of her.'

Clearly, Kannagi's mother was every bit the pattini Kannagi herself was. The newfound reverence for pattinis—devout and chaste women who did the most ridiculous things in the name of virtue—and the tendency of rabble-rousers to elevate these virtuous wives to a pedestal while tearing down all other women by denouncing them as prostitutes, made the likes of Chittu sick with fury. I didn't care as much because I had never sought out pedestals. People had dredged up old stories of the seven famed pattinis of Puhar and, like them, my mother couldn't stop talking about it.

'Can you believe the foolishness of a widowed woman, who fancying she saw her husband's image on the banks of the Kaveri, remained rooted to the spot even after the river overflowed the embankment and swept her away? Why do men insist on women acting like fools to earn their approbation?

'I particularly hate the one about the wife who supposedly used the full might of her chastity to change her appearance to look exactly like a monkey to avoid the lecherous gaze of men, and reverted to her original face only when her departed husband returned to her. The one who changed herself into a stone and stood on the seashore while awaiting her husband's return was every bit as stupid!'

I hadn't heard of these, but I remembered there was one whose mother in an unguarded moment had promised her hand in marriage to her maid's son and tried to renege on the agreement, but this girl who was a beauty had placed the paunchy pauper's foot on her head and accepted him as her lord, though she was born to wealth and could have had her choice of suitors. And of course, there was Adimandi, King Karikalan's daughter who forced the sea to return her dead husband, though Chittu said that she had merely saved him from drowning, which was commendable in itself, but the poets had added all the other embellishments to make women feel unnecessarily bad about not being able to manage the impossible task of resuscitating their dead husbands.

Now Kannagi had been added to the pantheon of pattinis from Puhar, and Chittu was infuriated. When Vasanta told us that work had commenced on a temple to be built to commemorate her achievements, by the seashore, my mother nearly had an apoplectic fit. Ilamjeliyan, the younger brother of the slain Nedunjeliyan, who was holding the fort at Korkai, the ancient capital of the Pandyas, had begun the arduous task of rebuilding Madurai as its new King. He too had commissioned a temple to be built in Kannagi's honour, most probably to dissuade her from burning the place down again. The Cheran king, Senguttuvan, was also building a temple for her, and had asked his younger brother, the poet and monk Ilango, to set down her story in epic format, in order that the miracles she wrought be preserved for all of time. Or so Vasanta said.

'Vasantamala!' Chittu shrieked at my poor friend. 'You are such a silly goose for believing and repeating all the nonsense you hear from people who are even sillier. What a pile of rubbish! And Madhavi, dry your eyes at once. If you keep crying like this and ruin what remains of your looks, I will have you whipped. See if I don't! And haven't I taught you the art of shedding tears without ruining your mascara? You shame me!'

'I did say that some of what is being said simply cannot be true!' Vasanta said. 'But there is no denying that the King and Queen of Madurai are dead and the city itself burned. The capital of the Pandyas has been razed to the ground. All sources have confirmed this much to be the absolute truth. As for the rest…they say that she has wrought miracles and is now being worshipped as a goddess everywhere.'

Chittu snorted rudely. 'We have been told to believe that Kannagi, tiny little mouse of a woman that she is, twisted her left breast till it came loose, then proceeded to pluck it right out from her chest and hurled it at Madurai, setting it ablaze. Her flaming wrath supposedly consumed the City of Nectar in its entirety. Even intoxicated fools ought to know better than to believe that breasts are detachable organs that can be tacked on and removed at will, to be used as explosive devices! The more improbable the story is, the more inclined fools are to believe it. And if we were to dispute these fables as falsehoods, they would be angered enough to kill us all! Men are so foolish and will convince themselves that a woman's breast can be plucked like a flower or fruit and used as an incendiary device. They love breasts so much and yet, they are so frightened by the power of the pointy pair, it is beyond pathetic.'

Vasanta was looking bemused. 'I am not sure what to believe anymore. But there is talk that our King Perumkilli, heir of the late Nedumkilli, who prevailed in the civil war, might go to war with the Pandyas to avenge the unjust execution of an upstanding citizen of Chola Nadu, but I hear Senapati Seyon is against it. We are yet to regain our full strength after the civil war and besides, Senguttuvan is waging war against the Northerners, and has asked for Chola troops to be sent to supplement his own. On account of the aid he rendered during the civil war, enabling King Perumkilli to secure the throne, the Chera King cannot be refused, and we can't afford to go to war with the Pandyas at this time.'

I did not care to hear about the political manoeuvring that was going on in the wake of poor Kovalan's untimely passing. 'What happened to Kannagi?' I asked shakily.

'All I know is that they now worship her as a goddess and refer to her as Pattini Devi. But as to what actually became of her...' Vasanta hesitated, 'no one seems to know. She had her say in the Pandya's court, won justice for Kovalan, and brought about the utter ruin of Madurai as well as the King, but there is very little consensus about what happened to her after that. The prevalent belief is that she returned to her dead husband and sat with his head in her lap, as she allowed the flames to take her too.'

Had she joined him in death? The thought made me so unhappy for so many conflicting reasons, my head ached. If only I were dead too!

'There are those who swear that a lady with a lone breast was spotted in Chera Nadu. She was worshipped by some tribal women who then saw her being reunited with her husband. Indra, King of the Heavens, humbly took up the reins of the chariot that took their souls to Amaravati.'

Chittu snorted again. 'It is far more likely that she was gangraped and torn to pieces by the Apathuvadigal, sworn to protect the Pandyan King. They are supposed to be a fanatical lot and every bit as brutal and bloodthirsty as the Velakkara battalion, their counterparts in Chola Nadu.'

She stalked off in disgust when that brought on a fit of weeping so intense, I thought my heart would burst. 'It is my fault, Vasanta!' I sobbed. 'He made the decision to leave Puhar because he was convinced that he could not stay faithful to his wonderful, long-suffering wife while I lived and breathed. He ran away to escape me. There can be no denying that. I am the reason he is dead, Vasanta! And if anything bad happened to Kannagi, it is my fault as well. I am the deceitful dancing girl who…'

'Stop it, Madhavi!' Vasanta made me halt my tirade. 'You are not responsible for this tragedy. All you did was love him truly, and to the best of your ability. And you are not a deceitful dancing girl. People who say these foolish things don't know better. He lost his fortune but that was never your fault. You spent more on him than he did on you. That is the truth. He decided to go to Madurai. How can you blame yourself for that? Tragedy overtook him and his poor wife. It is most unfortunate, but you did not have anything to do with it. We are but the playthings of fate, Madhavi. You must let go of this guilt before it kills you. For Manimegalai's sake. She too has lost her father, whom she barely knew. Remember?'

That made me cry. Everything made me cry and I simply could not stop.

∽

If people had hated me before, they loathed me now and there was a fanatical edge to their passion. Many were demanding that the time-honoured tradition of dedicating girls to the temple be abolished. All dancers were declared to be vermin who seduced men, broke the hearts of their poor wives and, having deprived them of all worldly possessions, drove them to their deaths.

No one invited me to dance anymore. Even Ayya had left for Chera Nadu with some of his promising pupils, much to Chittu's fury. He blessed me before he left. 'You are a rare treasure among women, Madhavi! Don't let anyone make you feel otherwise. History will remember you kindly. You gave people a glimpse of their deepest potentiality through your art and dance, inspiring them to ascend higher and higher to the be-all and end-all of human existence, which is to achieve oneness with the divine. Your very life is testament to the fact that all the wonderful things we seek, the emotions we cling to, our deepest desires and innermost longings will be realized in the most sublimely meaningful way imaginable if we can find the courage and conviction to love fiercely and give generously.

'Have heart! Tragedy has overtaken you, but it will not be enough to consume everything you stand for. There will be beauty, truth and peace in your life, because you have earned it. You will never be a cautionary tale, dear Madhavi. Forevermore, women will seek to emulate you. Stay blessed, child of destiny. May the Gods protect you and keep you, a jewel among women, safe from all harm, now and forevermore.'

I touched his feet and accepted his blessings with all the poise I could muster. But after that I could not leave my room for days on end. Praise hurt me worse than condemnation, though I knew I deserved neither. Chittu wanted me to meet Senapati Seyon and arrange an audience with the King to secure Manimegalai's future and mine. But I was adamant. I knew I had worn the bells and danced my last dance. As for Manimegalai, the dancing bells would never touch her feet. Kovalan's daughter's life would be what she made of it.

'For once in your life, listen to me, Madhavi. Now is not the time for you to mourn and grieve like a wilting widow. You must fight for us all. Hold your head high and dance like never before. We have done nothing wrong. Act like it. Did you know that they butchered the dasis just like the veshas, who were dragged out by the hair from the brothels, as if there was no difference between the two during the rioting in Madurai, blaming them as always for all the evils wrought by mankind? They are starting to do the same here in Puhar. We must fight back! Mark my word, when they have had their fill of burning and bloodletting, and purity, piety and pattinis, they will come crawling back to us. Because we offer so much more. In the end, pleasure is always preferable to pain.'

I didn't know it then, but it was the last impassioned speech she would deliver to me. Had I known, I might not have shut my ears, screamed for her to stop it, and stormed out of there in a tempest of rage.

It was hard to imagine a future for myself. But I knew that one day the tears would stop, and a path would be revealed to me. I was content to wait. And I did not have to for long. The decision was practically taken for me.

Kannagi's parents had given away all their wealth to charity and left on a pilgrimage. Kovalan's mother starved herself to death. On the day her funeral rites were performed, his father had donated what remained of his fortune to various notable causes and joined a monastery. A huge crowd had gathered and once the doors of the seven Indra viharas closed behind him, the mob came for us. Mercifully, Vasanta and Manimegalai were not at home. For once, the fates were kind to me. Vasanta had taken my daughter to Atisha's ashram, where he was delivering a sermon to the public, and they were out of harm's way. Led by the worst vermin in society, the mob invaded our property, smashing, looting, burning and destroying everything they could get their hands on. The chatram where the hungry were fed and the hospice where the sick were attended to, both built by Paati and maintained by Chittu and me at great personal expense, were burned down with everyone inside. And all the while they accused us of sinning! They killed the poor swans and urinated in the pond, drowning or beating to death many of our helpers who were tending the grounds and had tried to make a run for it.

I did not resist when they dragged me out of my chambers into the harsh glare of the sun. They were welcome to my property and my life and whatever else they sought to extract from me forcibly. I wasn't crying anymore. Nor did I feel inclined to beg for mercy. Not even when they tore off my clothes and started to tonsure my head, shaving off bunches off my hair unceremoniously and with minimal care. I waited for the blade to strike off my head.

But the Senapati's forces arrived on the scene then to restore peace and order. I have absolutely no idea what happened next. All I know is that they were too late to save Chittu. Nobody knew what became of her. The house burned and I was told that she burned with it. I like to think that she escaped. With her life and the precious possessions that she cared for so much. It might be that she now has pupils who are like daughters to her and obey her every whim without arguments. In fact, I am sure of it.

It might have been that I was floating between conscious and unconscious states, but I distinctly remember asking to be taken to Atisha's Buddhist monastery.

Atisha offered me refuge as I had known he would. He made arrangements for the Bikkunis to take care of me. The injuries sustained had not been life threatening, but it took me a long time to stop feeling like every inch of my body had been defiled and violated beyond recognition. But even more powerful than the trauma that was inflicted on me, in my already weakened state, was the realization that I had survived the worst that they had all managed to do to me. Paati and Chittu would have been proud.

Once I became aware of the truth, my recovery was almost miraculous. Atisha usually stopped by to check in on the wounded souls who landed up on his doorstep and sometimes we would talk about this and that. It was decided that once I was on my feet again, I would take holy instruction on the eight *Garudamma*s, embrace the five precepts, prove my commitment to the monastic way of life, and with hard work receive ordination from Atisha himself to become a Bikkuni. Once the decision was made, I found myself more at peace than I had ever been. Dear Vasanta came to see me often. She promised to take care of Manimegalai and make sure she made something of her life as long as it did not involve dancing to the whim of others.

I was no longer afraid. Of being alone and unloved. Especially once I realized that after everything I had been through, aloneness was not the worst thing to happen to me. In my spiritual quest across timeless eternity, I found myself more closely attuned than ever before to all the things I had sought. The things I had feared I might never find. Those things that I had worried would surely be lost to me, once I had them.

This time, I was able to float free as a bird across infinity, untroubled by crippling fear that I would lose it all. Dreams of loss and longing made way for a better future where I saw myself from the heights of spiritual well-being. Finally, I understood that my expectations would be fulfilled in the realms of deathlessness, where I would not have to settle for scraps of love and lust. It took a while, but finally I needed nothing, and that was when everything was within my grasp.

Leaving behind the chaos, I found an ocean of calm. And in the depths, I discovered finally my ability to give in, submit, capitulate entirely to the tranquillity, and trust the waves to take me where they would. To myself. To him. To everything else that awaited on the other side.

KANNAGI

Sorrow, Solitude and Surrender

I AM DYING. IT is a blessed relief to hear Yama's approaching footsteps, drawing ever closer. The God of Death and Damnation had been in a rush to claim Kovalan, he had delighted in the doom of the City of Nectar, but with me, he really drew it out. For the duration of infinity. Or so it seemed to me, even as I flail beneath the whiplash of unceasing torment.

I remember that Madurai had burned. Not that it mattered much. He was gone. The smell of charred flesh and the anguished shrieking of the miserable souls consumed by voracious Agni assaulted my nostrils and eardrums as I lay insensate on a reed mat. Having consumed its citizenry almost down to the last man, woman and child, and regurgitated their remains, the City of Nectar would be rebuilt on their blood and bones. It would live forever. How did any of that matter to me? Only he had mattered. And he had been murdered by a King, whom I killed. Not that it made a whit of difference. Or made any of this less hateful or bearable.

Aiyai lay by my side, dreaming her own dreams of death and devastation. When she woke, she was strong again. The ferocity of her spirit undiminished. Her appetite as zesty as it had been before. She still has the capacity to find joy, meaning and fulfilment in the meanest of circumstances. Like caring for a friend who had transformed into a fiend, who now lay immobile and unresponsive, afloat on a mat of misery that was not entirely of her own making, which did not make it any less miserable.

Kavundi is here too. Perhaps there was a crack in the mirror-like calm she always evinced, but it was hard to say with her. Aiyai took to hovering over me, while Kavundi kept her distance. They are my watchful guardians who are determined to fight off Yama's meandering approach with whatever weapon comes to hand—potions, poultices, tenderly prepared meals, songs and sermons, and the solidarity of sisterhood. We are at cross-purposes but I am grateful for their company.

They are not the only ones who are determined to keep to my side. Many are coming to my sickbed. Undeterred by my strange stillness, silence and lack of movement, they are flocking to my side in droves. Some to worship. Some to whisper their wishes into my ears. They touch my feet. Bring offerings of flowers, fruits, milk and meat. They seem not to be bothered by the utter unresponsiveness, which is the best I can conjure up for their plight. And mine.

'She is dying!' they wail and lament. Crying and comforting each other. Offering up whatever they can think of to reverse the gradual deterioration of my health. Hymns, prayers, invocations and loud offers of their own lives to save my own, their breasts to replace the one I had chopped off. I really wish they wouldn't.

'The Goddess is exiting her mortal coil to enter the realms of the immortals…' they console each other, determined to believe that immortality offers something that is better than mortality rather than more and more of the same. If Kavundi heard the irreverence in my delirious thoughts, she gave no hint of it. We communed in silence, in the solitary spaces between the dialogues and diatribes of the many tongues that wagged in the immediate vicinity. She did nothing and yet, she helped more than all the herbs and healing potions in the world.

'Why?' I kept asking. 'Why me? Why Kovalan? Why us? Why did we fall in love? Why were we torn apart? Why did we find our way back to the other's outstretched arms just so we could lose each other again? Why did he have to die? Why did I have to murder and burn and consume the lot of them in the flames of my wrath? Why wasn't it enough? To bring him back or kill me as well? Why did it all have to happen? Why? Why? Why?'

In the rarefied realm of unreality I have been banished to, where I hover between life and death, everything was possible, but nothing mattered. Here, there was no room for reason or rationale. Only the undiluted truth prevailed, in all its bitter glory. In the litany of visions birthed in this phantasmic terrain, I see Kovalan again. Or rather, Kovalan as he had been many lifetimes ago. I didn't care about that. It was enough just to see him again and walk by his side.

A humble oil monger, he had not asked for much. All he wanted was to supply oil to light the lamp at the temple of Kali, the dark Goddess he loved with all his heart. She granted him his wish, and that night the pujari allowed him to pour his oblation into a single lamp, the tiniest one in her temple. The others were lit with the oil procured by the King himself, for it was his prerogative. That night, all the lamps in the Kali temple were extinguished, though the wind was holding its breath in stifling anticipation. One alone burned. Brighter than the stars in the firmament. The infuriated King drew his sword and struck down the ecstatic oil monger, who had been so filled to the brim with bliss that he did not feel a thing, other than his love for the Goddess, who had judged his heart and declared it greater than a King's.

Kali was enraged. I saw the wrath in her eyes before they boiled over and obliterated everything in sight. Those enormous carp-like eyes...they were my own. Nedunjeliyan threw himself at my feet and begged for mercy. In reply, I bludgeoned him to death with an anklet that was so heavy, I dropped it, and the damn thing cracked open his skull, spilling out the meagre contents. 'And I shall do it again. And again. As long as it takes for you to understand that you cannot kill without just cause!' I shrieked at him.

I couldn't help but think that being a goddess was a wretched business. But there was no agitation this time. Instead, I lay still as the tangled threads of a thousand visions unspooled before me in a relentless rush...

That dear handsome face! I would never tire of it. He was a soldier. They called him Bharatan. The sword seemed too heavy for him to wield but he seemed to delight in the power he wielded. Like a boy with a toy he ought not to be playing with. His wife delighted him too. And why wouldn't she? When she was as beautiful and charming as Madhavi, men seemed to have little cause for complaint. How was she always so effortlessly beautiful? Her face and form were just the perfect proportion of curves and angles. She was slim-waisted with full lips that he must have liked to kiss or nibble on...

He served Vasu, the King of Singapura. All was well. For the longest time. They seemed so happy. Especially him.

I saw Kovalan or was it Bharatan...drag the protesting Sangaman before the King in chains, accusing him of spying. The death sentence was pronounced in stentorian tones. He wielded the sword, which was much too heavy for him. Clumsily and unsteadily. Till the job was done. Sangaman fell. His wife, Nili, beat her chest and tugged her hair, crying so hard it was difficult to make out what she was saying or decipher the dreadful imprecations she was hurling at the unrepentant killer's head. But I heard the words. 'You will pay... for what you did to my husband! Your wife will endure everything I have endured. And then you will be sorry!'

Nili cried for fourteen days and fourteen nights over the dead body of her husband. Then, she rose to her feet and ran. Making her way to the towering cliff, she hurled herself off the edge. I could taste her anger in my mouth and stomach. Her hatred imploded in my chest and everything in it was broken like her body, which lay smashed to little pieces on the sharp rocks below, before the waves washed them clean.

The vision ended. And the story should have too. Especially after a climax like that. But there was too much trauma released and it could seldom be contained within the stories. Eventually it always spilled over. Across multiple lifetimes.

Aiyai is constantly by my side, her pleas interrupting my pointless peregrinations on the hopelessness of the human condition. 'Don't die, Kannagi!' she pleaded. 'We will go together to Chera Nadu, where nobody knows us. They have cows in all the Kingdoms in the known world, don't they? I am sure they will have use for experienced cowherdesses. I will teach you everything I know, and we will manage together. We could even pick out bulls to look after and we will marry the ones who tame them. I'll marry the strong one with the kind heart and as for you, Krishna himself will turn up to win your hand. See if he doesn't! The four of us will find two adjacent cottages to live in, and we will be happy as can be!

'Did you know that the imperial Viceroy of Korkai, Ilamjeliyan, now rules over Pandya Nadu? He is your foremost devotee! Can you blame him? It is thanks to you that he now sits on the Pandya throne. He has committed himself to building a temple for the Pattini Devi—Kannagi. The spot for this grand venture has been finalized and it shall be consecrated with the blood of a thousand goldsmiths who shall be rounded up and sacrificed! The monarch must be mad, but his will shall be obeyed and implemented.'

The Wife and the Dancing Girl

Dear Aiyai. What an unbreakable spirit she has! I am pleased for her. Kavundi and she would make it to Chera Nadu. Aiyai would find her bull tamer and they would live together in a form of matrimony, *kalavu*, in secret. She isn't going to be as happy as can be because nobody ever is, but she will go on to be reasonably pleased with her lot in life.

She is still trying to get some response, any response, out of me. 'Kovalan's father has joined a monastery. His poor mother gave up her life. You will be pleased to know that your parents are doing well under the circumstances. They have embarked on a pilgrimage. Once you come back to us, we will try and find them! You would like that, wouldn't you?

'Did you know that the poet Ilango Adigal, the younger brother of Cheran Senguttuvan, has been commissioned to compose an epic on the life and times of Kannagi? The Kings of Pandya, Chera and Chola Nadus are all planning to construct temples to be dedicated to you! Isn't that exciting?'

I didn't think so. Would towering monuments built to commemorate a traumatized woman serve any useful purpose? As for the storyteller, I supposed he might churn out yet another fanciful story to be passed on from generation to generation. About a Goddess, who wasn't one. It would be a cautionary tale on the perils of loving too much. It would dwell largely on the importance of being virtuous to a fault because it suits everyone else. It would hammer home the merits of choosing sanctity and sacrifice over satisfaction, which is mostly a fool's move. It would be just the sort of story that Devundi had always hated. What would she make of it all, I wondered? She would not believe it! I didn't believe it myself.

Mostly, I remain lost in the precious visions. Swept along by swift moving currents I had no wish to resist.

A child of prophecy. Born to the Pandyan King Nedunjeliyan. The astrologers divined that the sweet little girl would bring about the death of the King and be guilty of the dread crime of patricide. She would also bring about the ruination of Madurai. On his orders, they hid her in a chest of mangoes and cast her into the river, which emptied into the sea. Manaykan and Masattuvan, merchant princes from Puhar, found the chest. The former took the daughter he had always wanted. The latter made him promise that she would be his daughter-in-law. The child grew up to be a loving wife, abandoned wife, happily married wife, unhappy widow and vengeful Destroyer of worlds.

Did any of it make sense? I suppose it did and it didn't. Who cared about all that when all was lost? Death alone was certain. For that, I was grateful. It was good to know that it would all be over soon. And it was also good to know that it was never finished.

My coming together with Kovalan was the reason behind every experience of pleasure and pain. Against all odds, our lives remained inextricably entwined across the aeons. For better or for worse. We were so different. But when we became one, we were just the same. He was the dream, and I was the reality. Even when I woke up to my reality, I could not remain unaffected by everything I had enjoyed with him in the dream. Which was just the way it should be. It was the way it would always be.

He was gone. Free to roam the cosmos. I would be gone too. And no matter what happened, I was certain of one thing alone. Somehow or the other, we would be in each other's arms again. Across every iteration of the infinite stories spanning countless lifetimes. From sleep into the dreams, from the dreams into waking, from waking up to reality and living and dying. Across the length and breadth of it all, we would always have each other. The pleasure of our union will always outweigh the pain of parting. And as long as this is so, I remain content. Even if it never ends. Especially since there is no ending in sight. Because our love was always going to be forever. I wouldn't have it any other way. And so it ends. Except it doesn't.

AUTHOR'S NOTE

I TEND TO MAKE heavy weather of authoring my books. But this was the book which kicked me in the keister. Hard.

It was only a matter of time before I wrote about Kannagi and Madhavi. As a Tamil *ponnu* born and brought up and currently residing in Tamil Nadu, theirs was a story I grew up with. My initial response to this epic was profound irritation with a side of fledgling feminist rage. It was impossible to understand why these two loved Kovalan so much despite his nonsense. And it was even harder to understand why Kannagi burnt down Madurai, an hour's drive from Virudhunagar, where I was born, and an hour-and-a-half's drive from Sivakasi, where I live. It is also where my fave aunt and sister make their homes and where you can visit the Meenakshi Amman temple, stuff your face with Konar *kari dosai*, and cool your flaming innards with *jigarthanda*. Naturally, I felt it was somewhat unreasonable of Kannagi to ignore the fact that the city and its King had done her a favour by getting rid of her philandering husband, and insisting on burning it to a crisp. Moreover, these pattinis are impossible to emulate. The text of the *Silapathikaram* leads us to believe that in a land filled to bursting with pattinis, evils like drought and famine, poverty, and defeat in battle would not happen. (Insert eye-roll emoji.)

Despite my inclination to dismiss the *Silapathikaram* as a lot of ancient bunkum, the story had gotten its claws into me and refused to let go. Besides, as much as I tend to hate it, I have always loved it. When I was three books old, I took a stab at retelling Ilango Adigal's magnum opus. My efforts were rewarded with hair-tearing and gut-wrenching frustration and failure, and while I did not exactly scream in anguish and call upon the heavens to witness the devastating debacle, I did give up and move on. In a huff. Twelve books, my own Bharatanatyam arangetram (thank you, Niranjana *akka*), one pandemic and one award later, I was ready to take another crack at my personal Mount Doom. The going was expectedly rough, and I suffered more setbacks than I care to relate but I plodded on with a degree of obstinacy that can only be described as nuts. I am not sure whether I succeeded in my perilous mission or not, but I am pleased that I refused to throw in the towel this time.

For whatever reason, women are rigidly classified as either the good girl or bad bitch—wife or whore. Never mind that no woman in the entire history of the universe and across time has been entirely one or the other. Perhaps that is why I had to write *The Wife and the Dancing Girl*, if only to do away with binaries and stick to a modicum of realism and hardboiled practicality, insofar as these things are possible. To make it about the women who may be wives or whores and both or neither. I saw no reason to unnecessarily venerate the one while excoriating the other. To let generations of little girls feel freer of the burden of patriarchal expectations that have traditionally been used to oppress and suppress the female of the species via a brutal system that legitimizes male desire even when it runs to depraved excess while stigmatizing, villainizing and, ultimately, exploiting female desire. To let them know that it is all well and good to grow up and be a lady but sometimes it is necessary, even imperative, to be a bitch. The jury is still out on the extent to which I was successful in implementing my vision for this book, but personally, I think

Kannagi and Madhavi have done a bang-up job of telling their own stories. Kovalan was a revelation too and, to my surprise, I learned to appreciate his decent qualities while still being a little impatient with him.

Be that as it may, I cannot wrap this up without conveying my immense gratitude to V.R. Ramachandra Dikshitar for his definitive work—*The Silappadikaram*, which was invaluable in helping me negotiate the timeless terrain. I might be a Tamil ponnu but my English is superior to my Tamil. Don't blame me. Blame the forward caste twits who made it impossible for my great-grandfather, Periasamy *thatha*, to study in an English medium school, after pocketing the (exorbitant) admission fees, and keeping viciously silent when his teacher flat-out refused to teach him. His father packed him off to the missionary school in Palayamkottai, but Periasamy thatha dropped out because they insisted that he convert. But he did teach himself to speak English and was most particular that his own sons study in a propah English medium school. My grandfather M.S.P. Rajah completed his education in Montfort school, Yercaud, and graduated from Loyola College. He was the first graduate in the family and was rightly proud of the fact. My father Ramesh Rajah, in keeping with family tradition, was educated in Lawrence School, Ooty, and later went to Columbia Business School, with the end result that his Tamil is far worse than mine. He was also most particular that his daughters learn to speak the Queen's English, and we were enrolled in Sacred Heart's Anglo-Indian Girls Convent, Yercaud, where the nuns and teachers taught us to do so. All this is to say that it proved impossible for me to read the Tamil epic in the language in which it was written, which is why I am grateful to all the fine folks who made the *Silapathikaram* accessible in English.

Thanks are due to Alain Danielou (*Shilappadikaram: The Ankle Bracelet*), Lakshmi Holmstrom (*Silappadikaram Manimekalai*), R. Parthasarathy (*The Cilappatikaram: The Tale of an Anklet*), and Gananath Obeyesekere (*The Cult of the Goddess Pattini*), for holding my hand and helping a notoriously direction-challenged me find her way. Much obliged to Kapila Vatsyayan for Bharata's *Natyasastra*, which I was able to read and enjoy thanks to her efforts, the late Lakshmi Vishwanathan (*Women of Pride: The Devadasi Heritage*), and Davesh Soneji (*Unfinished Gestures: Devadasis, Memory and Modernity in South India*) for their assistance in exploring the history and lore of the much misunderstood and maligned dasis.

Appreciate my Rupa family for not being typical Delhiwaalon publishing types and arguing that revisiting an ancient Tamil classic would not have pan-India appeal. Indebted to Kapish Mehra, Yamini Chowdhury, Richa Tewari, Sana Yaseen and Geetu Martolia for assisting this baby through the difficult labour and delivery.

Thanks to every single one of my readers. You guys rock and your feedback, be it kind or critical, is oxygen to a writer's lonely, insecure and anxiety-riddled existence.

Author pals—Vinita Nangia, Kavita Kane, Shinie Antony, Koral Dasgupta, Kiran Manral, Meghna Pant, KSD, Chitra, Ashwin Sanghi, Utkarsh Patel, Satyarth Nayak and Anand Neelakantan, who always lend an ear when I grouse and whine about the challenges of being an author and give me the benefit of their personal knowledge while keeping me entertained with insider gossip.

My dance class buddies—V akka, Sivasakthi, Achu Anni (also my trailblazing sister-in-law), Kanch, Radhiga akka, Sarni, Shru, Siva, Sri, CM, Swe, Niranch, Harsh, Swathi, Samyu, Varsh, Vila,

Shar, Aish, Durga, Janani—thanks ever so much for putting up with my many foibles. I know I am insufferable on occasion, but you guys are indulgent and affectionate to a fault. To many more stages, late-night conversations, and dance performances!

Hugs and love to Mum (Maheshwari), Dad and the siblings (Varsh, Ash and Ram), who have been dealing with my 'artistic temperament' for ages. Gowri Perims and Cookie, you guys rock my world. My mother-in-law, Savi athai, you are a blessing.

My grandparents, Raji perims, Vidya mama, Ras ayyamma, Sherin Joy, who are all gone but are dearly loved and sorely missed.

The daughters, Veda and Varna, and the husband, Chandu, who keep me grounded with their especial blend of snark and sweetness. You will find it cringe, but love you mostest, though you drive me right up the wall.

GLOSSARY

Disclosure: I worked on this reluctantly and grudgingly because my excellent editor felt it was necessary. I am guessing it is because there are quite a few Tamil words in this book and Tamil (one of the longest-surviving classical languages in the world) is spoken and understood mostly by Tamilians from Tamil Nadu, Sri Lanka, Singapore, and those who have undergone a deep, tectonic identity shift after reading this book, which has prompted them to study the language with a vengeance so that they may read the *Tolkappiyam*, Sage Agastya's incomparable text on Tamil grammar and one of the oldest extant works in Tamil literature (if you remember this reference from the chapter on Madhavi's arangetram, you have my eternal love), and the *Silapathikaram* in the language in which they were written.

Those of you who googled the words they didn't understand or got it thanks to context, good for you. Feel free to skip this.

adavu	A series of basic Bharatanatyam dance steps and movements at varying speeds which are the building blocks or units in a dancer's repertoire. These are the very first rhythmic movements a dancer is taught and have to be mastered before the dancer can progress to intermediate and advanced levels.
amma	Mom, mother, mater, mum, female parent.
anna dhanam	Donating food to those in need.
anthapuram	Female quarters—an all-girls hostel.

appa	Dad, daddy, father, pater, male parent.
appalams	Pappadam.
arangetram	A grand occasion that indicates that the dancer is qualified to ascend to the stage—first public performance.
Athai	Mother-in-law or aunt.
Ayya	Respectful form of address for an elderly male.
bhutam	Ghost, usually evil.
chatram	A charitable initiative where the less fortunate can find food and shelter.
chunnambu	Slaked lime.
damaru	Tamil word for damaru is *udukkai*—handheld, hourglass-shaped, double-sided drum favoured by Shiva.
ganikai	Royal dancer.
gopuram	Tall ornate tower found at the entry points in South Indian temples. Gopurams are multi-tiered with elaborate, intricately carved sculptures and other decorative elements. They can be seen from a distance and never fail to warm the hearts of devotees.
idli	You have to know what this means. You just have to. I insist.
ishta deivata	Favourite God.
jhimki	North of the Vindhyas, these earrings are known as *jhumka*s, which apparently mean 'little bells' in Hindi. They are characterized by timeless elegance and are worn to this day.
jigarthanda	It is a cool-drink-meets-dessert, which is the distant cousin of a falooda. It is not meant to be explained but merely enjoyed when you find yourself in Madurai.

kari dosai	Dosa or dosai is a varying degree of crisp pancake made from a batter of rice flour and ground pulses. Kari is meat (chicken or mutton).
kathirikai puli kulambu	Brinjal gravy dish made with tamarind and ground spices.
kavutham	A unit to measure distance.
kondai	Bun. Not the edible kind.
koodam	Hall.
kungumam	Red turmeric powder used to make the auspicious mark on the forehead.
Mama	Father-in-law or uncle. Sometimes used to refer to a pimp if you are being a potty mouth.
mandapam	Traditionally a pillared hall or pavilion in temples for devotees to gather for worship, dance and music performances. It can also be a temporary platform erected for weddings, religious festivals, or to showcase singers and dancers.
Manmatha	Refer to *Kama: The God of Desire* by one Anuja Chandramouli.
mayil kazhuthu	Refers to the specific shade of the peacock's throat. The exact colour (blue? green? bluish green? greenish blue? peacock blue?) may be determined by performing microspectrophotometry, imaging scatterometry and angle-dependent reflectance measurements. Or so Google-ji has led me to believe.
Muruga	One of the names of Kartikeya—Son of Shiva. Don't ask me who that is. If you want more details, buy my book *Kartikeya: The Destroyer's Son*.
nadaswaram	South Indian festivities usually feature this double-reed wind instrument prominently. It consists of a long tube which widens at the

	end (like a trumpet) and is made of wood or metal with finger holes and a mouth piece. The nadaswaram is traditionally accompanied by a pair of thavil drums. This combination is believed to be highly auspicious and is played at most Hindu weddings and temples.
nattuvanar	Teacher or guru who usually choreographs the dance pieces. They also wield the handheld cymbals during a dancer's performance and conduct the orchestra (*nattuvangam*).
natyam	Dance.
nityasumangali	Eternally auspicious. As the wives of God, it was believed the devadasis were spared the horrors of widowhood as their Lord husband was immortal. It gave them many perks and privileges not enjoyed even by women of royal birth.
paadini	Singer.
Paati	Grandmother or old lady.
paavadai	Here it is a long skirt. But it is also worn as an underskirt beneath a sari. Also, a pejorative term insinuating that a male is effeminate, if you are using offensive lingo that will not have the approval of your Amma or Appa.
pattini	Chaste woman—goody-two-shoes type.
pattu sari	Pure mulberry silk saris woven on pit looms with intricate designs, originating from Kanchipuram (Kanchi).
payasam	A sweet dish made by boiling milk, sugar, rice, vermicelli, insert preferred ingredient. North Indians would say *kheer*. English speakers would say pudding, I guess.
periya melam	Literally means big band featuring the singers

	and players of instruments like nadaswaram, mridangam and tavil.
pisaasu	A malevolent spirit believed to be evil incarnate. Bit of a hellraiser. Not to be confused with my younger sister.
ponnu	Girl.
pottu kattuthal	Pottu here (not to be confused with the Tamil word for *bindhi*) refers to a gold chain worn like a *thaali* or *mangalsutra* by the dasi after she is wedded to the deity. A similar ritual was *kathi kalyanam*, marriage to a deity represented by a sword.
rasam saadham	Rasam is a watery and spicy soup consumed with rice (*saadham*).
sadhaka puja	An act of ritual worship performed to mark the commencement of a dancer's training.
sadhir katcheri	*Sadhir aatam* was the ancient dance form believed to have been practised by the dasis. Bharatanatyam is its modern-day descendant. A *katcheri* refers to an assembly of dancers, singers and the audience gathered for a performance.
salangai puja	It is performed ritually to mark the auspicious occasion when the guru decides the dancer is ready to adorn her feet with the *salangai* or the dancing bells. She is no longer a novice and is all set to progress to intermediate and advanced skill levels.
samana	Convivial gatherings where food, drinks and conversation was shared.
seempaal	Colustrum—the first milk produced by the mammary glands of mammals.
silambu koodam	The place where the dasis trained.

sorkattu	A traditional method of learning and practising rhythm through the vocalization of particular syllables—*Tha, ki, ta. Tha ka dhi mi, ta*, etc.
sthapathi	Sculptor.
talaikkol	Staff or central shaft of the white umbrella held over a king's head, signifying his divine authority. Or a bamboo shaft. It was part of the rituals included in a dancer's arangetram.
thaikizhavi	Refers to the mother or foster mother of a devadasi, dancing girl. Also, an affectionate term of address for the matriarch. On an unrelated note, it is a hit song composed by Anirudh Ravichander.
thamboolam	Includes the ingredients required for chewing betel leaves and areca nuts with slaked lime. Believed to be a stimulant with psychoactive properties.
thatha	Grandfather. Old man.
thattukali	A wooden block, comprising a stick and base to direct the rhythm of the dancer.
vadagam	A fried snack.
veshti sattai	Dhoti and shirt set.
vetrilai potti	Literally betel leaves box.
vidwan	Connoisseur of art, dance and music, who is well-versed in the subject and lends their expertise to help shape the dancer.
yaal	An open-stringed polyphonous instrument resembling the harp. It was a regular feature in ancient Tamil music, mentioned in Sangam literature, and can be seen in temple carvings. Over time, it was replaced entirely by the veena.